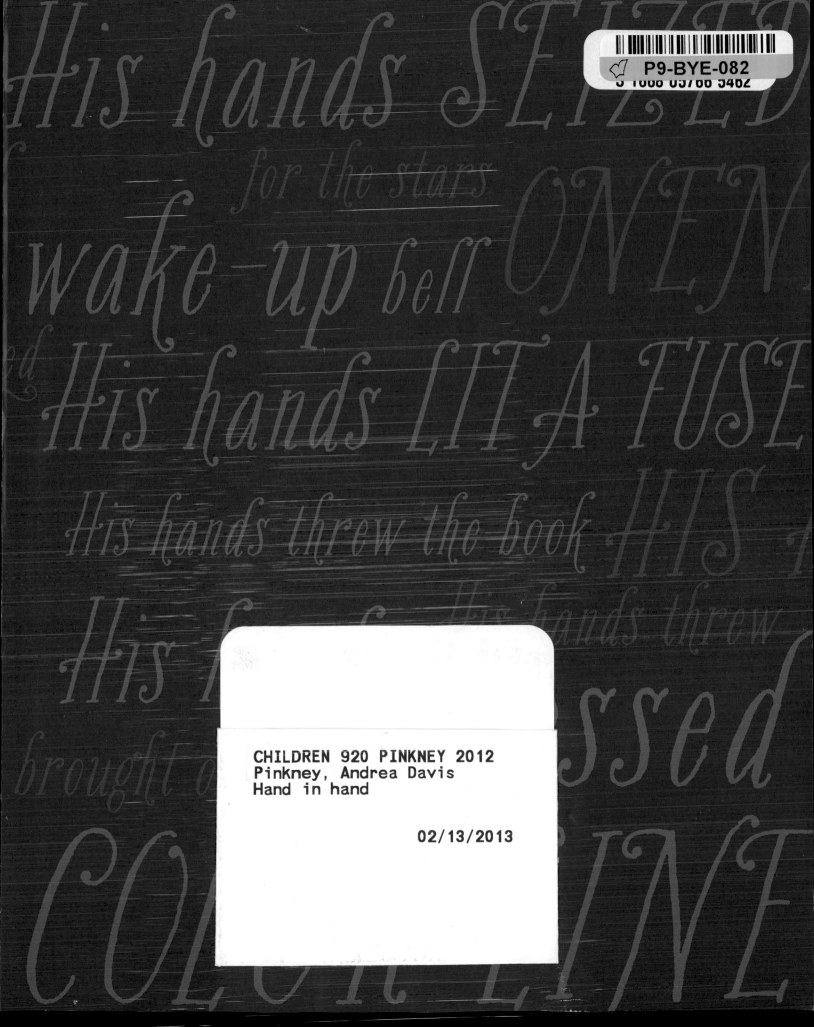

His hands SEIZED
for the stars
wake-up bell ONE
His hands LIT A FUSE
His hands threw the book HIS

His hands SEIZED

for the stars

wake-up bell ONEN

His hands LIT A FUSE

His hands threw the book HIS H

His hands

His hands threw

crossed

rought oneness

COLOR LINE

Hand in Hand

Hand in

Ten Black Men Who Changed America
Hand

BY Andrea Davis Pinkney   PAINTINGS BY Brian Pinkney

Disney 🌀 Jump at the Sun Books
New York

For PJ
—A.D.P

For Dad
—B.P.

Text copyright © 2012 by Andrea Davis Pinkney
Illustrations copyright © 2012 by Brian Pinkney

All rights reserved. Published by Disney • Jump at the Sun Books, an imprint of Disney Book Group.
No part of this book may be reproduced or transmitted in any form or by any means, electronic or mechanical, including photo-
copying, recording, or by any information storage and retrieval system,
without written permission from the publisher. For information address Disney • Jump at the Sun Books,
114 Fifth Avenue, New York, New York 10011-5690.
Printed in Singapore
First Edition
1 3 5 7 9 10 8 6 4 2
F850-6835-5-12196
This book is set in Cochin LT Std
The art was created with watercolor on 300 pound Arches cold press
Book design by Whitney Manger

Library of Congress Cataloging-in-Publication Data
Pinkney, Andrea Davis.
Hand in hand: ten Black men who changed America / by Andrea Davis Pinkney; paintings by Brian Pinkney.
p. cm.
Includes bibliographical references and index.
ISBN 978-1-4231-4257-7
1. African American men—Biography—Juvenile literature. 2. African Americans—Biography—
Juvenile literature. 3. Social change—United States—History—Juvenile literature. I. Pinkney, J. Brian, ill.
II. Title.
E185.86.P56 2012
973'.0496073—dc23   2011051348

Reinforced binding
Visit www.disneyhyperionbooks.com

Table of Contents

His hands SEIZED

for the stars

wake-up bell ONEN

His hands LIT A FUSE

His hands threw the book HIS HA

His hands threw

His hands

crossed

sought oneness

COLOR LINE

Reaching... Pulling...

These are the stories of ten bold men
who built a chain called *hand in hand*.

Each a link in this mighty strand:
>   *Reaching*
>   *Pulling*
>   *Believing*
>   *Achieving*

Working toward freedom
>   *Hand in hand.*

Brave souls, together strong.
Never stopped fighting.
Kept *speaking* and *dreaming*.
All for justice
>   *Hand in hand.*

Gripped iron courage
to withstand:

>   *Degradation*
>   *Segregation*
>   *Humiliation*
>   *Hard frustration*

Solid as one
>   *Hand in hand.*

Here are their stories,
courageous and true.

>   Their words,
>   their lives,
>   their unbreakable plan,
make this freedom chain

called Hand in hand.

Preface

*T*HIS BOOK WAS IGNITED by the beautiful hands of a black man. Or, as it were, the hands of several men whose complexions ranged from buff to midnight.

One summer, years ago, I was invited to attend a literacy institute at the University of Illinois at Chicago (UIC). The program had been developed by Dr. Alfred W. Tatum, literacy professor at the UIC, and director of the UIC Reading Clinic. Its purpose was to foster literacy and creative expression through writing in African American boys ages thirteen to eighteen. The program participants, who referred to themselves as "Brother Authors," began each day's three-hour session by standing and reciting their Preamble.

When I came to visit them, they were eager to share this introduction to their mission:

We, the Brother Authors, will seek to use language to define who we are.

We will become, and nurture, resilient beings.

We will write for the benefit of others and ourselves.

We will use language prudently and unapologetically to mark our times and our lives.

This we agree to, with a steadfast commitment to the ideals of justice, compassion, and a better humanity for all.

To this end, we write!

I was immediately struck by the fortitude and passion of these boys-to-men. Also inspiring was the posture with which they delivered their Preamble. The boys stood erect, proud, side by side, holding fast to their bright futures. They were of every beautiful hue that God must have conceived of when He stirred his palette to create the black race—amber, oak, mocha, red bark, vanilla bean.

These young men sought life direction in the books they read. They wanted to hear the stories of black men who had accomplished great things. They cared deeply about social justice, civil rights, laws affecting them and the African American community, the history of black people, and the tradition of achievement built by black men. They were hungry for role models. They wanted shoulders to stand on. They had high hopes as they approached adulthood. They affirmed themselves and one another.

There was never a question of *if* they could succeed—these kids had very straight-ahead ideas about *what* they would accomplish *when* they reached their goals. But as children who found strength through reading and writing, they wanted more books to reflect their ideals and to serve as stepping-stones to their manhood.

After spending time with these "Brother Authors," I knew I had to write *Hand in Hand.* Their determination—and the image of them standing united, side by side—left an indelible impression on me.

I'd grown weary of so much bad press and ignorant stereotyping of black males. I have become acutely aware of the negative impact this has, especially on boys who are developing their self-image. Even in its subtlest forms, this "bad press" can stitch a corrosive thread into a kid's psyche and cause him to believe he is inferior or flawed. Once this belief is established, it can be hard to turn around. Yet here was a group who refused to give way to such negativity. These boys restored my faith, and inspired me to get cracking on a book that celebrates black male achievement.

I wanted to create a testament to African American males, a comprehensive book that would also serve as a thank-you gift to all the positive black men who have touched my life and the lives of people I will never meet.

While this volume is comprised of ten different stories, when woven together like a chain, the individual accomplishments of these men link up to tell one story—a story of triumph.

Folks will no doubt ask why I've chosen the ten men featured in these pages. Selecting the candidates whose lives I would illuminate was one of the hardest aspects of *Hand in Hand*'s creation. This collection could contain hundreds of stories! There are so many black men who have made a tremendous impact on racial progress in America. My initial list was a long one, from which I created my own "black legacy time line."

It was important to span America's history, from the Colonial period to the Civil War to the turn of the century, World War I, the Great Depression, the Civil Rights movement, to our modern day. I found it essential to include men from varied sectors. And, rather than simply presenting a snapshot of each, I wanted the freedom to delve into the early lives, influences, and motivations that led to the accomplishments of the men in the collection. I was eager to explore the humanity that makes each man unique. Keeping the list to ten allowed me to do this. Also, each of these men had a hand in shaping America's progress, hence the book's title, *Hand in Hand: Ten Black Men Who Changed America.*

As I conducted my research and began to write, I continued to grapple with which men would "make the cut." The "Brother Authors" helped in this. The individuals I chose are among those whose names kept coming up on their "racial-pride radar."

Once I'd come to a final decision about which men would be included, it was time to determine the ordering of the stories. Who should come first, second, and so on? This was resolved by presenting the men chronologically by birth date.

The research on each notable figure took me on an incredible journey. While there exist countless books about African Americans and the ongoing quest for equality, few provide the breadth of personal detail that I wished to include in each man's story. In thinking about *Hand in Hand* as a cohesive chain—ten men, joined together, marching into the lives of this book's readers—I wanted to make sure I wasn't missing a vital "link" in any of the narratives.

I consulted many sources to assist in the creation of the biographies herein. It seems that each fact I uncovered sparked new questions, which led me to further research, more intriguing details, unforgettable facts, and patches of color that brought texture to the stories. I soon became consumed with the life particulars of these men and with so many discoveries about them.

Though the lives and accomplishments of these individuals span centuries and fields of endeavor, their remarkable stories underscore several common themes, important truths that affirm the power of black manhood:

Black men are builders.

Black men unify—and *are* unified.

Black men love to read.

Black men have ambitions, and the backbone to carry them out.

Black men are powerful public speakers.

Black men are charismatic.

Black men are smart.

Black men are skilled writers and effective communicators.

Black men are astute listeners.

Black men respect themselves and others.

Black men place family values in high regard.

Black men have good manners.

Black men are spiritual.

These virtues make for a hand-in-hand chain that is not only strong but significant. It is my hope that the qualities embodied in the stories of each *Hand in Hand* man will encourage young readers to build connections that will link them to their birthright of excellence.

—Andrea Davis Pinkney

His hands reached for the stars.

With the Big Dipper's cup
he scooped up
      the sky's mysterious ways.

Charted the moon, phase by phase.

Spent his days
marking the sun's steady climb.
      Astronomer ahead of his time.

Put his all into an almanac.

Helped abolitionists prove
      that being black

would not hold him back

from the Triple S genius he was:
      Scientist
      Scribe
      Surveyor of freedom

Snatched open the clouds of injustice
to let loose sweet rains of equality
that tumbled down in a torrent of words penned
      to Thomas Jefferson.

Socked it straight
to the secretary of state:

You declare one thing, but do another.
Owner of slaves, yet call me brother.

The pursuit of happiness encouraged his letter.

He wrote with a fury
until the sun set
on that threat

known as hypocrisy.

Benjamin Banneker

b. November 9, 1731, The British Colony of Maryland;
d. October 9, 1806, Baltimore County, Maryland

Surveyor of the Sky

———————

$\mathcal{B}$ENJAMIN BANNEKER WAS BORN under a lucky star. Came into this world a freeborn child, a blessing bestowed on few of his hue. In Colonial America, most black people were enslaved. But Benjamin's grandmother, Molly, was an indentured dairymaid from England who had obtained her freedom. Molly and Benjamin's mother, Mary, had both lived as free women in the colony of Maryland.

In 1730 Mary wed a former slave named Robert, a black man from West Africa. Robert had been granted his freedom by a master who let his slaves go if they agreed to become Christians. As soon as this offer was presented to Robert, he put his hand on the Holy Bible, said amen, thanked the good Lord, waved good-bye to his master, and gave freedom a hello hug.

Mary and Robert welcomed Benjamin a year after they married, in 1731. Then came Benjamin's three younger sisters: Minta, Molly, and a third little girl whose name is no longer known. The Banneker children had official papers that spelled out their freedom.

Mary and Robert saved enough money to buy a plot of land for growing tobacco. Their hundred-acre farm stood at the mouth of Maryland's Chesapeake Bay. The Bannekers named their place Stout, on account of their prosperous crops, and as a reflection of the hefty dose of love they had for each other and their children.

As soon as he could talk, Benjamin's grandma Molly started to teach him to read the only book she owned, the Bible. She also showed her grandson how to write. From the Bible, Benjamin learned everything from the begats to the Beatitudes. And by reciting all one hundred and fifty psalms, Benjamin discovered he could count.

Soon the boy knew numbers as well as he knew his name. For fun, he taught his sisters to count all ten fingers, every toe, and each of their new teeth.

Benjamin didn't have many friends his own age. His sisters were his only playmates. Because there weren't many other free blacks in America—and because Robert feared he could be thrown back into slavery—Benjamin, his sisters, and their parents tended to their land without much socializing.

They enjoyed their time together as a family. Working tobacco was no easy feat, but the Bannekers made the days go faster by singing as they worked.

In the spring it was Benjamin's job to pick slugs and bugs from the tobacco shoots. When August brought on days hotter than the hinges on the sun's front door, it was time for the tobacco harvest. Benjamin helped collect tobacco leaves, hang them to dry, then roll them into hogshead bundles.

These were big chores for a little kid. Benjamin turned his work into a game by telling his ma how many there were of anything worth counting—clouds, twigs, pigs, haystacks, horseshoes, beetles, blue jays. Soon Benjamin could add and subtract, and find the rhythms of arithmetic. Math was no chore for Benjamin. Numbers were fun. As Benjamin grew, so did his curiosity.

When the sun set each day, and stars pressed their diamond eyes through the curtain of the sky, Benjamin counted them, too. The beauty of those stars inspired Benjamin to wish, and to wonder:

When stars change their places in the sky each night, are they dancing while shining?

What makes the moon go from a ball of butter to an archer's bow, then leave the sky a blackened cape?

How does the sun know to rise each day, sit high at noon, and set at dusk?

These questions stayed with Benjamin. They were mysteries that he wanted to solve.

When Benjamin was grown, Mary and Robert let him run the family farm. He kept Stout going, building it into one of the heartiest tobacco enterprises along the Chesapeake Bay. By this time Benjamin enjoyed reading newspapers. Benjamin had taught himself geometry, algebra, and statistics. He was what nowadays we'd call a math-happy man. He even devised a plan for making tobacco farming more efficient by breaking the process into thirty-six steps.

Benjamin was a tinkerer, too. When a fence post or a hoe broke, he was quick to figure out how to fix it. If an oxcart wheel was missing a spoke, Benjamin did more than replace the wheel—he took all four wheels off the cart, constructed new ones with better traction, came up with a special design for the oxen's yoke, and trained the ox to step up his stride so the cart moved faster.

For most farmers, days were run by the rising and setting of the sun. Every waking moment was devoted to hauling, rinsing, rolling, and stacking tobacco leaves. When dawn broke, folks woke. When morning lit the day, farm chores were well under way. When the sun was highest in the sky, it was time for poached poultry, turnips, and collard greens—enough lunch to get through an afternoon of more hard work. As soon as dusk came, so did the stove's fire for baking an ash cake that would be served with molasses and milk before bed.

It occurred to Benjamin that his farm could function even more efficiently by putting the day's waking, hauling, rinsing, rolling, and baking on a clock's schedule. Clocks weren't common in the 1700s, especially for regular folks such as farmers. But Benjamin's way of approaching the world was far from regular. Though he had never seen a timepiece and didn't know how a clock worked, he set out to build one using wood pieces from Stout's timber shed. He borrowed a pocket watch, studied its innards, and got to work. This math-happy man drew clock plans, carved cogs, fashioned the clock's face and hands, and added a bell.

With just a few adjustments, Benjamin's clock worked perfectly. Its bell chimed at each hour. He could now wake before the dew even knew what to do. Or, though it wasn't likely, he could choose to sleep till noon.

Benjamin's clock was one of the few to be constructed in Colonial days. There were other clocks in big cities, but his was among the first to put farmers on a schedule that kept the rolling and wrapping of hogshead bundles running smoothly.

People from nearby farms heard about Benjamin's clock and came to see what to them looked like a magic box with a bell on top. No one knew it then, but that clock would keep accurate time for more than fifty years. And Benjamin's clock brought him and his parents new neighbors.

In 1771, the Ellicotts, a wealthy family, purchased seven hundred acres of land in a valley on the Patapsco River, not far from the Bannekers' farm. They spent many months building a gristmill on their property. One of the first things that caught Benjamin's attention was that the Ellicott family did not use slaves in any aspect of the mill's construction.

Benjamin also took great interest in the mill's complex structure and machinery that lifted and sifted grain. Over several years, he watched and waited as each phase of the mill's creation was completed. For the same reason he and his family had kept to themselves for so long, Benjamin didn't introduce himself to the Ellicotts—he didn't know if he could trust these white landowners. As Benjamin watched the mill's construction happen with the hands of white workers only, he and his father still had to be careful. Someone who didn't believe in freedom for black people could seek to destroy their papers, or bring harm to them.

It was the Ellicotts who made the first overture. John and Andrew III, the Ellicott brothers, wanted to develop the land surrounding their mill. They'd heard about the Bannekers' thriving tobacco crops and one day came to Benjamin's farm, asking to buy supplies that could help tame their acres. Benjamin's mother greeted them cautiously. John and Andrew III introduced themselves with warm smiles and open hearts. Mary Banneker learned they were Quakers, who, as part of their religious beliefs, shunned slavery. To the Ellicotts, the Bannekers were simply their neighbors. They didn't regard them as the "black Bannekers" or "the biracial Banneker family."

This was a big relief to the Bannekers, who gladly delivered farm supplies to the Ellicotts. As a neighborly gesture, Mary also brought them just-laid eggs, rhubarb pies, pails of milk still warm from her cows, and bread. These kept the workmen happy and well fed while they put the finishing touches on the mill.

George Ellicott, the son of Andrew III, was a math-happy man, just like Benjamin. His father put him in charge of surveying the Ellicott land for the purpose of building a road from the newly named Ellicott Mills to Baltimore.

Surveying was not easy. It involved making maps, plotting routes, and figuring out how a road could cut through wild brush. From his cabin window, Benjamin observed as George's road took shape. The project was going well. But Benjamin knew he could offer some good ideas for making the job proceed even more smoothly. Finally, Benjamin introduced himself to George. He shared his surveying ideas. The two men became instant friends. It was 1778.

Benjamin and George had a lot in common. They both liked measuring sticks, mechanical stuff, widgets, digits, and science. Benjamin showed George his clock and told him about the thirty-six steps he'd devised for tobacco farming.

George had a special interest in astronomy, the study of stars and planets. He didn't know anybody as passionate about this aspect of science until he met Benjamin. Soon, thanks to George, who eagerly kept giving astronomy tools to his new friend, every day seemed like Christmas to Benjamin!

First George arrived at Benjamin's cabin with a pedestal telescope. Then he brought a set of drafting instruments. Days later, George came to Benjamin's place holding a bundle of astronomy books, including *An Easy Introduction to Astronomy* and *Astronomy Explained upon Sir Isaac Newton's Principles,* both by James Ferguson, *A Compleat System of Astronomy* by Charles Leadbetter, and a set of lunar tables by Tobias Mayer. Benjamin and George started to study astronomy together. Using the tools he'd brought, George showed Benjamin how to pinpoint the position of the stars with careful numerical calculations.

They didn't get very far in fully mastering astronomy, though. George's father needed his son to devote more time to expanding the Ellicott enterprise. George was forced to get his head out of the stars and back on the road. That's when he brought his science buddy a gift that was big enough to wish him a Merry Christmas and Happy Birthday, combined.

George couldn't hoist this present on his shoulder. He needed workmen from his mill to help him make the delivery. Anybody who knew a thing or two about Mayer's lunar tables knew that a true astronomer *needed* a table to do his best work. George and his crew showed up with an oak worktable that looked as big as a bridge, once they got it inside Benjamin's modest cabin. The table fit perfectly at the windowsill, though. Its drop leaves kept the table contained when Benjamin wasn't using it, and expanded the table when Benjamin wanted to spread out his books, drafting instruments, and telescope. The table even had a drawer for holding his goose feather writing quills and a compass.

George promised Benjamin he'd be back soon and that the two of them would spend more time together figuring out James Ferguson's astronomy theories, interpreting Isaac Newton's know-how, unlocking Charles Leadbetter's lessons, and making sense out of Mayer's lunar tables. But Ellicott Mills was growing, and its development took up most of George's time. He had to travel frequently on business, so he was often away from home.

That telescope and those books were like horehound candy begging to be savored. After weeks of waiting for George, Benjamin was ready to burst. Though the tobacco farm kept him busy, Benjamin wanted to enjoy his gifts with his friend who shared the same love of science. He understood the importance of the Ellicott economy, but he was eager to learn. Finally he couldn't hold off for another minute. He cracked open one of the fattest books first—*An Easy Introduction to Astronomy.*

Benjamin pored over the pages of James Ferguson's book, taking in every detail he could. But there was nothing *easy* about this introduction. Mr. Ferguson was introducing how *hard* astronomy is. To understand even half the facts in all the books George had brought, a reader needed a brain stoked with double the kindling.

Benjamin read very carefully, taking one paragraph at a time, stopping to rub the strain from his eyes before continuing. The system of astronomy slowly started to come alive for Benjamin.

Tobias Mayer's book of lunar tables was the most complex of all the books. It showed readers how to locate star formations for every single day of the year. Mayer's lunar tables might as well have been the Bible, the very first book Benjamin learned to read. For Benjamin, those tables were gospel. They were the answer to Benjamin's prayers, and to the questions that had sparked up in him as a child. With Mr. Mayer's lunar tables and Mr. Leadbetter's *Compleat System of Astronomy*, Benjamin began to master the sky's mysteries. He learned the shapes and patterns of the constellations, when they formed, and how.

Benjamin was now math-happy and starstruck. With each of his books open on his table, he gave himself an assignment fitting for only the most accomplished astronomer. He set out to create a mathematical drawing of a solar eclipse, a rare phase of the planets when the sun, moon, and earth are lined up, one in front of the other, like three shiny coins. By reading his books, Benjamin learned that seeing a total solar eclipse in any one place is very rare. It only happens every three hundred and sixty years.

Benjamin carefully started drawing. He calculated. Consulted his books. Scribbled. Fell asleep at his worktable. Woke with numbers inked on his cheek from where he'd set down his head the night before.

He pulled his compass and ruler from his table's drawer.

Recalculated. Redrew. Slept some more.

When Benjamin checked his math, the calculations for an eclipse didn't add up properly. His drawing, known as a projection, did not compute correctly. Benjamin needed help, but George was still away on business.

Weeks passed. Benjamin lost sleep from dreaming about suns, moons, and rotating planets, spinning among a swirl of stars. Finally, his friend came back to town. George helped Benjamin find the errors in his calculations. As soon as Benjamin understood George's suggestions, he fiddled and fixed. The numbers came together properly. Benjamin's projection was now perfection!

This gave Benjamin great confidence in his abilities. Next he set an even greater task for himself—to create an almanac.

For farm families, an almanac was a book as important as the Bible. Its pages told folks when the sun would rise and set, which nights would shine with the moon's full face, and when a crescent moon would slice a scythe into the sky's black cape.

Farmers read their almanacs to know when spring would bring rain, which days would swelter with summer's hottest heat, when to expect autumn's chill to paint frost on trees, and how heavy winter's first snow would be.

This information helped farmers determine when to seed their soil, when to plow and harvest. It let them know when they'd have to pray for rain, or when they would be thanking the Almighty for sunshine after weeks of wet weather. To anyone raising livestock, almanacs gave pointers on hog habits and cow manners. Every almanac came with a calendar, showing holy days and festivals.

Like the Bible, some folks consulted their almanacs each morning for a daily dose of guidance. The best almanacs were packed with so many facts that readers could find answers to questions that helped them plan the daily doings of their lives and the months ahead.

Not all almanacs were the same, though. Some were more complete than others. Benjamin wanted his almanac to be the best. Having spent his whole life on a farm, Benjamin knew the important information needed for growing crops and raising critters. And with his careful attention to astronomy, Benjamin's calculations for the moon's phases and the stars' patterns were precise.

Benjamin devoted most of 1789 to plotting lunar cycles and star formations, noting each day's weather, and observing his farm's animals. He filled his almanac with everything that was essential to a farmer's success.

With a new year coming soon, Benjamin was eager to get his almanac printed for 1790. He sent his manuscript to several publishers, who each had the same reply—*no thanks, Mr. Banneker.*

Though Benjamin had triple-checked his calculations to make sure his almanac was free of errors, the publishers he contacted didn't fully trust the abilities of someone they considered an amateur. They weren't willing to take a chance on Benjamin.

Benjamin's faith in himself and his almanac was as black as a midnight sky with no moon.

But sometimes stars hide in the sky and then reveal themselves when someone needs to make a wish. This happened to Benjamin. Just as he was about to give up hope of ever getting his almanac published, a tiny diamond of hope pierced the dark.

In the final months of 1790, James Pemberton got word about Benjamin Banneker and his almanac. James was president of the Pennsylvania Society for the Abolition of Slavery, a group of people who believed black men and women deserved to be treated the same as white citizens.

To James and other antislave crusaders, Benjamin's almanac was a freedom flag. They waved Benjamin's manuscript high in the air so that pro-slavers throughout Maryland had no choice but to notice. Benjamin's accomplishment showed that to uphold slavery was to oppress black men and women whose talents were equal to, or superior to, any white person's. The almanac, a heavy bundle of pages, was a weighty statement on a black man's capabilities. Whether slave owners bothered to read it or not, Benjamin's book was as hard-hitting as a brick slammed in the face of injustice.

Benjamin's supporters were loud in their endorsements but too late to make a difference. It was now December 1790. There wasn't enough time to publish Benjamin's almanac for 1791. But Benjamin had gained such encouragement from his new abolitionist friends that he never stopped wishing on what had now become a sky filled with glittery constellations.

As he got busy calculating and note-taking for an almanac that he hoped would be published in 1792, a new opportunity came his way in February 1791. President George Washington identified a portion of Maryland and a section of land from the commonwealth of Virginia to be sectioned together to create a new capital of the United States. The president needed an expert surveyor to lay out this federal territory. George Washington chose Major Andrew Ellicott IV to do the job. Major Andrew needed a survey assistant. He'd become acquainted with Benjamin through the Ellicotts' family friendship with the Bannekers. There was no doubt in the major's mind that Benjamin was the perfect person to assist him.

To help the surveyors mark straight boundaries on the ground, they needed to chart the stars' locations in the sky. At the survey site, Major Andrew IV put Benjamin in charge of monitoring the astronomical clock, an instrument that let the surveyors know the exact time each survey of the sky's stars took place. This made math-happy Benjamin even happier. But he was eager to return to the creation of his new almanac. After leaving the survey, Benjamin went back to watching the moon go from a waxing gibbous to a full ball of light, from a waning gibbous, to a new black night.

While he worked by candlelight, using his astronomy tools, Benjamin got to thinking about the surveying he'd done for the nation's capital. He also considered what his new almanac would mean, once he'd secured publication for it. As the first black man to work on behalf of the president on a survey for a federal district, and as the only black person to accomplish the creation of an almanac, Benjamin knew he'd be met with a range of reactions. He'd be scrutinized and criticized by some, applauded and praised by others. No matter what anyone else said or did, Benjamin knew in his heart that he'd done well in completing two important jobs.

Benjamin wondered, though, if through these actions he'd really done enough on behalf of black people. With any luck, his almanac would be on bookshelves throughout Maryland and the surrounding states. But in those same places black Americans were enslaved. They were being forced to dust the spines on all kinds of volumes—including almanacs—that they couldn't read, because nobody had taught them how, and because it was illegal for enslaved black people to learn letters or numbers. And though Benjamin was born free, his own father had been a slave.

Benjamin had the ability to monitor a clock that helped lay the land for America's seat of government. And he had the skills to calculate an astronomy table to its teeniest tenth. But as brilliant as Benjamin was, he could not solve the huge problem of slavery. How, he wondered, would this new federal territory and his almanac serve to free his people?

Benjamin finished writing his almanac's manuscript in the summer of 1791. On the evening of August 19, Benjamin got started on another important bit of writing. With crickets chirping outside his cabin's windows, Benjamin sat at his large worktable and penned a letter to Secretary of State Thomas Jefferson. Benjamin's quill did not quaver. He wrote with a steady hand. The letter began:

Maryland, Baltimore County,
Near Ellicott's Lower Mills August 19, 1791.
Thomas Jefferson, Secretary of State

Sir, I am fully sensible of the greatness of that freedom,
which I take with you on the present occasion; a liberty
which seemed to me scarcely allowable, when I reflected
on the distinguished and dignified station in which
you Stand, and the almost general prejudice and
prepossession, which is so prevalent in the world against
those of my complexion.

Benjamin was telling Thomas Jefferson that he was a great man with a big responsibility. In 1776, Jefferson had written the Declaration of Independence, one of the most important documents in the creation of America, which said "all men are created equal" and that every person was entitled to "life, liberty, and the pursuit of happiness."

But the secretary of state did not live according to the promises he set forth in the Declaration. Jefferson owned slaves. The men and women who he counted as his property were equal as human beings, but as enslaved individuals, they were not afforded equality. And Lord knows, Thomas Jefferson's slaves—or anyone who was enslaved—sure didn't have liberty, or the freedom to pursue happiness. Because of slavery, black boys and girls who were born with intelligence and creativity couldn't learn to read, or do math. They would not have the chance to become scientists or writers, or, as Benjamin had done, enjoy the pursuit of their full abilities, as long as slavery kept them down.

In Benjamin's eyes, Jefferson was a hypocrite. He had signed his name to the Declaration, thus giving an oath to his intentions, but he was not living up to what he affirmed to be true.

Benjamin wrote and wrote and wrote. He reminded Jefferson that white people had once been oppressed by the British during the American Revolution. Now Jefferson was doing the same thing by participating in the practice of slavery. Benjamin's letter prodded the secretary of state to remember that not so long ago, he was living under unfair rule, and that at that time, when he himself was a victim of oppression, there was no doubt in his mind that this was unfair. Yet, here he was, turning tyranny onto black Americans.

Benjamin wrote:

> *Sir, how pitiable it is to reflect, that although you were so fully convinced of . . . equal and impartial distribution of these rights and privileges . . . you . . . at the same time [are] . . . detaining by fraud and violence so numerous a part of my brethren, under groaning captivity and cruel oppression, that you should at the same time be found guilty of that most criminal act, which you professedly detested in others, with respect to yourselves.*

As Benjamin prepared his letter to send, he enclosed a copy of the manuscript for his almanac.

Jefferson responded to Benjamin right away. He agreed with Benjamin, writing that black people have talents and abilities equal to that of whites, and that because of slavery they cannot fully realize these. His letter said:

Philadelphia, Aug, 30, 1791.

Sir, I Thank you sincerely for your letter of the 19ᵗʰ
instant and for the Almanac it contained. No body wishes
more than I do, to see such proofs as you exhibit, that
nature has given to our black brethren talents equal to
those of the other colors of men; and that the appearance of
the want of them, is owing merely to the degraded condition
of their existence . . .

Jefferson referred to black men as *brethren*—brothers. But Benjamin's letter begged the question, *What kind of brother enslaves another?*

Jefferson also wrote that he hoped someday an institution such as slavery that demeans people would not exist, and that black men, women, and children would have the opportunity to live up to their fullest potential:

I can add with truth, that no body wishes more ardently
to see a good system commenced, for raising the condition,
both of their body & mind, to what it ought to be, as far
as the imbecility of their present existence, and other
circumstances, which cannot be neglected, will admit.

Benjamin read Jefferson's letter again and again. It had been near to a miracle that a government official had written to a black man with such enthusiasm. Benjamin was pleased.

It seemed there were many powerful letters being sent and received in the summer and fall of 1791. While Benjamin was corresponding with Jefferson, James Pemberton kept up his pursuit of finding a publisher for Benjamin's almanac. He wrote to publisher William Goddard on Benjamin's behalf. James's letter told Goddard that he'd had the great pleasure of receiving the manuscript for an almanac written by the "Astronomical Genius of Benj. Banniker a Black man . . ."

James urged William to read Benjamin's almanac, and to publish it.

In addition to being a passionate abolitionist, James was a smart negotiator. In his letter, he made it clear to William that Benjamin deserved to be paid a good sum for the time and hard work he'd put into creating his almanac.

William wrote back saying, "I am heartily disposed not only to be just, but generous to . . . Benjamin."

The Pennsylvania, Delaware, Maryland, and Virginia Almanac for the Year 1792 by Benjamin Banneker was the talk of the town in December 1791, when it went on sale.

William Goddard, a smart businessman, knew he had invested in a good thing. He produced an enticing advertisement for the book, billing it as "BENJAMIN BANNEKER'S highly Approved ALMANAC."

The ad was true. That almanac was not only "highly approved"—it also proved highly that a black author's work was worthy. James McHenry, a senator from Maryland and antislavery activist, wrote an introduction for the almanac. This also sparked great buzz about Benjamin's book. In his introduction, James declared that the system of racial prejudice "must be relinquished."

The preface of Benjamin's almanac also underscored how special it was, and how powerful its creation by a black man. The almanac's editors wrote that they were "gratified" to publish "an extraordinary effort of Genius . . . by a sable Descendent of Africa" whose "specimen of Ingenuity" demonstrated that "mental Powers and Endowments are not the exclusive Excellence of white People . . ."

With these endorsements, Benjamin's book sold out right away. Aside from being the first by a black author, *The Pennsylvania, Delaware, Maryland, and Virginia Almanac for the Year 1792* was like no other book of its kind.

It included Benjamin's unique approach to stargazing and calculating phases of the moon. The almanac was such a hot seller that it created an immediate demand for a second edition for the following year.

Benjamin's 1793 almanac was as distinctive as his first. It contained an added bonus: Benjamin's letter to Thomas Jefferson and the secretary of state's reply.

With such interesting reading material included alongside his astronomy projections, folks specifically requested Benjamin's book. When

a farmer went to the local mercantile looking for an almanac, he made a simple request: "Give me the one by Banneker!"

At the same time that Benjamin's second almanac was published, the newly developed land he had helped survey years before was completed on January 1, 1793. It became the District of Columbia, or Washington, D.C.

Benjamin published an almanac every year until 1797, when he was sixty-six years old. His health was declining, and so were the sales of his almanac. Since Benjamin was no longer well enough to manage his farm, he rented portions of his land to neighbors for growing their own crops.

Slavery continued for sixty-six years after that. Thomas Jefferson never relinquished the practice of slavery for himself. But Benjamin Banneker had forced the secretary of state to examine his own conscience. Also, Benjamin's intellect and steadfast nature showed America that black men and women are indeed created equal.

Though Benjamin didn't live to see slavery's end, his deep desire for freedom was a dream that did come true for African Americans. It was a miracle brought about by many earnest souls wishing on heaven's brightest stars.

His hands, big as hams,

struck a blow
to slavery's ugly face.

    Fought
    by being self-taught:

Reader
Writer
Speaker
Seeker

In abolition's army
he led the charge to freedom.

Runaway slave
who escaped to the pages
of his own life-story:

Autobiography of My Colored Soul
        Beaten Red,
            Black,
               and Blue
                   by the White Whip's Lash

Oh, his oration!
Oh, his cadence!

Lion-tree leader,
told his tale with a roar.

Held all who listened in his mighty palm.

Inspired a nation divided
to believe in Emancipation's

                     promise.

Frederick Douglass

b. February 14, 1817 or 1818 (exact date unknown),
Talbot County, Maryland;
d. February 20, 1895, Washington, D.C.

Capital Orator

———❖———

*L*ATE ONE NIGHT, WHEN the moon was full of milk, and the sky was as black as molasses, a boy-child was born on the Holme Hill Farm near Chesapeake Bay, Maryland. His mama named him Frederick Augustus Washington Bailey. Frederick came from two worlds. His father was the color of that moon. His mother, Harriet, was as dark and as beautiful as that sky.

The baby was his mother's special Valentine's Day gift. And though she loved him with her whole heart, she could not stay with him. She was forced to work far from her child. That was the way of slavery. When the master said *Wake*, you woke. When the master said *Work*, you worked. And if working meant leaving those you love, you did it. Even if it broke your heart.

Frederick's mama died when he was seven years old. Though he'd known her only a short time, her love stayed with him.

Frederick never knew his father. He was sent to live with his grandmother until he was eight years old. Then Grandma Betsey took the boy to the Lloyd Plantation in Maryland, located miles from Holme Hill Farm. The plantation owner made Grandma Betsey leave without Frederick. He wanted Frederick to stay on his farm and work as his slave. Grandma Betsey had no choice in this. She couldn't even say good-bye to her own grandson. When Frederick realized what had happened, something changed within him. He now understood what slavery meant—that one person ruled over another. Right then, Frederick made a promise to himself. It was a promise to help end slavery.

Not long after his grandmother left, Frederick was sent to live in Baltimore, Maryland, at the home of Hugh and Sophia Auld, where he worked as a houseboy. Sophia embraced Frederick as if he were her own child. She taught him to read by showing him her Bible. And, oh, did that boy love letters. To him, they were like tiny dancers playing on paper— *P*'s, *B*'s, *U*'s, and *Q*'s.

Sophia loved watching Frederick learn. All those *P*'s, *B*'s, *U*'s, and *Q*'s spelled out joy to both of them. Sophia was a gifted teacher, and Frederick was an eager student.

When Sophia shared this good news with her husband, Master Hugh Auld, he stomped all over those *P*'s, *B*'s, *U*'s, and *Q*'s. He put a quick stop to Frederick's lessons. It was a crime for slaves to learn letters. But it wasn't the law that worried Master Hugh most. It was Frederick's desire. He hollered at Sophia. He told her reading would spoil Frederick and make him "forever unfit to be a slave." Hugh said Frederick should know nothing but the will of his master, and learn to obey it. He said reading would make Frederick want to "run away with himself."

Hugh's anger frightened Sophia. She stopped Frederick's reading lessons. She turned her back on Frederick. She slammed the door on their joy. Sophia Auld had become a slave to slavery.

Frederick learned a great lesson that day. Master Hugh's anger taught him that reading was powerful. If others believed that knowledge made him unfit to be a slave, he would work hard to get as much of it as he could.

While working for the Aulds, Frederick earned a little money doing errands at Master Auld's shipyard. With fifty cents, he bought a book called *The Columbian Orator*, a collection of speeches about liberty. In that book, there was a conversation between a master and his slave about slavery. The master told the slave why slavery was essential. In the story, the slave spoke as smooth as the finest silk when he told the master why slaves deserved to be free.

Frederick had to read secretly. At night he used *The Columbian Orator* and other books to teach himself. Frederick's only light was the moon, which poured its white-white onto the pages of Frederick's books. Over time, Frederick's knowledge grew.

Reading gave Frederick many ideas about freedom. He saw freedom all around him. The trees were free. The fireflies were free. So was the breeze that carried bugs and leaves. Even the master's chickens were free to roam as they pleased. But slavery still had a hold on Frederick. *He* was *not* free.

Not long after Frederick learned to read, the Auld family divided their slaves among households. In 1834, Frederick was sent to live in Talbot County, Maryland, with Captain Thomas Auld, one of the meanest Auld brothers.

When Master Thomas said *Work*, Frederick worked. But to the master's way of thinking, Frederick was not working hard enough.

There was no pleasing Master Thomas.

To make matters worse, Frederick began to let Master Thomas's horse run off to a nearby farm. Frederick wanted the horse to be free. He wanted the horse to be able to play in a pasture. Frederick often followed the horse, and they frolicked in the field together.

This enraged Master Thomas, who whipped Frederick several times

for taking these liberties. That didn't stop Frederick. He continued to let that horse roam.

Master Thomas had had enough. He worried that he couldn't control Frederick, so he sent Frederick to live with Edward Covey, a "slave-breaker." It was Covey's job to make Frederick more obedient by wearing him down. And Covey . . . whew! He was *evil*.

He stood over Frederick while he worked. He made him chop wood till his back was about to break. When Frederick stopped to take a rest, Covey smacked him with a branch. During his first week on the Covey farm, Frederick let Covey's team of oxen run wild. Covey beat Frederick hard for this.

As the months passed, Covey did all he could to "break" Frederick. He kicked him. He punched him. He tied him to a tree and whipped him. This went on for almost a year. Covey's cruelty was starting to work on Frederick. Frederick was beginning to break, but he was determined to withstand Covey's abuse.

Though Frederick had been beaten, he stayed strong. When Master Covey came at Frederick again, Frederick refused to back down. Now *he* was the one punching and kicking. Frederick and Covey fought for hours, until Covey finally gave up. Frederick had broken the slave-breaker!

Frederick was still enslaved, but now he was free of fear. He knew that he could survive the harshest treatment ever. Through this experience, Frederick changed from a boy to a man.

Four years had passed. Master Thomas sent Frederick back to Hugh and Sophia Auld in Baltimore. Frederick met a free black woman named Anna. Frederick wanted to marry Anna but would not propose to her until he was free.

Now Frederick was more determined than ever to gain his freedom. By escaping to the North, where black people were not enslaved, Frederick could be free. He borrowed money to buy a train ticket from Baltimore to Philadelphia, Pennsylvania.

One of Frederick's friends let Frederick use his "sailor's protection"—a paper that said he was a free seaman. Frederick dressed as a sailor and got on the train. He worried the whole way. If he was caught, he would be killed. He did not fit the description on the paper. And his sailor clothes didn't fit right, either. But Frederick was fit to flee. After all that he had endured, he was ready to run.

A true blessing smiled on Frederick that day. The train's conductor didn't even check his papers. He hardly noticed Frederick. There were even passengers on the train who recognized Frederick, but they kept quiet when they saw him.

As the train sped through the slave state of Delaware, Frederick's heart raced, too. At Wilmington, Delaware, Frederick boarded a steamboat for Philadelphia. Then, that night, Frederick took another train to New York City. He traveled all night. He didn't sleep. There was too much excitement leaping up in him.

It was a ride he would never forget. From the window of the train, Frederick watched the sky and the moon. As the white in that moon tucked its face deep into the black pocket of the sky, Frederick traveled northward to freedom. It was September 4, 1838.

To make sure no one from his past would find him, Frederick changed his name to Frederick Augustus Douglass.

Frederick sent for Anna. She came to New York. They married, and over time had five children, three boys and two girls.

Frederick was eager to help other enslaved people. In August 1841, Frederick attended a convention of the Massachusetts Anti-Slavery Society. The event was held on Nantucket Island, in Massachusetts.

It seemed like the hottest day ever on Nantucket. There were nearly a thousand people crammed into that room. They were abolitionists, men and women who believed slavery was wrong and fought to end it.

Frederick stood quietly at the back of the meeting hall. He was ready to listen. But when someone found out he was there, folks urged him to address the group. Some had heard Frederick preach at a nearby church. They knew that he could deliver a speech like nobody else. They wanted to hear the story of his life in slavery.

Frederick was apprehensive, but the crowd encouraged him.

Even though Frederick was six feet tall and strong, he was nervous in front of so many strangers. But he remembered the promise he'd made to himself when he was a child—the promise to help end slavery. He could now do this by telling his story.

When Frederick stepped to the platform, his knees wobbled. His shoulders trembled. So did his size-fourteen feet.

As scared as Frederick was, he spoke with conviction. He told the people about Master Hugh Auld forbidding him to read, and about the cruelty he'd suffered with Edward Covey.

Every person in that place listened closely to Frederick. The room was quieter than the air itself. No one wanted to miss a word. When Frederick finished, the crowd clapped and cheered. Some people even cried. Many had never heard a former slave tell of his experiences. Of course they knew that slavery was wrong, but hearing Frederick tell his story so clearly reinforced how terrible slavery was.

Those listening loved Frederick's speech, but it filled them with hatred. After hearing Frederick, they hated slavery more than ever. When leaders of the Massachusetts Anti-Slavery Society asked Frederick to join their group, he immediately agreed to become a member.

He traveled to cities and towns, to farms and churches, telling people about his life in slavery. He no longer trembled when he spoke. He delivered his words with power. When he preached, it was as if thunder was stomping its feet. Many times those who listened rose to *their* feet to support Frederick.

Not everyone welcomed Frederick's oratory, though. In some places he was booed, shooed, and pushed off the podium. But no one could deny Frederick's reputation. With his mane of hair and mighty delivery, folks called him a "lion-tree" of a man. Others said he was a "colored king." Some named him "the capital orator."

By speaking so openly about his life, Frederick was risking great danger. If one of his former masters tracked him down, he would surely be killed or forced back into slavery.

Despite the risk involved, Frederick wanted to spread his message by setting it to parchment. In 1845, Frederick wrote his life story. He didn't shy back from any of the facts. He put it all down. He named his past masters and their plantations. He detailed his escape, his preaching, and his whereabouts. He let his pen loose, with the whole who's who. It was more than a story. It was a sermon in script. It told of the spirit's ability to overcome the worst.

When Frederick was done, he showed his writing to his abolitionist friends. He was proud of his work. He had written nearly five hundred pages! But his antislavery friends frowned. One told Frederick to throw his manuscript into the river. Another said, "Burn it quick!"

They were sure that once Frederick's autobiography was released, every Southern slave catcher in the land would be after him. But Frederick refused to destroy his writing. He gathered his pages and made them into a book entitled *Narrative of the Life of Frederick Douglass, an American Slave.*

Frederick's book was published in May 1845. It became a sensation! People from as far away as Europe purchased the book. To make sure he would be safe in his freedom, Frederick traveled to England, where slave catchers couldn't get him. According to British law, all men and women living on British land were free.

Frederick traveled to England and Ireland, sharing his story and explaining America's slave system. The people were outraged by what they heard. Like Frederick's followers in the United States, they made a pledge to speak out against slavery.

Although he had the support of the British, Frederick was eager to return home. There were still so many enslaved people in the United States. Frederick wanted to help them. Unfortunately, slave catchers would be waiting for him as soon as he stepped back onto American soil.

But good luck was with Frederick.

Before he returned to America, two friends he'd met in England raised enough money to buy Frederick's freedom. They sent $710.96 to the Auld family. That's how much Frederick was worth to the Aulds. Even though he had written a book that had sold vibrantly. Even though he was a respected speaker and leader. To the Aulds, Frederick was property.

That was the way of slavery. A man was not a man. He was an object that could be purchased, same as a bridle or an ax.

On December 5, 1846, the Auld family signed the papers that declared Frederick Douglass truly free. No matter where Frederick went, blood-hounds could no longer be ordered to sniff him out. No slave-breaker could try to destroy him. And he would never be forced to address another man as his master.

In the spring of 1847, Frederick returned to America, ready to celebrate his freedom through teaching, preaching, and writing. He settled in Rochester, New York.

On December 3, 1847, Frederick began publication of *The North Star*, a weekly antislavery newspaper. Part of the paper's motto was: "Truth is of no color." And, truth be told, men and women of *every* color read that paper.

On April 12, 1861, the Civil War began. Oh, that war. So much fighting. So much fire. So much dying. It was a war between the states. It was a war about everybody wanting their own way.

The Southern states, called the Confederacy, wanted to keep slavery alive. The Northern states, known as the Union, wanted to see slavery die. The United States was divided. Each side fought viciously for their cause.

Frederick knew that if slavery continued, America's states would not stay united. Now, more than ever, slavery had to end.

As the war raged on, Frederick waged his own battle. In his lion-tree speeches, he insisted on the absolute, immediate end of slavery. When he wrote articles, his quill pressed hard on paper. There was one word he used again and again in his writings: Freedom.

On January 1, 1863, those words came true. President Abraham Lincoln issued the Emancipation Proclamation, a document that called for the freedom of all slaves in the Confederate states.

Frederick was in Boston on the night the proclamation was read. He waited with thousands of people who had packed Tremont Temple. Frederick wrote about that special night: "We were waiting and listening as for a bolt from the sky . . . we were watching . . . by the dim light of the stars for the dawn of a new day . . . we were longing for the answer to the agonizing prayers of centuries."

It was inching on to midnight when a messenger shouted the good news. "It is coming! It is on the wires!" Lincoln's pronouncement came on a telegram. It said, ". . . I do order and declare that all persons held as slaves . . . are, and henceforward shall be, free. . . ."

Whoops and yahoos filled the temple. It was a night of jubilation. Even Frederick Douglass, stately as he was, let his tears run free. He had kept his promise to himself. Through courage, determination, and work, he had helped end slavery. He had fought hard for a new day. And now the day had come.

Frederick called January 1, 1863, "a new and glorious era in the history of American liberty." As soon as the Emancipation Proclamation was official, black people packed their croaker sacks and marched off their masters' plantations with their heads held high. No good-bye. Not even a glance behind.

The Civil War kept on. African Americans were free, but they still faced discrimination. Black men were not allowed to fight in the war. Frederick was certain that the North could win if African American men joined the Union army.

He demanded that black men be permitted to fight as soldiers. He appealed to the government. Through his writings, he told them ". . . this is no time to fight only with your white hand and allow your black hand to remain tied. . . ."

Soon after the Emancipation Proclamation, Congress authorized black men to join the Union army. The first black unit of soldiers was the Massachusetts 54th Regiment. When the governor of Massachusetts asked Frederick to help recruit black soldiers, Frederick got right to work.

He went straight to his desk in Rochester, and wrote with a roar. His article was entitled "Men of Color, to Arms!" It said, "A war . . . carried on for the . . . enslavement of colored men, calls . . . loudly for colored men to help suppress it."

He implored black men to "go quickly and help fill up the first colored regiment from the North."

Frederick wrote and wrote. He told African Americans, "This is our golden opportunity." Two of Frederick's sons, Lewis and Charles, went to the army office and signed up. They were followed by their brother, Frederick Jr., and thousands of black men who went to war eagerly so that they could fight for equality.

But the war's "golden opportunity" soon lost its shine for black soldiers. They were paid half the money white soldiers received. Nobody gave them proper combat training. They had to fight with broken weapons. They could not become officers. Worst of all, when black soldiers were captured by Confederate troops, they were killed.

These injustices angered Frederick. He asked to meet with President Lincoln so that he could enlist the president's help. In August 1863, Frederick Douglass and Abraham Lincoln met for the first time.

When Frederick arrived at the Executive Mansion, there was a long line of men waiting to petition the president. Frederick was the only black man there. He brought a good book to read. He thought he would have to wait all day long. But Frederick never even opened his book. After two minutes, one of President Lincoln's aides called him in.

President Lincoln stood up as soon as Frederick entered the room. He said, "Mr. Douglass, I know you; I have read about you. Sit down, I am glad to see you."

When Frederick told the president about the treatment of black soldiers, the president listened carefully. He promised Frederick that black soldiers would receive the same pay as white soldiers. He assured

Frederick that he would quickly sign any recommendation made by the secretary of war to promote black soldiers to officers. And the president explained an order that he had already signed that aimed to prevent Confederates from killing black soldiers.

Frederick was impressed by Lincoln's sincerity. He later wrote, "In his company I was never . . . reminded of my humble origin, or my unpopular color." Frederick felt that Abraham Lincoln was someone he could "love, honor, and trust, without reserve or doubt."

Abraham Lincoln felt the same way about Frederick. After their meeting, he told a friend that Frederick Douglass was "one of the most meritorious men . . . in the United States."

In August 1864, Abraham Lincoln asked to see Frederick Douglass again. The president was worried that the North wouldn't win the war. He feared that to end the war, he would have to sign an agreement with the Confederacy to promise that slavery could continue. The president

was very tired. But he wanted to be re-elected in 1864 so that he could continue trying to gain peace and bring the nation together.

He asked Frederick to come up with a plan for safely leading black people out of the South if the Union were to lose the war. Frederick saw that the president cared deeply about preserving freedom. He wanted the president to win re-election.

Frederick came up with a plan right away. But when Union troops won victories, first in Atlanta, then in Savannah, Georgia, Frederick's plan wasn't needed. With the North in a strong position, Abraham Lincoln won the presidential election of 1864.

Frederick met with the president for a third time in March 1865. He had come to Washington, D.C., to hear Lincoln's second inaugural address. Frederick was proud to be "a man among men" at the inauguration.

After Lincoln's speech, Frederick went to the Executive Mansion to attend the celebration reception. He was dressed in his finest clothes—waistcoat, cravat, starched shirt, and shined shoes. His hair was a swell of cotton, a halo that made him stand out in the crowd.

When Frederick stepped up to the door of the president's home—a door he had entered twice before—he was immediately stopped by guards. He told the guards there must be a mistake. He knew the president would let him in. The guards shook their heads. Frederick asked them to tell Mr. Lincoln that he was there. As soon as the president found out that Frederick was being held at the door, he told the guards to escort him inside.

Abraham Lincoln was not much for smiling, but he smiled as soon as Frederick entered the East Room. "Here comes my friend," Lincoln said. He shook Frederick's hand. "I am glad to see you." The president asked Frederick how he liked his inaugural address. He said, "There is no man in the country whose opinion I value more than yours."

Frederick pressed his hand to the president's shoulder. "Mr. Lincoln," he said, "that was a sacred effort."

On April 9, 1865, the Civil War ended when Confederate forces surrendered to the Union at the Appomattox Court House in Virginia.

A week later, Frederick received terrible news at his home in Rochester, New York. President Abraham Lincoln had been shot and killed. This was a sad day for Frederick, but he was grateful for all that he and the president had accomplished together. Although his good friend was gone, Frederick soldiered on. He continued to champion voting and citizenship rights for all people and became a pioneer for women's rights.

Through determination and dignity, Frederick Douglass had carried the message of freedom to many. Some say he was the most famous black man of the nineteenth century. He was certainly one of the most influential black leaders of his time.

He was a lion-tree of a man.

A colored king.

The capital orator.

Frederick Augustus Douglass.

His hands dug

Up from Slavery.

Yanked the weeds
sprouted from seeds
sewn on the Civil War's battleground:

Once emancipated, stay enslaved to common labor.

But this grassroots griot
fed his people the true story.

He believed black men and women could rise
by starting down on their knees
to build, brick by brick,
the foundation for a school
to call their own.

Tuskegee —
the all-black Institute for an "industrial education."

A kind of learning that comes
with Grade-A elbow grease
to teach
its lessons.

Eager Educator.
The "Great Accommodator."

Preached the Gospel According to Booker T.:

To achieve racial harmony
Black people should take pride
in skilled service-work

rendered with the utmost dignity.

Booker T. Washington

———◆———

b. April 5, 1856, Hales Ford, Virginia;
d. November 14, 1915, Tuskegee, Alabama

Polished Pioneer

❖

*F*OLKS PREDICTED RAIN ON the day Booker T. Washington was born. But the sky was as clear as a mirror, inviting spring to reflect its beauty over the wooded acre where Booker's log cabin stood.

When Booker's mother, Jane, took a first look at her child, she saw determination in his gray-green eyes. Though her son had been born into slavery, she prayed the boy would someday be free.

Booker never knew his father. The townspeople suspected he was a white man, because of Booker's light eyes and hair the color of a cinnamon stick.

Booker and Jane were the property of James and Elizabeth Burroughs, slave owners who treated Booker, his older brother, John, and his younger sister, Amanda, with as much kindness as one who owned another could. Still, Booker and his family were among the Burroughs's possessions, in the same way Elizabeth's teakettle and James's hoe were among the items they had purchased and could sell if they chose.

James was a tobacco farmer. He may not have been the richest man in Franklin County, but he and his wife and their daughters lived comfortably. It was easy for the Burroughs family to rest after a long day. They had Booker, his mother, and other slaves to pick and roll the tobacco leaves, haul the haycocks, shine the brass and silver, bust wood, and cook.

As a little boy, it was Booker's job to fan the flies from the table at mealtimes, while James and Elizabeth and their daughters enjoyed corn cakes in the morning, salted fish in the afternoon, and roasted sweet potatoes before bed. Booker got to be so good at swatting, that flies, mosquitoes, and all the other wingy bugs started to fear his fast little hand.

Booker's mother worked harder than hard as the plantation cook. She shucked corn, defeathered poultry, hoisted iron pots and pans, and spent most of her days sweating by the fire as the meals she prepared boiled and baked on top of hot coals. The Virginia heat didn't help. One of the worst parts was peeling onions. The sharp smell rising off them made Jane cry. But really, it was the sad reality of slavery that yanked the tears from her eyes. She wanted a better life for herself and her children. And she wanted to be free from the horrors of being enslaved.

When Booker was four, his mother married Washington Ferguson, a slave from a nearby plantation. It was illegal for slaves to marry officially, so to seal their love, Jane and Washington jumped the broom, a tradition used during slavery to acknowledge a couple's lifelong commitment to each other. They were not allowed to live together. Washington's master was very mean. He wouldn't even let Washington see Jane. Washington had to sneak away from his plantation to visit his wife in secret. As a young boy, Booker hardly knew his stepfather.

At night, when Jane returned to the slave quarters after a long day of preparing food for the Burroughs family and cleaning up after them, she was glad to be with her sons and daughter. Though she was more tired than a wrung-out dishcloth, she always managed to spend special time with Booker, John, and Amanda, telling them about her day, teaching them prayers and spirituals.

Even with his mother's comforting ways, Booker sometimes tossed and turned before sleeping at night. He and his family lived in a tiny ramshackle cabin. They slept on smelly grain sacks. To make it worse, their stomachs often growled at night from hunger. It was not easy for Booker to have sweet dreams when all he'd eaten was gruel left over from the slop that had been fed to Master Burroughs's hogs earlier that day.

Booker's fly-swatting hand grew strong. When his fingers were big enough to hold James's hoe, Master Burroughs sent him to the fields to work. Booker's little sister, Amanda, took her place as the child who was the family bug-shooer at Master Burroughs's dining table.

Booker's chores now included hauling heavy buckets of water to the hog troughs, feeding those critters (with the same slop he would be eating for dinner), then taking the remaining water to the men working in the fields. When the sun rose each morning, Booker watched Master Burroughs's daughters leave for the town schoolhouse. During the afternoons, when he only had strength enough to yawn, Booker saw the Burroughs girls return home with their schoolbooks and giggles. One day, Master Burroughs gave Booker a new job—carrying his daughters' books to school for them. Booker bid good riddance to the water buckets and farm hogs, and took up bundles of schoolbooks in both arms. As soon as the girls entered the schoolhouse, Booker found himself a crate, stepped up, and peeked inside the school's tiny window.

The voices of the students reciting their lessons filled Booker's ears like music. Not even a church choir sounded as sweet as the rhythms of boys and girls reciting the alphabet, counting together, reading poetry. When Booker remembered this years later, he said being allowed inside the schoolhouse to study and learn would have been "about the same as getting into paradise."

But for enslaved children, paradise was as far off as the highest cloud. Teaching slaves to read or write was illegal. Booker's mother wanted her children to be educated, but it was too dangerous. They could be sold away from her if it was discovered that they knew letters. Jane warned Booker many times: his job was to *carry* schoolbooks, not *care* about them. And she told him that he was never to look too closely at the schoolbooks. Like the flies he had once swatted, he was to chase away any thoughts of wanting to read. If by chance he came to recognize a letter—or worse, a word—as the result of hearing the white kids in school or opening a book, he was to fling it away immediately.

Booker was now nearly six years old, and getting a mind of his own. He didn't want to disobey his mother, but every time he gathered schoolbooks for carrying, or came near the schoolhouse, he was tempted to look, listen, and learn. It was like a breeze on a hot-as-blazes day. Booker couldn't help but let it blow.

In 1862 as the Civil War raged, President Abraham Lincoln looked for ways to weaken the economy in the Southern states so that the fighting would end. The South depended on slaves to keep its commerce alive. President Lincoln knew that the best way to cripple the South would be to put an end to slavery. On September 22, 1862, he announced the Emancipation Proclamation, a document stating that as of January 1, 1863, all slaves living in the Confederate states would be granted their freedom.

As midnight drew near on December 31, 1862, Booker and his family huddled together in their tiny cabin, waiting for news about Lincoln's Emancipation. Two days passed with no word. Finally, Master Burroughs gathered his slaves in front of his house. He stood on the porch with his wife and daughters while a government official on horseback announced the news—they were free.

It didn't take a sack of onions to make Jane cry. When the word *free* rose up, so did her happy tears.

Soon after the Emancipation Proclamation was issued, Booker's stepfather, Washington, fled to West Virginia, where he found work as a packer in the salt mines of the tiny town of Malden. He sent money for Jane and her children to join him. In Malden, Jane got a job as a cook and maid. A maid who *made money* for the work she did. To help make ends meet, young Booker and his brother, John, had to work. Like their stepfather, they earned money shoveling crusty salt into rickety barrels. This was hard work for a kid. Though he was glad to be free, Booker missed carrying books for the Burroughs girls and seeing inside their classroom to consider letters, words, and spelling.

As a free black child, it was now safer for Booker to learn to read. Jane saw how eager her son was. The boy's eyes were always scanning anything that had letters dancing on its label—a bag of sugar, a tin of tea, a flour sack. With the money she'd earned as a cook, Jane bought Booker a surprise—a Webster's spelling book. Booker stared and stared at Webster's pages, taking in the beauty of letters. Slowly, Booker taught himself the alphabet.

But he wanted to learn more. When a black school opened in Tinkersville, a town just down the road from Malden, Booker begged his parents to let him enroll. His stepfather refused, though. Allowing Booker to take time during the day to go to school instead of work was a luxury they couldn't afford. Thankfully, the Tinkersville school also held classes for kids at night. As soon as Booker learned this, he was at the school's front door, waiting, while dusk turned to darkness. On that first evening, Booker received a gift. When his new teacher, Mr. Davis, welcomed Booker, he asked him to stand and tell the class his first and last names. Up to that point, Booker, like many children who had been enslaved, hadn't considered having a last name. Everyone had just called him Booker. Having spent his entire boyhood swatting flies, slopping hogs, carting books, and packing salt, a last name wasn't needed.

Now it was time to take pride in who he was, from the first to the last. Booker didn't blink when his teacher asked him to introduce himself. He rose from his seat. He spoke proudly when he made his stepfather's first name his new last name—Booker Washington. (Years later, Jane told Booker that he also had a middle name—Taliaferro. This is how he came to be known as Booker T. Washington.)

With gritty salt crystals in his pockets and socks, Booker left the mines each day and went straight to school. Though the schoolhouse was in Tinkersville, the boy did more than tinker. He was serious about getting an education. When his stepfather saw Booker reading the newspaper during the few free moments he had for lunch at the salt mines, he finally allowed Booker to go to school during the day.

Booker loved school. But when his family felt the pinch of not having his salt mine salary, Booker was forced to go back to working during the day. Someone had taken his job in the salt mine, so Booker now had to shovel coal in a coal mine. Going from salt to soot was no fun. Booker did not like walking to Tinkersville every night with blackened clothes and smudges on his cheeks and fingers.

One day at the coal mines, while reading his newspaper during a short break, Booker heard some men talking about an all-black school in Virginia called Hampton Normal and Agricultural Institute, a place that trained students to become teachers. Right then, Booker made a quiet decision: his coal days would soon be over. He would attend Hampton.

But there were just a few things standing in Booker's way. First, he had no idea where Hampton was, or how to get there. And, to enroll at Hampton Institute, students needed more than desire to attend. The school charged tuition. Booker needed money to be at Hampton.

This didn't stop Booker. While in the coal mines, he put a rhythm to his shoveling that sounded like *Haaampt-on . . . Haaampt-on . . . Haaaampt-on . . .*

It seems that backbeat encouraged Booker to find a job that could help him earn the money he needed. When he heard of a job opening as a houseboy for General Lewis Ruffner, one of the richest men in town, he applied. General Ruffner offered Booker the job, with a salary of five dollars a month. This was more than double what he was earning at the coal mines. But Booker sure had to work for that money. The most grueling part was putting up with the general's wife, Viola, who was more demanding than a cranky baby with a double-wet diaper. Viola screeched all day. She wanted what she wanted—now. It was Booker's job to clean, straighten, dust, fetch, lift, press—anything that needed doing in Viola's home. The one advantage was that Viola had a lot of books, and she shared them with Booker.

By 1872, Booker was sixteen. He'd had enough of polishing Viola Ruffner's doorknobs, painting her fence posts, and answering the demands from her snippy tongue. He was sick of her never-ending get-for-me, do-for-me attitude. His own attitude was: *Hampton, here I come.*

During the years he'd worked for the Ruffners, Booker had learned how to get to Hampton, which was the town in Virginia where the school was located. He still didn't have enough money to afford transportation to the school or the tuition. But his desire had stayed as strong as ever. He told his mother and stepfather that he was going to Hampton, no matter what. Though Booker had been living with the Ruffners, he was still in Malden, near his parents. Jane and Washington did not want their son to leave town, but they were proud of his ambitions. They bragged about him to their friends, because the boy had the determination of a hungry bloodhound. When Malden's black community got wind of Booker's dream, they collected pennies, nickels, and even dimes in a sack. Every time somebody threw in a coin, they pressed it into their palm to rub in good wishes for Booker. Soon there was enough money, rubbed with plenty of blessings, to send Booker to Hampton, nearly five hundred miles from his home.

On October 5, 1872, Booker stood in front of Hampton Institute in Hampton, Virginia. The school was one of the biggest brick buildings he'd ever seen, not like the humble schoolhouses he knew from his childhood. Years later when he remembered this day, he wrote: "I felt that I had reached the promised land."

As soon as Booker clanged the knocker at Hampton's front gate, he was made to take a special kind of "entrance exam." The school's principal, Mary Mackie, looked from Booker's matted hair to his cracked shoes. He was a mess. After so much travel, his clothes were dirty, and he had not combed his hair. There was one tidy thing about Booker, though—his diction. He spoke clearly and with conviction when Mary asked him why he'd come to Hampton, and what he expected to learn. Booker impressed her with his answers. Still, "Lady Principal," as she was called, wanted to test Booker's spirit. She shoved a broom and a rag at him and demanded that he sweep and dust.

Booker got right to work. This was his Hampton "entrance exam."

At that moment, Booker was thankful to have worked for Viola Ruffner. His experience at the Ruffner home had taught him to be mindful of every dust speck and cobweb. Now, on his very first day at Hampton, he cleaned like a machine. When Lady Principal came to inspect, she took one look and welcomed Booker to his new school. To afford Hampton's tuition on an ongoing basis, Booker worked as the school's janitor.

Soon after he'd passed the sweep-dust test, Booker met the head and founder of Hampton, a white man named General Samuel Chapman Armstrong. The general was as strict about cleanliness and hygiene as Lady Principal was. He insisted that every button and shoe-toe shine. Lint, stains, fingernail dirt, and teeth gunk were not tolerated. General Armstrong believed clean outsides helped students' minds be clear and unhindered for learning. General Armstrong had served as an officer in the Civil War, and he ran Hampton like the infantry.

The educational philosophy at Hampton was that black people needed to become "civilized," that black men and women required lessons in the building of character rather than in academic subjects.

Hampton students learned what Armstrong called "the routine of industrious habits." At the core of Hampton's curriculum were courses that stressed hands-on work, and the idea that students could derive their self-esteem and moral integrity through labor. So, boys and girls at Hampton spent their time perfecting the skills needed to become blacksmiths, seamstresses, carpenters, tanners, and the best janitors. Instead of pencils and paper, students needed thimbles, leather cutters, handsaws, and long-stringed mops to ace a test. Though Hampton also taught students to become teachers, this was not its primary purpose.

There was a reason for General Armstrong's methodology. He believed that the best way for black people to gain respect among white people in the South would be for them to learn a trade and to be as clean and kempt as possible. This would show white people, General Armstrong believed, that black people could be trusted and didn't pose a threat. He also believed, incorrectly, that black people lacked the intellectual capacity to learn academic subjects such as math, languages, history, and science. In the general's eyes, these were a waste of time for black students.

Though his thinking was backward and very limited, the general was a kind man who had the best intentions for his students. He truly believed he was doing the right thing for them.

This idea that race relations could improve if black people focused not on academics but on hands-on trade work and craftsmanship made a deep impression on Booker. During his three years at Hampton, he became enamored with General Armstrong. Booker internalized Hampton's "dignity in labor" philosophy and made it his own. General Armstrong became his mentor.

What General Armstrong—and the very impressionable Booker T.—failed to see was that many black people hungered for more than learning to push a mop or pound out a horseshoe. Black students possessed the desire and ability to excel in the study of algebra, the Middle Ages, Greek, Latin, English composition, and how clouds form.

In June 1875, Booker graduated from Hampton Institute. He was chosen to be one of Hampton's commencement speakers. He addressed his listeners with passion and grace. Folks said his speech was delivered with the conviction of a lawyer. It was clear to everyone that Booker had a talent for public speaking, and that while he'd fulfilled General Armstrong's goals as a Hampton student (in addition to receiving his teaching certificate, Booker had become an excellent janitor), Booker had talents that extended beyond menial labor. He was ready to show students what he knew.

After graduation, he returned to Malden, where he taught at the Tinkersville school. Folks were glad to have him back in town. He was a keen example of a local man who'd gone on to further his education. Booker brought what he'd learned at Hampton to his students. He taught them the importance of cleanliness, from washing behind their ears to dusting their shelves. He stressed the importance of dressing impeccably, making sure their shoes were shiny, their buttons gleamed, and their bow ties were arrow-straight.

It was one thing to be clean, but Booker also taught his students that in order to become accepted by white people they should become "so skilled

in hand, so strong in head, so honest in heart, that the Southern white man cannot do without him." By focusing on becoming indispensible laborers, Booker's students could become not only tolerable but also valuable to those who had previously looked down on them.

Booker taught at Tinkersville for several years, driving home this philosophy to his students—and to himself. He was like no other teacher the students and faculty at Tinkersville had ever known. They admired him in the same way that Booker had admired General Armstrong. To the folks in Tinkersville, Booker was a bright light with new ideas.

In early 1879, when Hampton was celebrating its tenth anniversary, General Armstrong invited Booker to return to the school as a teacher. Booker was pleased to accept. He taught courses in civil government that were part of the students' overall industrial education. His classes were among the most popular at Hampton. Everybody wanted to learn from *the* Booker T.

One day in 1881, General Armstrong received a letter postmarked from Tuskegee, Alabama. The letter had been sent by a group of men and women who were opening a black school in Tuskegee. They asked the general if he could recommend a white man to serve as principal of the school. News of the school brought a smile to General Armstrong's lips. It also made him happy because he knew, without a doubt, that the best man for the job was Booker!

He replied immediately, letting the developers of the Tuskegee school know that no white man could fill the shiny shoes of a new principal better than Booker. Soon after General Armstrong wrote to Tuskegee, a telegram came back. It said: "Send him at once."

So, at the end of the school year, Booker packed his bags and headed to the hills of Macon County, Alabama, to embark on his new opportunity. In his mind, he had visions of tall brick buildings and manicured lawns. He couldn't wait to get his hands on the new writing tablets and chalk, and the tools needed to teach the industrial skills he'd come to see as valuable for black students.

In June 1881, when Booker arrived at the place in Tuskegee where this new school was supposed to be, all he saw was crabgrass and dandelions. There *was* no school! Months before, Booker had been told that the state legislature had passed a bill that would provide money to build a school. He assumed the school would be waiting for him when he got there. However, once he was in Tuskegee, Booker found out that, although the bill had passed, it would take months for the state funds to become available. Also, the funds could only be used to pay teachers' salaries—not for land, construction, books, or school supplies.

Standing on a plot of dried-out land, Booker wiped the perspiration from his forehead and thought about what to do next. He knew that to get this school started, he would have to do more than just be its principal. He would need to find a better location for the school and figure out a way to construct some buildings.

Booker wasted no time. First he wrote to Hampton Institute, asking for any books and school supplies they could spare to help him get the new school under way. It was clear to Booker that the school needed an ample parcel of land. The parched plot with its spiky weeds would not do.

Booker was on a mission. He walked and walked and walked all around hilly Tuskegee, looking for land. When he came to a hundred-acre farm, just south of town, he knew this was the place. There were some small buildings on the property that could be used as classrooms. The structures needed a lot of refurbishing, but Booker saw their potential. Luckily, the farm was for sale. Unluckily, the farm's owner, William Bowen, wanted his money right away.

Between what he'd spent to travel to Tuskegee and the money he was paying to live in a boardinghouse, Booker was nearly broke.

He was rich in some respects, though. He possessed something that packed tremendous value. Booker T. Washington had a wealth of charm. He put on his cleanest and neatest suit, spit-polished his shoes, huff-shined his fingernails, and made his way around Tuskegee, shaking hands, smiling, and telling people about his plans for the new school. He went to banks, bakeries, quilting bees, and horse auctions, explaining his vision.

Many white residents of the town wanted to see the black school built. The Civil War had ravaged their community. Large groups of freed slaves had left Tuskegee for other Southern towns where they had successfully found work. Tuskegee's economy was suffering. People hoped the new school could help bring it back.

Booker also visited black churches, asking congregations to help. Excitement began to spread. Because of the tough economic times, not many folks were able to lend money, but they had good ideas and gave Booker lots of encouragement. Members of the African Methodist Episcopal (AME) Church donated a shack that stood alongside their main building. This was enough to get Booker's school started. Just a little over a week from the day he arrived in Tuskegee, Booker opened the Tuskegee Normal and Industrial Institute in the African Methodist Episcopal Church shanty. It marked a humble beginning, but it was impressive that Booker got his school up and running so quickly. Kids and their parents lined up at Booker's boardinghouse to enroll in his new school. He had to stay busy to get the real school built. He was principal, teacher, and fund-raiser, all in one.

After several months, Booker received the state funding needed to buy the Bowen farm. As soon as it was purchased, Booker put his students and faculty to work, clearing twenty acres of land, planting vegetables, chopping down dead trees. Booker had two words to say to anyone who complained about the muscle and sweat it took to build his school: *bye-bye.* He was putting to practical use his belief in the power of manual labor. The work paid off. By November 1881, student enrollment had nearly tripled. People came from towns all over to attend the Tuskegee Institute.

Booker drove home the educational ideals he'd fostered at Tinkersville and Hampton—that there is beauty and dignity in labor. In addition to teaching students the skills for farming, housekeeping, tinsmithing, and carpentry, the Institute offered courses in brick-making. Day and night, students were required to form bricks that would be used to build, from the ground up, the buildings that would eventually compose Tuskegee's campus. It was at Tuskegee that Booker's belief in "industrial education" as a means for solving racial tensions began to gain widespread attention.

Many conservative white people loved the idea of black people focusing on skilled labor and service work rather than on higher intellectual pursuits. Some of these people thought this was an effective means for "keeping blacks in their place."

With his school slowly coming along, Booker returned to Malden in the summer of 1882, where he married Fanny Smith, a young lady who had been a student of his both at the school in Tinkersville and at Hampton Institute. As autumn approached, Fanny and Booker returned to Tuskegee together.

By 1883, Booker had much to be grateful for. His daughter Portia was born. That same year, the Tuskegee Institute had become the talk of politicians in Washington, D.C. Several United States senators embraced Booker's ideas and sought his advice on race matters.

Sadly, Fanny died a year after Portia was born. To help cope with the loss of his wife, Booker poured himself into further developing his institution. Through his hard work (and the elbow grease of his students, who maintained a brickyard, continued to construct buildings, and kept every aspect of the school neat and tidy), the Tuskegee Institute expanded to a 540-acre campus that included vegetable gardens rich with collards, tomatoes, and carrots; barns filled with egg-laying chickens; cows full of milk; a water tower that was the highest structure in the county; and a printing press that allowed students to publish their own journal, the *Southern Letter,* a bulletin that told of developments at Tuskegee.

The school kept growing. Student enrollment increased, along with the faculty. One teacher, a bright young instructor who had come from Hampton, had a keen understanding of how to raise funds for the school. Her name was Olivia Davidson. She organized fund-raising events for the school and encouraged students to knock on doors to solicit donations.

Booker appointed Olivia as Tuskegee's first lady principal. In 1885, Olivia and Booker were married. They had two sons, Booker T. Jr., and Ernest. Under Olivia's leadership, the school became the premier educational facility in the South for black students. As the institute expanded, so did Booker's reputation and passion for his school. Once again, though, Booker suffered the loss of his wife. Olivia died in 1889.

Fortunately, another wonderful woman came into Booker's life soon after Olivia's death. Margaret James Murray, a lady with a strong command of grammar and excellent diction, arrived at Tuskegee to teach English. Soon after, Margaret was named Tuskegee's principal. She and Booker married in 1892. They had no children of their own, but adopted Margaret's niece, who had become orphaned.

By this time, when the Tuskegee Institute was just a little more than ten years old, Booker T. Washington was renowned for accomplishing great things on behalf of the black community.

He had gained the attention of many influential white people, and he invited them to tour the school's campus. When these men and women saw everything Booker had accomplished, they sent him large sums of money to help support the institute's efforts.

In the eyes of his students and fellow teachers, it seemed Booker had a kind of magical power. He came to be known by his students and faculty as "the Wizard."

Booker had a way of making people feel comfortable in his presence, especially Southern white people who may have previously been uneasy around black folks. As his teachings gained popularity, Booker traveled throughout the South and also to Northern cities delivering public addresses about the virtues of black progress through industrial education.

Booker loved the podium. And audiences loved to hear him speak. To warm up his listeners, he often started his addresses with humor. But sometimes his jokes were about black people. Racist white people thought this was funny, but Booker started to alienate some of his black brothers and sisters. When he talked about the importance of black people focusing their efforts on manual labor, this made some of them even angrier. Booker started to gain detractors among black Americans, especially black intellectuals. With whites, though, Booker's speeches hit the jackpot. He would often leave a speaking venue with a commitment from white philanthropists to send thousands of dollars to help Tuskegee continue to grow.

Despite the differing opinions about his philosophies, one thing was certain. Everywhere Booker went, he mesmerized audiences with his passion.

On September 18, 1895, Booker gave the defining speech of his career. It was a scorching-hot day in Atlanta, Georgia. Even the trees begged for a breeze to cool their leaves. Booker didn't mind the heat. As always, he wore a starched shirt and a vest with buttons that gleamed. The Cotton States and International Exposition, a large fair, had just opened. People came from all over to see the sights and to hear Booker speak. When it was time for Booker to proceed to the stage, he knew this would be an important moment for him and his future. Thousands of people had gathered. They were black folks, white politicians, farmers, storekeepers, educators, ditchdiggers, doctors, and dignitaries, all looking forward to hearing what Booker had to say.

His speech started off slow and folksy. Once he'd captured the full attention and trust of his audience, Booker ramped up his delivery. He told the crowd that black people would gain empowerment as a result of "severe and constant struggle rather than artificial forcing." He reminded black listeners that it was a foolish bunch of "folly" to press for equality.

Lots of white people nodded in agreement; so did some of Booker's black followers. But other black people, especially Northern intellectuals, frowned.

He said, "No race can prosper till it learns that there is as much dignity in tilling a field as in writing a poem. It is at the bottom of life we must begin, and not at the top."

The heat of the afternoon started to rise. The atmosphere was stifling.

Booker had started his speech with hands in his pockets, but soon he was articulating with his cadenced voice, palms raised to make his point. Next he held up his hands so that everyone could see all his fingers. He said, "In all things that are purely social, we can be as separate as fingers . . . yet one as the hand in all things essential to mutual progress." This remark brought a lot of hands together in applause.

When Booker was done with his speech, thunder clapped throughout the exposition grounds. It wasn't the clouds making noise. It was people applauding and stomping their feet with appreciation for what Booker had to say. His address, known as the Atlanta Compromise, had instantly catapulted Booker to an even higher level of notoriety. News about his speech spread quickly. Magazines and newspapers reported on its effectiveness and on Booker's talents as an orator. Periodicals printed Booker's remarks so that those who didn't attend the exposition could read the speech for themselves. Even President Grover Cleveland read it. He wrote a letter to Booker, telling him, "Your words cannot fail to delight and encourage all who wish well for your race."

But a whole bunch of black folks weren't so keen on Booker's words. They started to call Booker "the Great Accommodator," accusing him of belittling black people and working against the good of black progress for the sake of gaining funds for his institute and getting closer to whites in high places.

Booker stood by his beliefs. He continued to gain widespread attention. He had become a controversial and influential civil rights leader. With so much interest in his accomplishments, and the growing debate about his values, Booker felt compelled to share his personal story.

In 1901 he wrote *Up from Slavery*, his autobiography, in which he tells of his life as a child with the Burroughs family, how he taught himself to read, and what it took to become the leader of one of America's foremost black schools. Booker poured his whole soul into writing about his experiences. Like his speeches, the narrative in *Up from Slavery* had an accessible tone. Booker's writing made readers feel they were walking alongside him, talking to a good friend. His stories of hardship and victory made readers root for him. *Up from Slavery* resonated with readers, whether they were rich or poor, black or white, Northerners or Southern bred.

The book was translated into Chinese, Arabic, German, Swedish, and Zulu. There was even a Braille edition for blind readers. *Up from Slavery* is still used in classrooms today to help teach the history of civil rights.

With the popularity of Booker's autobiography, his beliefs gained more attention. In the fall of 1901, President Theodore Roosevelt, a fan of Booker's, invited him to dinner at the White House. On October 16, Booker shook President Roosevelt's hand and met the First Family. They all enjoyed a simple supper prepared by White House cooks. Booker was impressed by the starched table linens, polished silver, and sparkling crystal. He'd come a long way from fanning flies at his master's dinner table. When dessert was served, the president asked Booker for his advice on how to solve the race question in America. Booker further explained his views on black self-reliance and compliance as the answer to the troubling problems of race in the United States.

Though the dinner between the two men went smoothly, it didn't settle well in the stomachs of many people. Southern whites didn't like the idea of a black man breaking bread with the nation's president. Even open-minded white people saw the president's invitation as going too far. It was one thing to let a black man speak from a podium; it was another to have him eat from the First Lady's china. Newspapers were filled with scathing editorials about the dinner.

Booker's detractors, black and white, increased after his meal with the president. Despite the success of the Tuskegee Institute and Booker's persona as a leader, race relations remained at a low point. More black people took issue with his ideas, and his opponents became more vocal in their criticism. In the minds of some people, it was as if the Wizard was filled with more hot air than a passenger balloon with a basket on the bottom. When Booker made speeches or was quoted in newspapers, his critics accused him of *talking* a lot but not *saying* much of any real value.

But as a man who, with his own hands, had crafted the bricks that built an entire institution from a dry patch of weedy land, Booker T. Washington was not going to be halted by negative opinions. He still had many followers, and when he set out on a series of state speaking tours in 1905, he was greeted—and treated—like a celebrity.

Many people had read *Up from Slavery* and felt they *knew* Booker T. Washington. There were times when his train eased into the station in Boston, New York, Philadelphia, or Chicago, and Booker couldn't see his way past the train's exit door. Men, women, boys, and girls crowded to get a good look at the Wizard. They waved flags. They cheered. They chanted his name—"Booker T.! Booker T.! Booker, Booker T.!" Sometimes entire brass bands showed up to play for him.

For Booker, one of the most satisfying aspects of his speaking tour was the reception he received from white millionaires who were eager to donate money to the Tuskegee Institute. John D. Rockefeller and Andrew Carnegie, two wealthy businessmen, were especially impressed with Booker. Mr. Rockefeller, an oil magnate, donated enough money to construct a new building on Tuskegee's campus. Mr. Carnegie, a steel baron, wrote a check that provided funds for a two-story Tuskegee Institute library. Once the money from these wealthy patrons was in the bank, Booker's students pulled up their starched sleeves and started mixing the mortar that would secure the bricks they'd made themselves. Then, brick by brick, they erected what became Rockefeller Hall, and the library that housed thousands of books, including *Up from Slavery*.

Mr. Carnegie expressed his own sentiments, which echoed the feelings of many, by writing that Booker T. Washington was "The modern Moses, who leads his race and lifts it through education to even better and higher things. . . . History is to know two Washingtons, one white, the other black, both fathers of their People."

Booker T. Washington proved that there was dignity in hands-on work. Through his commitment to building a firm foundation for black education, he achieved one of the highest ideals any race of people could hope for—empowerment through learning.

The campus of Tuskegee Institute became a national landmark in 1965. Two decades later, the school earned university status and was renamed Tuskegee University. It is still one of the most noted historic black universities in the United States.

His two hands

      brought oneness
to the souls
of black folk.

      Used his pen
again and again
to spell out *The Crisis:* N-A-A-C-P.

      Defined the color line.

High-hatted scholar

Headstrong historian

      Dotted the I in intellectual.
Put the handle on Pan-Africanism.

A#1 of the Talented Tenth

Ever the eloquent

Dapper

Devoted

      Wove his truth into the fiber of his being:

One thing alone I own, and that is

                       my soul.

W.E.B. DuBois

b. February 23, 1868, Great Barrington, Massachusetts;
d. August 27, 1963, Accra, Ghana

Erudite Educator

———◆◆◆———

WILLIAM EDWARD BURGHARDT DUBOIS, later known by most as W.E.B., came into this world with the best of the best of both his parents. His mother, Mary, was a silent woman, but strong inside. She believed deeply in hard work and striving for what you wanted. W.E.B.'s father, Alfred, was a vagabond poet who liked adventure, literature, and a good debate.

Mary had beautiful skin the color of dark coffee, and meaty arms for hugging her son tightly. Alfred was a butterscotch-colored man with a big mouth for telling the world about his dreams of travel. Alfred left Mary and baby W.E.B. soon after W.E.B. was born, and never came back.

W.E.B., who was a caramel-colored combination of both his parents, missed having a father as he grew up, though some of his daddy's traits had become a part of him. Little W.E.B. was whip-smart and loved to read. He went to school in a wooden schoolhouse surrounded by the Berkshire Hills in Massachusetts. Those mountainous peaks, and his mother's belief in aiming high, encouraged W.E.B. to aspire to the greatest heights. He was the only child of color in his small school, but this didn't bother W.E.B. or his teachers. By the time he entered Great Barrington High School, he had become a star student. His brilliance shone in the provincial town in which most folks lived a simple farmer's life. They had no need for sophistication.

W.E.B. was the opposite. He was a boy with complex ideas. As a teenager, he was reading books written for grown-ups. While other kids spent Saturdays hauling wood on their families' New England farms, W.E.B. parked himself at the local bookstore, where he browsed the shelves, found books that he liked, and read till closing time. One day, Johnny Morgan, the man who owned the store, allowed W.E.B. to take home a set of books about world history and its leaders. He told W.E.B. not to worry about paying for the books. Those history volumes were like a good friend to W.E.B. He read them in the morning. He read them when the afternoon sun stretched its pointy fingers through the branches of Great Barrington's pine trees. There were books that included stories about Samuel Adams, Shaka Zulu, and Sophocles. W.E.B. could not part with Mr. Morgan's books. He even read them long after his mother told him to snuff his late-night lantern and go to sleep.

Mr. Morgan could see that W.E.B. was destined for great things. He helped W.E.B. get a part-time job selling subscriptions for the *New York Globe*, a black newspaper. W.E.B. eventually paid Mr. Morgan for the history books, which he would end up keeping, and hauling from place to place, for the rest of his life. While he was still a teenager, W.E.B. became the Great Barrington correspondent for the *New York Globe*, and a reporter for the *Springfield Republican*. This was the start of his expressing himself through writing.

He began to see that newspapers were powerful tools for social change. In the articles he wrote, he urged black people in the community to attend town meetings and to take part in local politics. After school, W.E.B. went to these meetings. He was one of the only kids in the place. Whenever W.E.B. attended one of these gatherings, he was as wide-eyed as a hooty owl. He paid close attention, studied the mannerisms of the speakers, learned the art of oration and the craft of debate. He was also one of the few folks of color in the room. Still bright. Still eager. Still sharp as the point on the reporter's pencil he kept tucked behind his ear. As inspiring as these assemblies were, W.E.B. started to wish there were more people who looked like him and his mother at the meetings—more brown-skinned people.

When W.E.B. received an invitation to attend a picnic in Rocky Point, Rhode Island, for the black communities of New York, Connecticut, and

Massachusetts, he was among the first guests to arrive. It was as if this gathering was tailor-made for W.E.B. The sweetest part of the picnic wasn't the pies. It was the people who came in every black, brown, and peanut-butter hue under the good Lord's sun. He later called the picnic an experience that demonstrated "the whole gorgeous gamut of the American Negro."

This beautiful array showed W.E.B. that if black people wanted equal rights, they needed to organize themselves. It was 1883. W.E.B. was just fifteen years old. He was so inspired that he immediately formed the Sons of Freedom, a small club in Great Barrington dedicated to civil rights.

The following year, W.E.B. graduated from Great Barrington High School. He was one of thirteen students in his graduating class, and the first black child to ever graduate from the school. He was chosen to give the commencement address, which he did with the might of ten men. Using the skills he'd developed writing for newspapers, the speaking techniques he'd observed at his town's political meetings, and the grace he'd inherited from his mother and father, W.E.B. spoke about Wendell Phillips, an abolitionist who had died earlier that year. When he concluded his speech, every student, parent, and teacher stood to applaud him. His mother, Mary, clapped loudest of all.

For W.E.B., the commencement speech confirmed that he had two special gifts—writing and public speaking—that he could use to put an end to injustice. But even a gifted student can benefit from going to college, and to W.E.B., a college education was more important than an all-day standing ovation. He wanted to attend Harvard College, one of the premier institutions in the nation, and one of the most expensive colleges in the world. Harvard, located in Cambridge, Massachusetts, was a little more than one hundred miles from W.E.B.'s home and was the place where rich people sent their kids to school. Mary didn't have the kind of money it took to send her son to such a highbrow place. What she did have, though, was the belief that miracles happen. Her faith was worth more than the winning ticket in a million-dollar raffle. She knew her son's chances for attending, and affording, college were as good as anyone's who had a strong conviction that prayers make intentions possible.

In addition to his mother's support, W.E.B. had several things that made him unique among his classmates. Few others had the desire to continue their educations, none possessed W.E.B.'s fortitude, and he was the only one who had the backing of Frank Hosmer, the principal of Great Barrington High School; Edward Van Lennep, the head of a local private school; and the reverends C. C. Painter and Evarts Scudder—all of whom worked to raise money for a scholarship that could pay for W.E.B. to attend college.

Gathering the funds took time. A year after W.E.B. graduated from high school, a good amount of money had been raised, but not enough for Harvard. The four townsfolk who had helped raise the funds told W.E.B. that he could afford the tuition at Fisk University, an all-black college in Nashville, Tennessee. W.E.B. and Mary were disappointed. Seeing as he was such a bright student, his mother had dreamed of and prayed for Harvard's top-notch education for her son. W.E.B wanted a college that challenged him intellectually.

Sometimes prayers are answered in ways that the ones doing the praying don't expect. There were advantages to Fisk. It was in the South, the place where there was an abundance of "the whole gorgeous gamut of the American Negro." W.E.B. would no longer be the lone black student among his classmates. And, he hoped, he would have the opportunity to find ways to bring his people together, to galvanize them.

W.E.B. began to look forward to what Fisk had to offer. But months before he was to leave home, his mother died. When it was time to go to Nashville, W.E.B.'s heart was heavier than the iron hatchets his former classmates used to bust wood. His suitcase was heavy too. It was filled with the set of history books from Mr. Morgan.

As his train rushed from the North to the South, W.E.B. watched the piney woods turn to hanging moss, and he experienced two emotions at the same time. He was sad to say good-bye to his mother, and excited to greet what lay ahead.

When W.E.B. arrived at Fisk, it was immediately apparent that several things were different about him. For one, he talked funny. Most of the other students were from Nashville and other Southern towns nearby. To them, this Northerner's New England accent sounded downright proper. Second, W.E.B. was very handsome—despite the fact that

his ears stuck out. And third, because of his smarts, W.E.B. was able to enroll as a sophomore. So the seventeen-year-old sat in class with kids older than he was.

To W.E.B.'s way of seeing things, though, he fit right in. This was the first time in his schooling that he was one among many black students. He got right to work. It didn't take long before folks on campus knew his name. W.E.B. showed everyone how sharp a mind he had. He excelled in every area of study—Greek, Latin, History, French, English Composition. He even aced the two hardest C's on everyone's course list—Chemistry and Calculus.

He impressed the folks at Fisk as more than just a bookworm. He *became* a book, a walking encyclopedia. An *intellectual*. He not only read and read and *read*, he often led robust classroom discussions about the reading assignments. When W.E.B. wasn't studying, he served as the editor for the university newspaper, the *Fisk Herald*.

Life at Fisk wasn't all wonderful for W.E.B. The South had a dark side. In New England, white people had been tolerant of black people. There were so few people of color in his hometown, and he had been such a shining example in so many ways, that no one bothered W.E.B. or his family. But in the South in the late 1880s, bigotry and race hatred loomed.

W.E.B. learned of violent acts against black people by the Ku Klux Klan, a white supremacist hate group.

One summer W.E.B. saw the effects of racial oppression firsthand. He was teaching summer school to poor black students in a rural Tennessee town. Each day he noticed how downtrodden they were. Many of them attended his classes in an effort to improve their circumstances, but they couldn't overcome the day-to-day realities of low wages and poverty brought on by racism. While instructing these men and women, W.E.B. learned something no book could teach him. He came face-to-face with how scarcity prevented black people from reaching their full potential. He made a commitment to use his skills to throw off what he called "the Veil that hung between us and Opportunity."

When W.E.B. returned to college in the fall of 1887 for his senior year, he wrote with fury in the *Fisk Herald*. In one of his noted *Herald* editorials, he wrote that he was redoubling his efforts and committing himself "toward a life that shall be an honor to the race." Stepping up on every hen crate, soapbox, and bleach barrel he could find, he used his public speaking abilities—and his thick-leather lace-up shoes—to pounce hard on prejudice.

In 1888, W.E.B.'s graduating year, he was once again chosen to give the commencement address. This time he spoke about a man he'd learned of in one of his many books, the German chancellor Otto Eduard Leopold von Bismarck, who had managed to lead the people of Germany despite their many differences and the dissension that had risen among them as a result. W.E.B. compared the chancellor's success in uniting the people of Germany with what needed to be done by and for black people in America. He told everyone at Fisk that black people needed strong leadership, and that to overcome oppression they needed to join together with unity and purpose.

Though this was W.E.B.'s parting message at Fisk, it was also his personal intention for a new beginning he hoped to forge.

During his time at Fisk, W.E.B. had kept on praying that someday, somehow, he could enroll at Harvard. Just a few months after his Fisk graduation, W.E.B. learned that his prayers had paid off. An envelope arrived addressed to him, bearing Harvard's return address. Inside was a letter with Harvard's motto inscribed on top. The motto was a Latin word W.E.B. knew from his studies—*Veritas*, which means *truth*.

Truth was the perfect way to begin what the letter had to say. Harvard was writing to invite W.E.B. to join its student body! The university had come to recognize his exceptional abilities. Also, the college was looking to add more black students to its population. And the best bit of truth was that Harvard would offer W.E.B. grant money so that he could afford the school's tuition!

W.E.B. read the letter several times to make sure it *was* true. The tuition money would be granted to him if he agreed to enroll as a junior in the undergraduate class. University officials believed that Fisk's curriculum was inferior to that of Harvard's and that the only way W.E.B. could meet their academic standards would be to go back two years. Even though W.E.B. had been the smartest student in his high school, and had skipped a grade when he entered Fisk, in the eyes of Harvard his education didn't measure up.

This was the sad truth of the matter. But W.E.B. accepted Harvard's offer and planned to show the university the *undeniable truth*—that he had what it took to succeed in any class they put him in.

One area of special interest to W.E.B. was philosophy, the study of how different people and cultures view the world. He was intrigued by the fact that the word *philosophy* comes from a Greek word that means "love of wisdom." That's what W.E.B. wanted—a college that could help him delve deeper into his passion for gaining wisdom through knowledge.

At Harvard, that's exactly what W.E.B. got. As at Fisk, he was immediately recognized for his study habits and intellect. W.E.B. excelled in every subject he took—History, Science, English Composition, Economics. Higher learning in the Ivy League was a high-IQ dream come true. W.E.B. couldn't wait to take tests. When exam week came, he was as eager as a happy heart. If a professor assigned a ten-page paper, W.E.B. delivered twenty pages of crisp prose and thoughtful ideas.

Harvard's academic program had a lot to offer, but the people at

Harvard were not as friendly to W.E.B. as the course work. He missed the familiarity and comfort of the fellow black students he'd found at Fisk. He kept mostly to himself, focusing his time and energy on getting the best grades he could.

When it was time to graduate, Harvard's commencement committee came calling. They couldn't deny W.E.B.'s ability to express himself well. He would be graduating with honors in philosophy and was invited to be one of six undergraduate student speakers on graduation day.

This being W.E.B.'s third commencement address, he knew how to inspire a crowd. But this wasn't just any audience. This was a group who had set him back two grades and was now bringing him up to their podium to speak.

And did W.E.B. ever speak! His address focused on Jefferson Davis, a man who had a strong belief in slavery, and who had served as president of the Confederate States of America. Though W.E.B. was firmly against slavery, he pointed out that Davis provided a good example of a leader who was strong in his convictions, but whose selfish and shortsighted thinking oppressed an entire group of people and thereby wounded everyone who lived under his leadership. W.E.B. gave his speech with measured poise. It was so well received that *The Nation* magazine praised W.E.B. as a scholar of good taste.

As soon as Harvard bestowed W.E.B. with an undergraduate degree, they were keen on keeping him at the university for more study. Through a series of scholarships, W.E.B. pursued a graduate degree, then a doctorate from the university. As part of his doctoral studies, he traveled to Europe, where he attended Friedrich Wilhelm University in Berlin, Germany.

Being in Europe changed W.E.B. For the first time, he was living in a place where black and white people were true equals. W.E.B. didn't have to put up with ignorant attitudes about race. He enjoyed living in a place where he was regarded as W.E.B. the scholar, or W.E.B. the thinker, or W.E.B. the orator, rather than W.E.B. the *Negro* scholar, or W.E.B. the *brown-skinned* thinker, or W.E.B. the orator with crinkly hair. He later wrote that he enjoyed being seen as an equal, rather than "as a curiosity or something subhuman."

Being viewed first as a man, rather than a *black man*, showed W.E.B. that equality among people was possible, and it inspired him to think differently about race relations. He grew hopeful that race equality could happen in America.

In 1894 W.E.B returned from Europe with a new attitude—and a new appearance. The fashions of Germany and its neighboring countries appealed to him. When he arrived back in America, he turned some heads as he strode down streets he had once walked. W.E.B. was more handsome than a fresh-cut paycheck. He wore a high silk hat, bow tie, and spats. White gloves hugged his delicate hands as he hailed taxis and waved to people with his cane. His waxed moustache invited people to read his lips as he spoke with the manners and inflection of a proper European gent.

Starched collars and creased slacks couldn't shield W.E.B. from the bigotry that had grown up from American soil during the two years he'd traveled abroad. While he had progressed in many ways, America had *regressed*. By the time W.E.B. had returned, he was disturbed to discover that racial hatred of black people had increased. Lynching was at its highest rate ever, and there were daily reports of other hate crimes against black people.

Adding to this, the nation's economy had declined, which affected the grant money W.E.B. was receiving for his education. The funds he needed in order to continue at Harvard had run out. Rather than finish his doctoral studies, W.E.B. was forced to find work right away. And jobs were hard to find.

He'd discovered that the best way to keep learning and to earn a living at the same time was to teach. Fortunately, W.E.B. had gained a good reputation for his many talents. In 1894, Wilberforce University in Ohio invited him to teach Latin and Greek. *Veritas* was one of the first Latin words he shared with his students. In the evenings, W.E.B. continued to work on his Harvard doctoral dissertation, which he entitled "The Suppression of the African Slave Trade to the United States of America," a passionate paper about the history of slavery beginning as far back as the 1600s.

While he wrote, it didn't matter to W.E.B. that he was no longer on Harvard's campus. He could write and study anyplace there were books and a quiet room. W.E.B. completed his dissertation and sent it to Harvard. The university could not deny his hard work and fortitude. He was awarded a PhD in history in 1895, the first black man to receive a doctorate from Harvard. With so much time spent studying at Harvard, W.E.B. had given new meaning to the term *advanced degree*. In earning Harvard undergraduate, master's, *and* PhD degrees, he had also advanced the perceptions of those who believed black people were incapable of such accomplished scholarship.

W.E.B. was excited to share all that he'd learned, and he looked forward to expanding his life even further. In 1896 he married Nina Gomer, a dark-eyed beauty who loved W.E.B.'s intellect and charm. Soon after his marriage, W.E.B. became a professor at the University of Pennsylvania, then at Atlanta University, where he organized a series of annual conferences that focused on the hardships and racial struggles faced by black people in the United States. Prejudice continued to worsen in America, and W.E.B. wanted to stop it. By 1897, this goal was especially important to W.E.B. Nina gave birth to a son, Burghardt. W.E.B. and Nina wanted their child to grow up in a world that was free of racial discrimination.

He used the conferences at Atlanta University to gather information that could help improve the lives of black citizens and also bring races together. Over several years, W.E.B.'s conferences examined what was called "the Negro problem"—the pains and trials that plagued black people due to the oppression they faced as Americans living in a racist society. About racism W.E.B. would later say, "The ultimate evil was ignorance, and its child, stupidity."

A prevailing theme kept cropping up each year at W.E.B.'s conferences: black people were divided in their philosophies about race. Some did not want to be part of white society; they wanted to exist as a unique whole, apart from white folks. Others didn't believe in racial separation. They wanted to be fully assimilated into mainstream white society. W.E.B. saw both sides. He believed it was possible to be black, to fully identify with one's black heritage, and to also be an American who was part of a larger culture, which meant being included in a white world as well.

While W.E.B. had hoped to instill these values in his son, sadly, the opportunity never came. Baby Burghardt died in 1899 after drinking water that had been contaminated by Atlanta's sewage.

While mourning the loss of his son, W.E.B. tried to keep busy to ward off his grief. He prepared an exhibit on black life in America to be shown at the Paris Exposition. The exposition, held in 1900, was a bright and colorful world's fair with people from many nations attending. W.E.B. was excited to return to Europe. The streets of Paris were filled with happy people who had come to enjoy the fair. W.E.B.'s exhibit won a grand prize at the exposition and enlightened people's views on the issues facing black people. With such a positive reaction to his exhibit, W.E.B. was encouraged to explore further possibilities for social change. He met a group of men and women who, like himself, had broad and intriguing ideas. These people looked beyond the parameters of the United States for advancing the causes of people of African descent. There were black people all over the globe. Why, they wondered, can't these people from every nation work together toward equality?

This group of thirty-two friends held a meeting in London, England, where they created the Pan-African Association. When it was time to name a chairman, they all looked to W.E.B. There was no doubt that he was the man who could best promote the idea of worldwide unity for black people. W.E.B. took on this role with a passion. This was his opportunity to bring black people together in every nation to work as a unified group. The concept was called *Pan-Africanism.* W.E.B. became known as "the father of Pan-Africanism." He embraced the notion as only a father would, with care, hope, commitment, and the love that it takes to help something grow.

When he returned to the United States, W.E.B. shared the philosophy of Pan-Africanism whenever and wherever he could. He wrote essays about Pan-Africanism for the *New York Times* and other periodicals that reached a broad range of people. His essays sparked all kinds of discussion, debate, and change. W.E.B. was making people think about things they hadn't considered before.

In 1902, a publisher asked W.E.B. if he wanted to put all of his essays together into a book. W.E.B. didn't have to think twice. The next year his collection of fourteen essays, entitled *The Souls of Black Folk*, was read by scholars, farmers, preachers, and teachers from Maine to Mississippi, from Nigeria to Normandy.

In his book, W.E.B. articulated the struggle of being black and a citizen of the United States. W.E.B.'s essays explained the sensation of a man's or woman's soul torn in half between opposing worlds. In one essay he wrote, "One ever feels his *twoness*—an American, a Negro; two souls, two thoughts, two unreconciled strivings; two warring ideals in one dark body."

In another essay he wrote, "The problem of the twentieth century is the problem of the color line." This statement was one that would later be used to describe the split between black and white people, a divide that would come to be known as *segregation.*

One of W.E.B.'s most controversial essays was an attack on Booker T. Washington. Booker and W.E.B. had many things in common. They had both come from meager beginnings and were self-made men. Each had captured the attention of black and white Americans as a result of their views on race. Both were effective public speakers and authors. W.E.B.'s *The Souls of Black Folk* was as widely received as Booker's book, *Up from Slavery*. But Booker's views were very different from W.E.B.'s.

He believed that the best way for black people to get along with white people would be for black folks to squash their desires for equality. To Booker's way of thinking, black people could get ahead by *not* mixing with white people and by *not* seeking to be members of white society. Booker didn't believe black people should vote or work to get jobs held by white people.

Booker's views made W.E.B. as angry as a hornet whose nest was being rattled. To W.E.B., Booker's ideas were backward. He accused Booker of having "an old attitude of adjustment and submission."

When readers opened W.E.B.'s book, they were greeted with a chapter entitled "Of Mr. Booker T. Washington and Others." The essay took great offense at Booker's views. It called his theories "a gospel of work and money" that neglected "the higher aims of life," and that shifted "the Negro problem to the Negro's shoulders."

W.E.B. had worked for much of his life to help black people gain respect and equality through education. He held firm to the belief that, while there was only a small percentage of blacks in America who were college educated—about one in ten—these people held the keys to doors of opportunity that could advance the entire black race. He called this group of highly educated men and women "the Talented Tenth." It was through knowledge, not industrial training, that black people would gain power, W.E.B. believed. The Talented Tenth, he said, possessed the true skills needed to lead black people forward.

In 1905, along with several others who were opposed to Booker T. Washington's ideas, W.E.B. founded the Niagara Movement, a group that did not believe in Booker T.'s views on accommodation. Booker and W.E.B. remained rivals for years, and they never agreed on how race relations could be bettered, but over time they came to respect each other's differences.

Even with everything W.E.B. and others were doing to rally against hate, race crimes were still happening. Thankfully, as the number of assaults against black people grew, so did the number of men and women who wanted to help stop them. And more white Americans were joining the cause for civil rights. In 1908, William English Walling, a white journalist, witnessed a race riot in Springfield, Illinois, and it troubled him deeply. He immediately wrote an essay about what he'd seen, urging people to come together against these kinds of injustices.

His essay issued a plea and set forth a challenge. William believed that if a strong group of people—black and white—came together to form an organization that would fight for equal rights for black citizens, brutality against African Americans could end. Others agreed with him. The advancement of black people was needed for positive changes to happen.

Mary Ovington, a white woman, was inspired by the ideas in William English Walling's essay and by the Niagara Movement. She was the first to come forward with a solution. She organized a conference to discuss what actions could be taken. The conference was held on May 31, 1909, in New York. William English Walling came, and of course W.E.B. DuBois was there, filled with enthusiasm. New York was already a busy town, but when the sixty conference attendees arrived, the city took on new excitement. The conference room was filled with anticipation.

Oswald Garrison Villard, an activist who had once supported Booker T. Washington's philosophies, was now in favor of moving black people forward by encouraging them to strive for the highest social and intellectual ideals. Oswald was very outspoken. He told those gathered that they needed to build an organization that should be called the National Negro Committee. Everyone agreed, especially W.E.B. and William English Walling.

The group talked and talked and talked. They met several times after the meeting in May and settled on a new name for the committee. It would be called the National Association for the Advancement of Colored People (NAACP). W.E.B. DuBois was given the important job of director of publicity and research. He would be responsible for spreading the word about the organization, and also gathering information that could help it develop. In his new role, W.E.B. knew that he had to take immediate action. He was thrilled that the NAACP now existed, but there was one important aspect of it that needed to change. The organization's mission was to foster the progress of *colored people*, yet the only *colored person* who occupied an officer position was W.E.B. DuBois!

As director of publicity and research, W.E.B. used the power of his writing to spread the good news about the NAACP's initiatives. He knew that the best way to reach many people was by offering them a monthly journal that addressed the NAACP's primary purpose. In November 1910, the first issue of the NAACP's official magazine was printed. It was called *The Crisis*. The periodical included articles about improving race relations, book reviews, opinion pieces, profiles on notable black people, and editorials by W.E.B.

The Crisis caught on immediately. It was read by Southerners, Northerners, famers, financiers, liberals, conservatives, members of the Talented Tenth, and Booker T. Washington himself. Folks were eager to read about the NAACP's activities, whether they were in favor of them or not.

The Crisis encouraged people to become NAACP members. Membership grew to one hundred thousand people of all races.

W.E.B. edited *The Crisis* for twenty-four years. He worked hard to make the NAACP an international organization. Through his efforts, he showed the world that black people were a powerful force when they came together for a common good.

But not everyone took kindly to W.E.B.'s actions. By the early 1950s, the U.S. government was paying close attention to anyone they deemed a threat to America's ideals. The government had launched an anticommunist campaign in an era known as McCarthyism. They targeted W.E.B. because of his socialist beliefs, questioning his allegiance to American values. This disappointed W.E.B. greatly, and increased his desire to visit nations outside the United States. From his travels in Europe as a college student, he had learned that understanding different cultures could open his eyes to new possibilities for tolerance.

In 1958 he traveled to the Soviet Union, where he was immediately embraced by the people. He received an honorary doctorate degree from Moscow University, and the Lenin Peace Prize, an honor reserved for the most distinguished scholars. When W.E.B. met Soviet Union premier Nikita Khrushchev, W.E.B. suggested that the Soviet Union establish

a center devoted to the study of African culture. Khrushchev was so impressed by W.E.B. that he agreed to open the Institute on Africa in Moscow.

The following year, W.E.B. went to China, where he visited with Mao Tse-tung, chairman of the People's Republic of China. Mao Tse-tung had heard many great things about W.E.B.'s work in helping people of color gain equality. When Mao Tse-tung met him, he joked, "You are no darker than I am. Who could tell which one of us is darker?" The two men enjoyed spending time together, sharing their experiences as cultural leaders.

W.E.B.'s next trip was to Ghana, West Africa, at the invitation of Ghana's new president, Kwame Nkrumah. It was 1960. W.E.B. and Kwame became friends right away. They shared many common beliefs about brotherhood among people of all races. W.E.B. felt perfectly at home in Africa.

As with many places W.E.B. had visited outside the United States, skin color didn't matter in West Africa. There was no color line, no *twoness*. Black people of all shades were everywhere, and beautiful, and working together. This brought W.E.B. so much peace. When Kwame asked W.E.B. to move to Ghana, it didn't take long for W.E.B. to decide. He packed his silk hat, his collection of books, and his cane, and he made Ghana his home for good. It was as if the country had been waiting for him. The Ghanaian people regarded him as "Africa's father."

W.E.B.'s legacy is still alive today. The NAACP remains one of the world's most vital and visible civil rights organizations and has members from many nations.

W.E.B.'s book, *The Souls of Black Folk*, is required reading in Black Studies programs at many colleges and universities.

Most important, W.E.B. DuBois showed the world that it is the soul within that counts and connects us all.

His hands rang a wake-up bell
for Brotherhood.

When hatred's hot sun rose,
he roused the sleeping car
on the Railroad to justice.

Put it back on track.

Gave the Porters a lift
from the weight of racism's baggage.

Then fired the boss named Bigotry.

Organizer
Agitator
Union Maker
Labor Leader

Rabble-rouser radical!

Demanded decent jobs.
Fought for fair wages.
Won benefits befitting black workers.

A "New Negro"
who delivered the word
via *The Messenger.*

Then Marched it on Washington

straight to equality's front door.

A. Philip Randolph

b. April 15, 1889, Crescent City, Florida;
d. May 16, 1979, New York City

Always Striding Ahead

---

*H*E WAS A BABY who wriggled in his mama's arms. Wouldn't keep still, that boy. The child wanted to *move*!

His father, the Reverend James William Randolph, and his mother, Elizabeth Robinson Randolph, knew their son had what folks called "a striver's desire." As a toddler, he went after what he wanted. While grabbing for a rattle, he was preparing for when he was grown and would shake things up.

His parents named him Asa, after one of the great kings in the Old Testament. The name fit him rightly. He was a natural-born leader.

A-S-A—spelled the same *front ways* and *back ways*—was also the perfect name for a child who was:

Always
Striding
Ahead.

From the time Asa could walk, he was in front of other kids. His older brother, James Jr., had to run to keep up with him. Whenever another kid shouted, "Catch him if you can!" nobody took the challenge. It was hard to keep up with Asa Randolph.

Reverend James and Elizabeth recognized their son's gifts. Because he was good at moving forward, they insisted that he advance his mind by learning to read and write well. Because of his parents' high regard for education, Asa excelled at Jacksonville's Cookman Institute, the only academic high school in Florida for African American students.

Every afternoon, Asa and James Jr. had to come home right after school and read with their daddy. Reverend Randolph was a minister in the African Methodist Episcopal (AME) Church. He helped his boys strengthen their reading by poring over Bible passages. Asa and James learned many things from the Good Book's pages, mostly that in God's eyes, all men are equal.

Reverend Randolph also gave his sons books about the history of black people. He had been born in 1864, just before the Civil War ended. As the son of parents who had both been slaves, the reverend taught himself to read. He was determined to educate his sons about the struggles and triumphs of African Americans. As a minister, Reverend Randolph bolstered his sons' schooling by preaching about the virtues of black achievement. He also taught his sons the importance of good manners and proper dress. He showed them how to stand tall when addressing an audience, and how straightforward language is the best way to encourage people to listen while you talk. The reverend reminded Asa, who was soft-spoken, that one's words ring loudest when delivered with confidence and sincerity.

These lessons stayed with Asa and James, who, like their father, took to books and public speaking. As much as Asa's parents enjoyed seeing their sons read, they would not let them go to the local public library, which was segregated. At home, the Randolph boys had their pick of books, and they could relax and read in any room they chose in their small house. In the town library, the rule was blacks on one side of the stacks, whites on the other.

Some kids might have bemoaned spending hot afternoons with Bible passages, black history pages, and living-room sermons from their daddy. But for Asa, reading was fun. And watching his father speechify showed him how to speak publicly with conviction. These skills made Asa a star at school. He impressed his teachers, Miss Lillie Whitney and Miss Mary Neff. They encouraged Asa at every opportunity. When it was time to audition for school plays, Asa always landed leading roles in Cookman's productions. In the school choir, Asa's confident baritone voice outsang everyone else's.

When Asa graduated from Cookman Institute in 1907, he was valedictorian of his class, and he was chosen to deliver the graduation speech. Asa stood as straight and proud as the cypress trees that graced Cookman's property. He was eighteen years old, more than six feet tall, and skinny as a broomstick. But he spoke with the eloquence and power of a full-grown man. Cookman was a modest school, but when Asa talked about racial equality, he lit up the place.

On that day, his family were the ones who were front and center, sitting in the first row, cheering on Asa.

Asa's parents didn't have enough money to send him to college. But Reverend Randolph had a plan for his youngest son. He wanted him to follow in his footsteps and become a minister. There was no doubt that Asa had what it took to bring a podium alive and to inspire people. But while growing up, Asa had often heard his father say that clergy people were *called* to the ministry. This is how Asa knew he wasn't meant to be an ordained preacher. As hard as he listened, nothing seemed to *call* him to ministerial work.

After graduation, Asa stayed in Jacksonville, where he continued to attend Sunday services at his father's church and to sing in the AME choir. During his father's sermons—and when the choir rocked "This Little Light of Mine"—Asa silently prayed for guidance and a light of his own to show him the way.

Good employment opportunities were limited for black people in the segregated South. Even when African Americans could find jobs, they were paid less than white people and treated unfairly. This bothered Asa, who worked several odd jobs.

At the local grocery store, he was the best bagger. At the drugstore, he was a clerk with charm. At a nearby insurance company, Asa made sure his customers felt special. He always worked his hardest. But the jobs were boring and didn't motivate Asa. When payday came, Asa sighed at the sight of his measly paycheck. He saw no future opportunities in any of the places he worked, and he wanted to be somewhere other than Jacksonville.

In his spare time, when his father preferred him to read the Bible, Asa read plays by William Shakespeare. He came to love Shakespeare's use of language so much that he learned the lines from many of his plays. The beautiful words played in Asa's thoughts while he worked at monotonous jobs.

On weekends, Asa performed with a local drama group. Folks in town got to know his name and came to see him. When Asa was onstage, he felt alive. His secret dream was to become a professional actor.

In spring 1911, Asa made a decision that would change him forever. He used his talents for elocution to land a job as a kitchen worker on a steamship that was sailing to New York City. He told his parents he'd only be gone for the summer, but when that boat pulled away from the harbor, Asa knew he was kissing Florida good-bye.

Days later, Asa arrived in Harlem, where the streets were paved with black pride. Harlem was known as "the capital of black America," and on every corner, African Americans held their heads high. Black people didn't just work in stores and hotels and restaurants—they owned them. When Asa went to the library in his neighborhood, he could roam the stacks and read as he pleased. When he asked for his own library card, nobody blinked. When he checked out history books, story collections, and Shakespeare's plays, the librarian only had one word for him: *Enjoy!* And that's what Asa did. He savored those books.

Asa worked as a janitor, dishwasher, and porter. These positions were as uninspiring as the jobs he'd held in Jacksonville, but Asa had his library books and the pulse and excitement of New York City to spark his imagination. Harlem was going through a renaissance. There was black creative expression everywhere, in the form of art, poetry, culture, and music.

Asa's appreciation for the theater and his love of Shakespeare grew. And he'd never lost his admiration for the church. He joined Harlem's Salem Methodist Church's drama club, where he performed in Shakespeare recitals. During this time, Asa went from a soft-spoken amateur to an oratory professional. When Asa spoke the words of *Julius Caesar,*

Othello, The Merchant of Venice, or *Hamlet*, he understood what his father had meant about being *called* to do something that made your soul sing.

Asa wrote to his parents to tell them of his desire to become a full-time actor. He received a reply quickly. The response, written by his father, was short but not very sweet. His and Elizabeth's feelings about their son going into show business was summed up simply: *No!*

To Reverend James, acting was a waste of Asa's abilities. It was frivolous business, not respectable work. His letter told Asa that even though Asa may not have wanted to become a preacher, he was destined for greater accomplishments than those of an actor.

It was around this time that Asa returned to a book he'd encountered a few years earlier, *The Souls of Black Folk* by civil rights leader W.E.B. DuBois. *The Souls of Black Folk* was a series of essays denouncing segregation and promoting black empowerment through education.

DuBois's essays moved Asa deeply. *The Souls of Black Folk* changed him. While Shakespeare's language made Asa's soul sing, DuBois's *The Souls of Black Folk* went deeper—its essays *sank* into Asa's soul. They made him realize that perhaps his father had been right about his being called to a higher purpose. Though he didn't want to be a minister, he could minister to people, and help African Americans gain equality, through his God-given abilities.

Asa came to see that if he was seeking an audience and standing ovations, he needed to stand *for* something. He recalled the words of Hamlet, one of Shakespeare's most noted characters, a tragic prince who struggled with questions of when to proceed with an action, and what is right and wrong. Asa had delivered the words of Hamlet's most noted soliloquy— "To be, or not to be, that is the question"—many times, but now Hamlet's words articulated the path Asa had been seeking. For Asa, the question wasn't "to be, or not to be," but rather, *what* to be and *how* to be it?

In Harlem, Asa met many young black men and women, who, like him, were well-read, bright, and eager to learn. They told Asa about New York's City College, where classes were free. When Asa enrolled at City College, it was as if the glittery hand of Harlem was presenting him with a beautiful package wrapped in a bow. Asa's college classes seemed to have been made especially for him. History, economics, political science, and debate society were among his favorites. Asa read and read and read his textbooks, sometimes two or three times. He excelled as a college student. But college wasn't all about course work for Asa. He started to make friends with students who were deep thinkers, who had exciting ideas for bringing about social change.

At City College, Asa learned about the principles of socialism, the belief that if everyone in a society is working equally, no one person, or group of people, should be entitled to more wealth—or stuff—than anyone else. In a socialist society everyone shares goods and services to the same degree. Everybody has equal amounts of everything—food, clothes, shoes, soap, juice. And there's equal access to the same doctors, banks, dentists, butchers, bakers, and schools. Some socialists believe that common workers should organize themselves into groups in order to gain more control over their nation's industries and government.

Asa was immediately struck by socialist ideals. What a great way for black people to be equal, he believed, especially black workers. But it was 1913, and socialism was a radical idea for many to accept. In some respects, socialism was like Shakespeare's language—it sounded good, but many found it hard to grasp. At City College, Asa enjoyed debates with his classmates about socialism's advantages. Through further reading, Asa became convinced that a socialist society was the answer to how black people could gain political power in the United States.

One night at a Harlem party, Asa was introduced to Lucille Campbell Green, a beautician who shared his ideas about socialism. Asa and Lucille got married just months after they met. They never had children. Asa called Lucille his "beautiful, gregarious, elegant, fashionable, and socially conscious wife."

Not everyone was as smitten with Asa and his views on socialism as Lucille was. When Asa shared his beliefs, some saw their value. At the same time, though, he encountered many doubters. In 1914, Lucille introduced Asa to Chandler Owen, a black sociology student at Columbia University, which was a few blocks from City College. Chandler put the red-hot in radical. He was outspoken, freewheeling, mouthy, and confrontational. Asa liked Chandler. On the day they first shook hands and said hello, they ignited a powerful friendship. One of their favorite meeting places was the library. Asa had found a buddy who loved reading as much as he did.

After they had finished their day of classes, the two men pushed into crowded rush-hour subway cars to get downtown where labor meetings and socialist rallies were held. When Asa and Chandler listened to speakers talk about socialist concepts, and how these could provide a road map to freeing black people from economic oppression, they embraced socialism even more wholeheartedly. They both joined the Socialist Party of America.

Socialism was making its way uptown, too. In Harlem, there were a few street-corner speakers who tried to convince Harlemites of socialism's value. These speeches were met with only moderate enthusiasm. Through his father's oratorical home-training and his time on the Shakespearean stage, Asa had learned that it's not only *what* you say, but *how*, that convinces people. It seems Chandler had already learned this lesson.

He and Asa gathered up some book boxes that had been left in the alleyway near their favorite library. Where some street preachers stood on soapboxes, Asa and Chandler elevated themselves by using the crates that once held the gems that had gotten them to this point.

They were ready to shout socialism's promise, and they did. With Asa's skills for forming an articulate argument, and Chandler's brassy-pants way of driving home a message, the two became a dynamic speaking team.

When they parked themselves on the corner of 135th Street and Lenox Avenue, they were more effective than a hallelujah chorus in delivering the merits of socialism. Whenever they spoke, they put an even higher rise in Harlem's renaissance. Soon subway trains were packed in the opposite direction. Downtowners were coming uptown to hear Asa and Chandler. The sidewalks were filled with young people who were fired up by these radical orators.

"Tell it, Asa!" they shouted.

"Speak on, Chandler!" they enthused.

Sometimes people put their praises to music. "Preach it!" they sang.

And yes, Lord, Asa and Chandler did preachify.

Many of those gathered were men and women who considered

themselves "New Negros," young radicals who took pride in being militant forward-thinkers. One of these listeners was William White, president of a black waiters' organization. William had an idea. He wanted to create a publication that would be read by black waiters, one of New York's service professions largely occupied by African Americans. He presented his idea to Asa and Chandler and asked them to help launch the periodical. Asa and Chandler said yes immediately. This was their chance to extend their ideas from the pavement to the printed page. Together they founded a publication called *Hotel Messenger*.

Asa and Chandler worked all hours, writing, editing, observing waiters at their restaurants, sharing their stories, and bringing light to the unfair treatment of black laborers. Asa changed his name to A. Philip Randolph for his byline.

Like true journalists, Asa and Chandler told it like it was, reporting on real happenings as they occurred. Mostly they reported on issues of pay, work hours, and the physical demands of being employed in a service profession. In one article, they told of an argument that had erupted between a group of junior waiters and more experienced head-waiters. William didn't like this kind of reporting. He felt it was not the best use of the journal, so he fired Asa and Chandler, and the *Hotel Messenger* folded.

On the day in August 1917 when they left William White's office, carrying their notes and issues from the now-defunct *Hotel Messenger*, Asa and Chandler said good-bye to each other on the corner. Asa's shirt collar created a ring of sweat around his neck as he walked to his apartment. Summer's heat was unrelenting. The hot air coming up through the subway grates didn't help.

Then, like a cool breeze that clears away the thickest humidity, Asa was struck with a realization. Even though the *Hotel Messenger* would not continue, he was even more committed to helping black workers. The answer to his own questions of *what* to be and *how* to be it was waiting right in his very own hands.

What he was meant to be was an advocate for black workers. *How* to be this was simple, but it would not be easy.

Getting fired fired up Asa and Chandler. They were still among the hottest neighborhood speakers in Harlem. Their socialist views were very controversial and always sparked colorful debates among the crowds they drew to the street corner where they preached.

The *Hotel Messenger* had gradually gained the attention of African Americans who were employed in places other than hotel restaurants. Store clerks, subway operators, washroom attendants, and other laborers had taken an interest in the articles. When these people and members of the "New Negro" faction learned of the publication's demise, they were disappointed. Asa and Chandler kept getting requests for the return of a publication that spoke to the needs and opinions of black workers. One of these "New Negroes" gave them a typewriter (William White wouldn't let them take the one they'd been using in his office), and they got started on a new monthly magazine.

Just weeks before Thanksgiving 1917, the residents of Harlem, and black workers throughout the city, got something they were truly grateful for. *The Messenger*, Asa and Chandler's new publication, was a welcome sight on the newsstands of New York. It cost fifteen cents, and was a nickel and a dime well-spent. Asa and Chandler called *The Messenger* "the first voice of radical, revolutionary, economic, and political action among Negroes in America."

The Messenger was a controversial mix of pieces that spoke out against lynching, shunned racist practices perpetrated upon black workers, and promoted socialist opinions. The most contentious position of *The Messenger*, however, was its views on African Americans being enlisted to serve in World War I. The United States had entered the war in April 1917, and black soldiers were joining the ranks of the armed forces in great numbers. But these brave men were paid lower wages, had inferior weaponry and supplies, and, as in every other aspect of their lives as civilians, they were segregated, this time from white soldiers.

In *The Messenger*, Asa underscored these injustices, reminding readers that black men were being forced to fight on behalf of America while at the same time being considered second-class citizens by the very nation they were serving. Several issues of the magazine asked readers, Why should these men risk their own lives for a country that discriminates against them?

In 1917, it was considered unpatriotic to express views against the war, but Asa and Chandler didn't back down. People got scared of Asa's hard-hitting position on black participation in the war. His scorn of unfair labor practices also frightened people. But *The Messenger* was doing what all good newspapers do. It was telling the truth about conditions as they were. Still, by 1920, the U.S. Justice Department warned that A. Philip Randolph was "the most dangerous Negro in America."

This made Asa even more committed to his cause. (Years after the Justice Department's declaration, Asa said he didn't "give a fig" what the government thought of him.) What was really dangerous were the prejudicial practices endured by black citizens.

Whether people loved or hated *The Messenger*, Asa and Chandler stayed determined to keep its message strong. In time, though, its readership began to decline. In 1923, Chandler moved to Chicago, where he got a job as a newspaper reporter.

Though fewer people were purchasing *The Messenger*, it still had a strong pull on the attention of its devoted readers. One group of committed *Messenger* followers were the porters for the Pullman Company, a long-distance rail enterprise that employed mostly black men to serve people who traveled in deluxe sleeper cars.

Porters did practically everything for Pullman passengers. They hoisted luggage, shined shoes, helped ladies over puddles and ditches, cleaned the velvet-upholstered train seats, sang lullabies to train-sick babies, served breakfast, lunch, dinner, snacks, and anything else that a high-paying customer wanted.

But compared to the amount of work they did, porters were paid a piddly paycheck. If a porter got hungry while at work, he had to buy his own food with the small wages he'd earned. Porters worked around the clock, sometimes not receiving wages for all the hours they put in. These men had to be away from their wives and children for months at a time. If a porter got sick, he was not entitled to time off and he had to keep working. Also, porters received no medical benefits or pension, which would have allowed them to save money for when they were too old to work.

One of the worst parts about being a porter was the daily humiliation of being called "George." Whether your real name was Thomas, Ezekiel, or Joseph, if you were a black man working on a Pullman railroad car, white passengers addressed you as "George." This demeaning practice disregarded each porter's individuality and turned black men into faceless servants.

Imagine spending hours and days and months hearing:

"George, get me some water."

"George, my pillow's too stiff."

"George, fix my lightbulb."

"*Now*, George!"

Asa's brother, James, had worked as a porter. He told Asa all about the slights he'd faced. In 1925, the porters asked Asa to help them organize a union. White porters already had a union that guaranteed them pay increases and decent working conditions (and nobody called white porters "George" unless it was the name their mothers and fathers had given them).

Asa accepted the invitation of the black porters, but he knew there would be a long struggle ahead. Black porters had tried unsuccessfully to form a union in the past. There were too many risks. If a black porter expressed discontent with his job, he could be fired, or even lynched. Asa understood this, but he also knew that when banded together, the black porters would be a powerful force that could stand up to the Pullman Company. The men believed in Asa. They called themselves the Brotherhood of Sleeping Car Porters, or "the Brotherhood" for short. Asa was elected as their president.

The Pullman Company immediately refused the Brotherhood's request to form a union, and they did everything possible to sabotage the black porters' efforts. They threatened employees and Asa. They ignored the Brotherhood's continued attempts to negotiate. They even spied on Brotherhood organizational meetings to monitor their progress.

By the end of 1926, there were nearly six thousand men in the Brotherhood, comprised of workers in branches throughout the United States.

But the Pullman Company was one of the wealthiest industry giants in America. Going up against Pullman was like hurling train-track pebbles at a locomotive.

Asa didn't care how big Pullman's steam whistle was. He was not backing down. He was intent on building strength through unity to bring about changes. The Brotherhood continued to grow, but their cause suffered many setbacks. Under Asa's leadership, they tried to gain union status through the Railway Labor Act of 1926, legislation that had created a board to settle disagreements between large companies and their employees.

Asa wrote a letter to the railroad mediation board. He told them that he wanted to apply the Railway Labor Act to the dispute between the Brotherhood and the Pullman Company. The mediation board assigned a lawyer, Edward Morrow, to investigate the dispute. To succeed in his pursuit, and to apply the Railway Labor Act, the majority of the Brotherhood had to be in opposition to the Pullman Company's practices. A majority would warrant a dispute.

But many black porters were still apprehensive about speaking out publicly against Pullman Company practices. They were afraid they'd lose their jobs. When Edward contacted the Pullman Company, he was told that there was no dispute between the management and workers. The Pullman Company refused to enter into any mediation discussions. Pullman Company officials could not be forced to participate in mediation talks, so the Railway Labor Act didn't allow the Brotherhood to apply its practices for their gain.

When Franklin D. Roosevelt was elected president in 1932, things slowly started to get better for the Brotherhood. One of President Roosevelt's first actions was to improve labor laws so that more people could find and keep jobs at a time when America was facing an economic depression. But even with the president's efforts, it would take five more years for the Brotherhood to get their union.

Finally, on August 25, 1937, after years of pounding away at the Pullman Company and seeing the passage of new federal labor legislation that improved the lives of other union workers, the Brotherhood of

Sleeping Car Porters won a tremendous victory: representatives of the Pullman Company agreed to a large wage increase, overtime pay, fair work practices, and shorter workweeks.

Under Asa's leadership, the Brotherhood was the first group of black employees to sign a labor agreement with a major corporation. The struggle took twelve years. When it was finally over, black porters rode the trains with pride on their side, more money in their paychecks, and time off to partake of picnics and birthday parties with their families.

And, thankfully, passengers on Pullman trains started to refer to the porters as "Sir."

Asa's work with the Brotherhood of Sleeping Car Porters proved that when black people came together in unity—and stuck to their course— they were a mighty force. Asa was proud of what he'd accomplished on behalf of the Brotherhood, but there was more work to be done.

A continuing area of discrimination was African Americans in the armed forces. Since World War I, when Asa first protested this in his *Messenger* editorials, he felt strongly about the inequity of black men having to risk their lives on the battlefield for a country that was not serving them fairly.

In 1941, when World War II loomed, black soldiers were still forced into segregated ranks. Skilled black workers were also denied jobs in the defense industry. These men could have been helpful in producing war supplies, but they were denied opportunities because of their race.

As World War II raged abroad, Asa came up with an idea for a demonstration that was all about peace. His plan was to organize a massive march on Washington, D.C., to protest the segregation of African American soldiers and the denial of defense industry jobs for black workers.

In January 1941, Asa proclaimed that he would coordinate a nonviolent march that would "shake up America."

Asa's intention was to rally black people from all over the United States to do something simple, yet powerful. He said, "Leaders in Washington will never give the Negro justice until they see masses—ten, twenty, fifty thousand Negroes on the White House lawn!"

Asa marked his calendar for July 1, 1941. This was the day he scheduled the march. He was confident that if America and President Roosevelt witnessed thousands of black people pressing into Washington, it would show that when gathered in large numbers, African Americans possessed unmistakable might.

Folks from all over were ready to join Asa in his fight. Though the protest was to proceed nonviolently, the sheer volume of people would be unstoppable. In working toward the march, Asa said, "Nothing counts but pressure, more pressure, and still more pressure."

So, the pressure was *on*. And anybody who'd ever handled a pressure cooker knew that corn kernels pop faster when the kettle's heat is high. Asa wanted government officials to feel the heat and pressure of discrimination and move quickly to end it.

Asa enlisted the help of black porters to spread news about the march. Since these men were traveling the nation's rails, they were able to disseminate information quickly and easily among black communities from New York to Chicago to Los Angeles.

It didn't take much to convince people to support the march. On the sidewalks of Harlem, Asa got back up on his book crates and spoke about the importance of conducting a protest that included large numbers of people. "Let the Negro masses speak!" he preached.

Soon sisters were calling brothers to tell them about the march. They, in turn, wrote to uncles, nieces, aunts, in-laws, third cousins twice removed, and nephews, too, encouraging them to join the march come July. Churches hung "March On!" banners. Bakeries created "march macaroons." There was even a bookstore that changed its name to March Community Bookshop.

By spring 1941, Asa had upped his own ante. He was now striving to get one hundred thousand citizens to participate in the march. When government officials found out about Asa's plan, they got nervous. They were afraid angry people would forget the peaceful intent of the march and that *non*violence would somehow turn to *mob* violence.

This concern was enough to get President Roosevelt to take action. The president invited Asa to the White House on June 18, 1941, and attempted to persuade him to call off the march. Asa's response was simple. He would scratch the July 1 date for the march from his calendar if, at the same time, Mr. Roosevelt added a priority to his presidential to-do list.

Asa insisted that the president issue an executive order that deemed all racial discrimination within the war industry illegal. Asa expressed the urgency of getting this executive order completed in a timely fashion.

President Roosevelt listened to Asa, who spoke with a quiet force. The president could see by the tightness of Asa's jaw and the intensity of his gaze that he was standing firm.

Asa could tell by the way President Roosevelt fidgeted in his chair that he was feeling the two things Asa knew were needed to make the president "pop" into action—pressure and heat.

On June 25, 1941, President Roosevelt signed on the dotted line to promote equality. He issued Executive Order 8802, also known as the Fair Employment Act, which declared racially discriminatory job practices in the defense industry illegal. Three days later, Asa spoke on the radio, letting folks know there would be no march.

Those who didn't have radios heard back from their cousins, uncles, sisters, and brothers, who shared the news. Folks put away the marching shoes they'd shined for the trip to Washington. Instead, they'd be wearing these shoes to church to stomp their feet during the hallelujah chorus, where they'd praise the Lord for Roosevelt's Order.

Though Asa had cancelled his 1941 mass march on Washington, he had successfully, and peacefully, marched on up to the president on his own, and convinced him to make an important change to the law. Asa was pleased with this progress, but black citizens had not yet gained full equality.

As much as there was to celebrate about Executive Order 8802, in Asa's eyes, the Fair Employment Act only warranted half a hallelujah. While the order put an end to defense industry job discrimination, it didn't address segregation in the armed forces. Black soldiers were still kept apart from white soldiers, and racial tensions festered in communities throughout America.

To keep working against this dissension, Asa continued to preach on Harlem street corners, avenues, boulevards, bridges, back roads, and even in alleys. He staged a civil rights rally in New York City's Madison Square Garden on June 16, 1942. In a pamphlet he wrote to spur people to attend the Madison Square Garden assembly, Asa issued an urgent call: Wake up, Negro America!

This piercing imperative roused people to attend the rally.

More than twenty thousand black men and women filled Madison Square Garden to attend what Asa said was, at that point in time, "the biggest demonstration of Negroes in the history of the world."

The crowds at Madison Square Garden inspired Asa to keep up his ongoing fight for fairness. Progress was very slow. Years passed with Asa staying firmly committed to his cause. When World War II ended in 1945, President Harry S. Truman was in office. The president had plans for seeking re-election in November 1948.

Mr. Truman needed black voters to win the upcoming election. Asa and his supporters saw this as an opportunity. In July 1948, at the Democratic National Convention in Philadelphia, African Americans showed up with picket signs, civil rights songs, and a giant bunch of gumption. They got the president's attention immediately. His pen was ready to write. He issued *two* executive orders—the first one established the Fair Employment Board, a group that would stomp out racial discrimination in government agencies; the second put an end to segregation in the armed forces.

Asa had now persuaded two different presidents to sign their names to the cause for justice. Both times it was the power of so many committed black citizens rallying together that had swayed the presidents to take action.

Witnessing the collective influence of his people prompted Asa to return to his idea for a march. There was still a very long road ahead. After years of walking in the name of equality, Asa wanted to take even greater strides. But the time and circumstances had to be right. During the spring of 1963, Asa spent much of his time tending to his wife, Lucille, who had become crippled from arthritis. She died in April of that year. Lucille had been one of Asa's strongest supporters. She had always encouraged her husband to keep on keeping on with his pursuit for justice. Once she was gone, Asa knew what Lucille would have wanted him to do—march.

In the summer of 1963, the opportunity came. John F. Kennedy was the president. Martin Luther King, Jr., had emerged as a powerful civil rights leader, instilling the message of progress through peaceful action. More black and white people had become committed to social change. There was a feeling of hope among Americans.

Asa had waited long enough. America was ready.

In June 1963, Asa gathered some of the most prominent civil rights leaders of the time and proposed the March on Washington for Jobs and Freedom. Its purpose was to encourage Congress's adoption of President Kennedy's civil rights legislation, which called for the end of segregation in public places and fair voting practices. Asa also had his own want list: He wanted to see all public schools fully integrated. He wanted the government to provide job training and placement for unemployed black people. He wanted a law barring all job discrimination against African Americans.

Once again, Asa, with the help of many, spread the word about the march, which was to take place on August 28, 1963. As plans were being made, a groundswell of enthusiasm grew. Black babies who in 1941 had just learned to walk, were now all grown up and were eager to strut to D.C. But, like President Roosevelt, President John F. Kennedy tried to talk Asa out of going ahead with the march. President Kennedy had the same concerns that President Roosevelt had expressed. He feared the march would turn violent and that black people would bring unrest to the streets. President Kennedy called Asa for a meeting. At this point in his life, Asa could talk to presidents with the ease and sincerity of one friend talking to another.

Asa said to John F. Kennedy, "Mr. President, the Negroes are *already* in the streets."

After hours of talking, Asa gained President Kennedy's trust. The president agreed to let the march proceed.

On August 28, 1963, two hundred and fifty thousand people—black, white, and every beautiful shade of brown in between—gathered at the Washington Monument to march their way to the Lincoln Memorial, where civil rights speakers would address the crowd.

Asa, James Farmer, Martin Luther King, Jr., John Lewis, Roy

Wilkins, and Whitney Young, who were some of the leading civil rights activists of the time and known as the Big Six, walked arm-in-arm leading the marchers.

Though a quarter million people had come to the nation's capital, in many respects, this march was Asa's march.

He'd dreamed of it. Organized it. Made it happen.

When Asa and the rest of the Big Six came forward, Asa stood with the pride of ten men.

People called out to greet him. "March, Asa!"

Asa sure did march. He had sturdy shoes with strong soles, and a heart filled with conviction.

Once everyone arrived at the Lincoln Memorial, they waited for the words of Martin Luther King, Jr., who would give his unforgettable "I Have a Dream" speech.

But it was Asa Philip Randolph who delivered the afternoon's opening remarks.

He said, "Let the nation and the world know the meaning of our numbers."

On this day, Asa gave meaning to the legacy he'd built upon a name that fit him rightly.

Spelled the same *front ways* as *back ways*—for a man *always* reaching forward, while at the same time staying rooted in the history of his people.

A-S-A
Always
Striding
Ahead.

His hands threw the book

at school segregation.

Argued *Brown vs. Board of Ed.*
Knocked "separate-but-equal"
on its crooked head.

Landmark Lawmaker

Legal Mind Supreme

Ardent Advocate

Ace Attorney

Thurgood stood
for the *good* of his people.

Put black students at the head of the class.
Gave them the chance
to raise *their* hands
high in the air.

So that every teacher *everywhere*
could call

on Justice for All.

Thurgood Marshall

———◆◆◆———

b. July 2, 1908, Baltimore, Maryland;
d. January 24, 1993, Bethesda, Maryland

Mr. Civil Rights

EVEN THOUGH THURGOOD MARSHALL was born two days before the Fourth of July, he was a child with the spark of a firecracker! Maybe it was his great-grandfather's legacy that ignited Thurgood's feistiness. Thurgood's great-grandfather was a slave who would not be kept down by slavery's wicked ways.

When Mr. Master got mean, Thurgood's great-grandfather kicked and screamed. On days when Mr. Master weighed him down with melon sacks and grain barrels, Thurgood's great-grandfather bucked them off.

No matter what Mr. Master tried, he could not control this man. Most plantation owners would have sold such a rebellious slave. But Thurgood's great-grandfather made that difficult, too. He'd become so strong-willed that Mr. Master couldn't sell him. Nobody would buy the guy. Mr. Master had no choice but to set Great-Grandpa free. He told him to get gone. To leave the county and never come back!

But Great-Grandpa refused to leave. Rather than flee to his freedom, he walked down the road, built his own home, moved in, and started fixing up the place where he lived comfortably for the rest of his free life.

This determination must have been in Thurgood's blood, because he was as bold as they come. Thurgood got his name from his father's daddy, also a rebel with a good cause. During the Civil War, when Thurgood's granddaddy on his father's side of the family wanted to join the Union army, officials insisted that he needed two names. In a moment of quick thinking, he told the army intake worker his name was Thorough Good.

Many years later, when Norma and William Marshall welcomed the youngest of their two sons in 1908, they kept their family's legacy alive by naming the boy Thoroughgood. By second grade, Thoroughgood was thoroughly sick of having to spell such a long name. And he was tired of his classmates challenging each other to say "Thoroughgood" three times fast. He convinced his parents to shorten his name to Thurgood.

Thurgood liked being the only child in his school, and town, and everyplace he went, with a name like his. He was a one-of-a-kind kid with a way all his own. The boy wore knee-pants and hard shoes. He carried a comic book in both his back pockets, and was good at snapping gum.

In school, Thurgood was the class cutup. He could turn a teacher's lesson into a joke so funny that even the teacher couldn't keep a straight face. Thurgood was an A+ prankster, too. If someone got stuck to a chair from a puddle of glue, or if a doodlebug landed in a lunch box, all eyes turned to Thurgood.

A true trickster, the one who makes the best mischief, is the one paying the closest attention. This was Thurgood. He always had his eye on details and his ears pricked for the right moment to take action. He was rowdy, but focused.

After one prank too many, Thurgood's grade-school principal punished him. The principal took Thurgood to the school basement and clobbered him with an assignment that was not for weaklings. He made Thurgood memorize, line for line, a passage from the United States Constitution, a wordy document written in 1787 by America's leaders, outlining the laws that would govern the country and its citizens.

Mr. Principal made his punishment clear. Thurgood could only return to his classroom once he knew the passage by heart. Thurgood got right to it. Being as feisty as he was, he was sent to the school basement again and again. Each time, he had to memorize a new passage of the Constitution. Thurgood's friends started to think that he secretly liked reading the pages written by the founders of the United States, and that he misbehaved so that he could be sent to what kids called the "D.C.D."—the Dreaded Constitution Dungeon.

Thurgood took to reading the Constitution as if it contained an important code worth knowing. It was filled with big words and high ideals, but Thurgood stuck with it until he could recite what he'd read.

When other students were sent to the D.C.D. with Thurgood, he helped them memorize the Constitution's articles, sections, branches, and oaths. He explained what the words meant as far as he understood them. By the time Thurgood was done with grade school, he could recite the entire U.S. Constitution, preamble and all.

From "We the people," to freedoms and rights, to powers and presidents, Thurgood knew that document as thoroughly as he knew his own name. He could also list all the men who'd signed the document. Everybody from George Washington to Benjamin Franklin.

There were two parts of the Constitution that made Thurgood think hard. The Fourteenth Amendment stated that all Americans were entitled to equal rights. The Constitution's Fifteenth Amendment further supported the Fourteenth by declaring that U.S. citizens could not be denied the right to vote "on account of race, color, or previous condition of servitude."

What Thurgood saw in the living conditions around him was very different from what the Constitution said was the law. In Thurgood's West Baltimore neighborhood, and in most other towns in America, black people were kept separate from white people on account of race and color.

It seemed the men running the government in Thurgood's time had different ideas about equality than those that were written in the Constitution. Despite this early vision of fairness for America's citizens, there was nothing fair about the ways African Americans were being treated as he was growing up.

Thurgood witnessed this every day as he walked to his all-black school and watched white children go to their all-white school, where, by law, black students were not allowed on account of race and color.

Thurgood wondered, Where is the equality in that?

Without even going to the D.C.D., Thurgood started to study the Constitution. He showed it to his mother and father, who told him it was fruitless to challenge segregation. They explained that the only way to successfully fight against the law was when you were sure you could win.

And to become a winner, you had to understand how the game was played.

Thanks to Thurgood's father, William Marshall, Thurgood got to watch the legal process and learn how winning happens in front of a judge and jury. He was able to see firsthand the "game" of what goes on in a courtroom. On the days Thurgood's father was not working at his job as a country-club waiter, he spent his free time at the local courthouse, observing lawyers as they defended their cases. When Thurgood was a teenager, his father took him along, and the two of them paid close attention to the details of trials in action.

Though Thurgood's father had little formal education, he was a smart and high-spirited man. When William was selected as the first African American in Baltimore to serve on a grand jury, he was a juror who spoke his mind. The first thing he noticed was that before the case started, when attorneys interviewed the other jurors, all of whom were white, the jurors asked if the person being tried was black or white. In William Marshall's mind, this made no difference. If the person was guilty, he or she was guilty. If the person was innocent, he or she was innocent. The man or woman's skin color had no bearing on whether he or she had committed a crime or not.

During juror questioning, William raised his hand. He told the courtroom his opinion about questioning the race of an accused citizen. When he spoke up, the courtroom got quiet. The only noise in the place was the annoyed breathing of other jurors who did not take kindly to William's views. But the head juror, the foreman, agreed with him. Before the trial had even started, William experienced a courtroom win. At that moment, the race questions ended and the trial proceeded.

This was how William Marshall "played the game." William understood that winning could come in the form of small but important victories that would eventually lead to bigger wins. He taught Thurgood to think carefully about all sides of a situation, to question, to debate, and to clearly articulate his point. He encouraged him to prove his ideas solidly, leaving little room for opposing views to crack the firm foundation of his argument. William didn't tell his son to become a lawyer, but he sure did put him on the path.

Thurgood's mother, Norma, wanted Thurgood to be a dentist. But

Thurgood had already been bitten by the legal bug. He wanted to sink his teeth further into the Fourteenth and Fifteenth Amendments of the Constitution, which, years after he'd moved on from grade school, still pestered him like an unchecked cavity. The Constitution indicated that the United States was to be a land of equality for all people. But America did not abide by this.

In high school, Thurgood continued to visit the local courthouse with his father. Part of his education about unjust practices came outside of the courtroom, where, every day, he saw examples of discrimination on the city's trolley cars, in restaurants and banks, and at the local public swimming pool, where black kids were not allowed to swim.

Thurgood graduated from high school in 1925 with one goal in mind. He wanted to attend college. Many colleges and universities were segregated, leaving few options for black students. That didn't stop Thurgood. He enrolled at Lincoln University, America's oldest black college, located in Chester County, Pennsylvania. As soon as Thurgood arrived at Lincoln, he met others who were as ambitious as he was, and who were eager to get a good education. His classmates included Kwame Nkrumah, the future president of Ghana, West Africa; a student named Cab Calloway, who would become a famous bandleader; and a smart poet named Langston Hughes, whose poems were already the talk of the town.

Langston and Thurgood became friends. They were different in many ways, but both had big goals for the future. Langston was quiet and bookish. He wrote to express himself, and penned beautiful poems that other students enjoyed pondering and interpreting.

Thurgood was loud, but he also loved to read. He spoke his views and made sure there was no question about their meaning. And young Thurgood Marshall liked to party. He took pride in being a member of what his classmates called "the Weekend Club," a bunch of students who, come Friday night, were long gone from Lincoln's campus, spending time having fun under the bright lights and in the dance halls of Philadelphia, the nearest city.

When Sunday rolled around, Thurgood was back on campus, cracking open his textbooks, getting his homework done for Monday morning. He was able to find the balance between studying and partying, but eventually realized that the Weekend Club was a fast track to no place worth going.

While in college, Thurgood experienced prejudice on several occasions. If he wanted to take his girlfriend, Vivian Burey, out for a meal, they were made to enter by the soda shop's back door, order their milk shakes and fries, and leave just as soon as the waitress handed them their food. This was no way to impress a young lady, especially one as smart and as beautiful as Vivian, who was a student at the University of Pennsylvania. But Thurgood's charm and good looks made any date worthwhile. After a brief courtship, when Thurgood asked Vivian to marry him, she said yes right away.

At Lincoln University, all the professors were white. This bothered many of the black students, who wanted to see more teachers who looked like themselves. Langston Hughes was among the most passionate about wanting the faculty to be integrated. He was as vocal about the matter as Thurgood. The issue was presented to school officials, who, after two years of debate, added black professors to their faculty.

By Thurgood's junior year at Lincoln, he was a star student, devoted husband, and fully retired member of the Weekend Club.

Thurgood remembered the cases he'd witnessed in courtrooms with his father. He understood the power of persuasion and brought this to Lincoln's debating team. Thanks to Thurgood's ability to influence others, the team became one of the most notable debate societies on the black college circuit.

In 1930, Thurgood graduated from Lincoln University with honors. His mother still hoped he'd become a dentist, but it was too late for that. He presented a compelling argument for why he'd make a lousy dentist but an excellent attorney. With an impassioned delivery, Thurgood told his mother that because of his knowledge of the Constitution, and all the time he'd spent in courtrooms with his father, he'd be better at digging into law books than drilling into molars.

After seeing her son speak with such conviction, Norma hugged him tightly. Thurgood had done exactly as his father had taught him. He'd left very little room for debate. Norma had to admit that her son had the gift of articulation.

Thurgood applied to the University of Maryland law school in Baltimore. Under Maryland's segregation laws, Thurgood wasn't even eligible to be a student at the university, an all-white institution that had never accepted a black person. But all those days in his grade school's D.C.D. had cemented the Constitution in Thurgood's memory. When he pulled his University of Maryland rejection letter from his mailbox (which came very soon after he applied), the words from the Fourteenth Amendment rang loudly in his mind:

No State shall make or enforce any law which shall abridge the privileges . . . of citizens of the United States, nor shall any State deprive any person of life, liberty, or property, without due process of law; nor deny to any person within its jurisdiction the equal protection of the laws.

The state of Maryland was doing a good job of ignoring these words. There was no doubt about it. They were cutting off Thurgood's *privilege* of going to the law school of his choice, and *depriving* him of the freedom to attend. The university was firm on its position. There was no room for discussion, debate, or due process. In the 1930s, folks tended to look the other way when standards of racial fairness were questioned. So it was easy for the university to sidestep the law.

Thurgood didn't waste time dwelling on this slight. He applied to Howard University Law School, an all-black college that had a stellar reputation for shaping leaders in many fields, including law, medicine, dentistry, engineering, and architecture. The admissions committee at Howard University knew a good candidate when they saw one. They accepted Thurgood immediately.

Thurgood grabbed on to his law courses and books like a man seizing a life preserver. He wanted to change the way *life, liberty, and property* were upheld for African Americans. This mission *was* life to him.

Thurgood studied late into the night, coming to know the power of the law and how he could use it to change the state of race in America. As a law student, Thurgood never forgot the lessons he'd learned in courtrooms with his father. He held tightly to the one word that was essential for a lawyer representing a case: *win.*

Thurgood was brash, outspoken, handsome, and one of the hardest working students at Howard University. Charles Hamilton Houston, vice-dean of Howard's law school, took an immediate liking to Thurgood. Charles was an active member of the National Association for the Advancement of Colored People (NAACP), and often argued cases on behalf of the Baltimore branch of the nation's leading civil rights organization. He became Thurgood's mentor. While still a student, Thurgood worked alongside Charles on the strategy, research, and presentation of arguments for upcoming NAACP cases. This gave Thurgood firsthand experience.

Charles believed that winning was more than a matter of *learning* the law; winning was brought about by *practicing* the law, using existing laws to support an argument.

He told Thurgood that the best lawyers are those who "get with the people," become leaders in their communities, listen carefully to the experiences of everyday folks, then bring these real-life situations into a courtroom to assert their power. Charles's lessons were ones that even the heftiest law books couldn't teach. These were the life lessons Thurgood would put into practice.

In 1933, Thurgood graduated from Howard University Law School first in his class. Soon after graduation, he opened his own small law firm in East Baltimore. He was eager to serve Baltimore's black residents who needed legal help.

On his first day of business, he dusted his law books, then waited for the phone to ring. But the only sound anywhere close to ringing was the chirp of crickets welcoming spring. Black folks were often afraid to bring suit against white people. In the segregated South it was dangerous for African Americans to exercise their legal rights. Some white citizens felt threatened by black citizens who were using the law to seek justice. This caused these people to retaliate against African Americans.

As a result, legal clients were scarce for Thurgood. He stayed patient. In time, his phone did ring. Often, those in need were black townspeople who'd experienced job or housing discrimination, or had been victims of beatings by the police.

Most of the people who sought Thurgood's services couldn't afford to pay him. They compensated him with homemade pies, hams, yams, collards, cukes, and Baltimore crabs wriggling in barrels, set down on the

doorstep of his law office. Thurgood wasn't the richest attorney in town, but thanks to his clients, he was one of the best-fed lawyers in Baltimore County.

In addition to paying Thurgood in kindness, Thurgood's clients were giving him the opportunity to *practice* the law. He prepared for and argued each case as if he were being paid more than a million dollars to represent what he believed was right.

Because of his work on behalf of everyday people—barbers, butchers, tailors, maids—Thurgood got to be known as "the little man's lawyer." His impact, however, was far from small. He gained a reputation as one of the most effective—and affecting—attorneys representing black clients.

Soon, it got to be that if someone in Baltimore needed legal representation, the immediate response was, "Call Thurgood Marshall!"

Even white judges who saw a black person in court trying to fend for themselves would counsel them to find Thurgood.

While the line of needy people trailing from Thurgood's front door grew, so did his desire to use his legal skills to help not only individuals but also the black community.

Leaders of the Baltimore branch of the NAACP had the same wish. They wanted a young, vibrant attorney to represent the organization's legal causes.

They wanted Thurgood Marshall.

In 1934, when the NAACP local branch offered Thurgood a job as part of their legal team, he accepted immediately. This gave Thurgood the opportunity to once again work alongside his Howard University mentor, Charles Houston. It also inspired him to "get with the people" by visiting black churches, social clubs, and Sunday picnics to talk about the importance of racial unity. Charles supported Thurgood in this effort, sometimes joining him in rallying support for the NAACP by encouraging Baltimore residents to become NAACP members. Their speeches in black neighborhoods also inspired African Americans to turn to the NAACP in times of need, and to trust the organization's ability to bring positive changes to the race problems plaguing the city's black residents.

Thurgood and Charles had the law on their side, and with the two of them working together, they also had a double dose of brainpower that served up a one-two legal punch. Among their first cases was defending the NAACP in a lawsuit brought against the organization by a group of merchants whose stores stood along Pennsylvania Avenue in Baltimore's business district. At the advice of Thurgood and Charles, black people launched a boycott of the stores that would not hire black employees. When the shopkeepers' lawsuit was slapped on to the NAACP, Thurgood and Charles got right to work. Thurgood prepared the research for the case. Charles presented the case in court, delivering an argument so sound that not even an ant could find the tiniest crack in its truth.

At the trial, when the white judge handed down his verdict, he also handed Thurgood and Charles his hearty congratulations on their winning presentation. He ruled in favor of the NAACP. From that day on, the stores on Baltimore's Pennsylvania Avenue hired black workers.

Thurgood and Charles were just getting started. One major area of concern in Maryland, and in most states, was segregated public schools.

By law, black children and white children attended separate schools. In 1896, in a case known as *Plessy v. Ferguson*, the Supreme Court ruled that racial segregation was legal when facilities for blacks and whites were "separate but equal."

This seemed to make sense in theory. But when it came to real people in real-life situations, the doctrine of "separate but equal" didn't fully hold up. Facilities for black Americans were, for the most part, not equal to that of white people. They were inferior. Also, the "separate but equal" idea was in direct conflict with the Fourteenth Amendment of the Constitution.

Thurgood knew that "separate but equal" was a misguided idea.

Most folks just went along with segregation and didn't question it. But there were those who wondered, like Thurgood: *How can separating people be equal?* It had always been that way, and nobody dared to challenge this system. Though Thurgood and Charles were excellent at building unshakeable arguments for their cases—while at the same time cracking through walls of long-held racist beliefs—even they knew that attempting to bust open the unjust segregation of public schools would be a nut that could only be cracked with a legal sledgehammer. A change of such magnitude would take time.

It was 1935. The two lawyers had a strategy. Rather than go whole hog on fighting the segregation of public primary schools, they'd start by attacking discrimination against black graduate students. They reasoned that African Americans looking to integrate colleges and universities posed less of a threat to the larger population of families who had kids in grade school. There were considerably fewer black students in college than in grade school, and even fewer pursuing advanced degrees.

Donald Gaines Murray was an African American college graduate who wanted to attend the University of Maryland law school, the same segregated law school that had turned Thurgood away on the basis of race. When Donald applied, Raymond A. Pearson, the university's president, shot back a rejection.

The university's position was that Donald could get a law degree at the Princess Anne Academy, an all-black college, also in Maryland. Raymond asserted that Princess Anne Academy could provide Donald with a "separate-but-equal" education. But Princess Anne Academy had no law school. It was certainly separate from the University of Maryland, but given that it could not prepare Donald to become a lawyer, what, Donald wondered, was equal about it?

Donald applied to the University of Maryland law school a second time. His application might as well have been a boomerang—it came back with a *thwack*!

This time the college president was forced to admit the real reason the university would not accept Donald. It wasn't because it was possible to get an "equal" education at a nearby black institution. It was because the University of Maryland had never admitted black students, and they sure weren't going to start now.

Thurgood was eager to win a case against the law school that had also shot back his application. But he also wanted to win it for Donald, and for every future black student applying to the University of Maryland. And he wanted to demonstrate that no matter how you sliced it, there was no "separate-but-equal" in this pie.

With Charles Houston, Thurgood built his legal argument around the "separate but equal" idea and the equal rights of America's citizens stated in the Constitution's Fourteenth Amendment.

In the case of Donald Murray, there wasn't much to debate. Since Princess Anne Academy could not offer Donald a law school, it was *un*equal. But the "separate-but-equal" question as it pertained to education had never been argued in court.

Thurgood changed that when he stood in front of the judge assigned to the case known as *Murray v. Pearson* and said, "What's at stake here is more than the rights of my client. It's the moral commitment stated in our country's creed."

Creed, indeed! Thurgood told it like it was. After hearing these remarks, Judge Eugene O'Dunne of the Baltimore City Court issued an order: Raymond Pearson had to unlock the door of discrimination at the University of Maryland law school, open that door wide, and let Donald Murray in. And he had to *keep the door open* just as fully for any black student who wanted to follow in Donald's footsteps.

The judge issued his order on June 25, 1935. On that day, after Thurgood and Charles left the courthouse, Thurgood danced a happy jig-step on Baltimore's sidewalks. He and Charles had won a major civil rights battle against the institution that had barred his entry just a few years before. Also, with this victory, they had set the stage for the future of equality in education, proving that "separate" isn't always "equal."

After working with Thurgood on the *Murray v. Pearson* case, Charles Houston became the first special counsel to the NAACP national office in New York. In 1936, he called Thurgood to invite him to serve as his assistant. Thurgood was in New York almost as soon as he got off the phone with Charles. Two years later, when Charles resigned from the NAACP, Thurgood took his place.

Thurgood had become one of the most talked-about black attorneys in the nation. He was strategic, smart, and walked with a swagger. He made people feel comfortable by speaking with the ease of a friend but the conviction of a leader. In addition, Thurgood was handsome as all get-out. With his good looks and charisma, he could have passed for a movie star.

Even though folks were talking proud about Thurgood, he was not ready to sit back and soak up the praise. Their talk, talk, talk was nice to hear, but Thurgood had a lot more talking of his own to do. There was still so much that he wanted to say in the courtrooms of America.

In 1939, Thurgood was appointed director-counsel of the NAACP Legal Defense and Educational Fund. In this role, Thurgood oversaw all the legal activities of the NAACP.

Working for the NAACP was gratifying for Thurgood, but it had some drawbacks. As America's leading civil rights organization, the NAACP and those working on its behalf were targets for hate groups such as the Ku Klux Klan and white segregationists who were out to get black people, especially those who were in positions of prominence.

As a black civil rights leader, Thurgood was often in danger. There were times when he slept in his clothes in case he had to flee from a lynch mob attacking his home in the middle of the night.

When Thurgood traveled to small Southern towns, he would stay at a different home each evening so that white racists could not keep easy tabs on his whereabouts. Despite these unsettling circumstances, Thurgood stayed focused on the cases he represented. He never lost sight of his goal, which was to win cases and thereby advance civil rights for black Americans. Also, with each case he won, Thurgood was setting legal precedents that could be used as ammunition for future cases.

Thurgood worked diligently to prepare for his time in court. Some nights, while traveling with fellow attorneys from one town to another, Thurgood would sit in his car with his typewriter on his lap, crafting notes for a case that was to start in the morning.

As director-counsel of the NAACP Legal Defense and Educational Fund, Thurgood argued cases in the same courtroom he had visited as a child with his father.

Working for the NAACP also afforded Thurgood the opportunity to argue cases before the United States Supreme Court, the highest court in America. This was a major accomplishment for any attorney. It allowed Thurgood to further sharpen his legal skills. He argued cases ranging from unfair evictions to falsely accused robberies.

Thurgood's many victories in court had earned him the nickname "Mr. Civil Rights."

By the early 1950s, Thurgood was ready to put his accomplishments to the test. The time had come for challenging "separate but equal" in public schools.

In America, many schools were as divided as a half-moon cookie. There were all-black schools and all-white schools, and the two did not mix. But unlike the equal sweetness on both sides of a half-moon cookie, schools for black students were not nearly as satisfying as schools for white students. This was the sour reality of school segregation. This was the law, known by many as Jim Crow, a law that often overshadowed the Fourteenth Amendment's promise of equality for all Americans.

Because of neglect by white school officials and lack of fair government funding, many black schools were inferior. Books were shabby and stained, and older than Grandma Moses. If a black child wanted to learn about participles, prehistoric animals, or Plato, he or she had to piece together textbooks with missing pages.

Black schools often lacked basic supplies such as pencils and paper. In some African American schools, desks and chairs were rickety and caked with enough wads of gum to patch the cracks in a broken bathtub. Some black schools were no more than tar-paper shacks, with one cramped room for all of their students. In black schools that were housed in sturdier buildings, the wall clocks were broken. So was the plumbing. So was the confidence of the students who were forced to learn under inferior conditions.

All-white schools received adequate funding from local school district officials. As a result, they often had superior facilities—a lunchroom, sports equipment, new books, and the luxury of a library, which many black schools could not afford.

African American teachers were paid less than white teachers. Black students often had to walk miles to get to school when a white school was closer to home.

There were some good things about black schools, though. Because they had been forced to endure limited resources for so long, black teachers were creative in their teaching. They could find ways to stretch the pennies allotted them by the government for school supplies. And, as part of their education, black students got something white students didn't—lessons in black history.

Still, Thurgood understood that *black* history was *American* history, and along with algebra, geography, and English, black and white children should be seated at desks, side by side, learning these subjects together.

In 1951, Thurgood took on a case known as *Oliver Brown v. Board of Education of Topeka*. The case began when Topeka, Kansas, resident Oliver Brown, the daddy of eight-year-old Linda Brown, tried to enroll his daughter at Sumner Elementary, a white school close to their home. Because she was black, the principal at Sumner wouldn't let Linda enter the school building. Instead, she had to take a five-mile bus ride, then walk through a dangerous railroad yard to get to the school she had been attending, Monroe Elementary. Oliver worried about his daughter's well-being. It wasn't fair that she had to wake up each morning before the birds to get to an all-black school, when there was a white school just blocks from her home. Oliver filed a lawsuit against the Topeka Board of Education. He lost his case but didn't give up. He joined forces with other parents from Delaware, Kansas, South Carolina, Virginia, and Washington, D.C., who had also filed suit. They called on the NAACP to help. Their cases combined to make one case, *Brown v. Board of Education*, which would be presented before the Supreme Court.

Thurgood knew this would be one of his toughest cases yet. But Thurgood was tough enough to tackle it.

In addition to being strong, Thurgood was strategic. To prepare for his case, he brought together an impressive mix of experts—educators, psychologists, sociologists, anthropologists—to help prove that separating students on the basis of race was harmful to their emotional and psychological well-being. He also set out to show the court that separate schools for black students were far from equal to those for white students.

The case began on December 9, 1952. Thurgood's opponent, John W. Davis, a white attorney, was one of the most notable lawyers in America. John was out to prove that segregation was central to American values, and that it was fair to both black and white people. John was an excellent debater and very convincing. His appearance was quite different from Thurgood's. John had hollowed, ruddy features, a sharp nose, and hair as white as new snow on a meadow. His track record as an attorney was solid. He won most of his cases.

Thurgood and John might as well have been in a boxing ring. In their remarks to the Supreme Court justices presiding over the case, they each landed hard legal punches.

BAM! John came on strong, arguing that segregation was needed to keep racial unrest from getting out of control.

BAM! Thurgood came back swinging, saying that black kids and white kids played together peacefully and that separating them in school served to undermine harmony between the races.

The case went on for more than a year. During this time, black parents prayed for change. Black students kept on keeping on with dog-eared textbooks and dog-tired feet, weary from their long walks to segregated schools miles from home.

In Southern towns, where segregation still ruled, white parents prayed, too. Those who didn't believe in integration asked the Almighty to keep their vanilla schools free from what they deemed the bitterness of dark chocolate.

In many civil rights cases that involved black versus white, people believed the white side would win. It had been that way for so long. But with his many Supreme Court victories, Thurgood had begun to change that. As the *Brown v. Board of Education* case unfolded, America waited and wondered, and hoped.

Finally, on May 17, 1954, the decision was issued. For most children it was the end of the school year. During the *Brown v. Board of Education* proceedings, their parents had explained what the case's outcome could mean for them. Now many kids wondered if they would welcome summer vacation with a celebration chorus or a sad dance of defeat.

When the Supreme Court's Chief Justice Earl Warren read the verdict, it seemed that every school kid, mother, father, teacher, preacher, doctor, farmer, and lawyer awaited his words from wherever they happened to be at that moment. In delivering the court's decision, Justice Warren first asked the question: "Does segregation of children in public schools solely on the basis of race . . . deprive the children of the minority group of educational opportunities?"

Yes! rang in the minds of many listeners.

As if he could hear the thoughts of every black parent in America, Justice Warren said, "We believe that it does."

But not everyone was happy about this opinion.

The dissenters cried, *"Oh no!"*

Justice Warren was not even done reading the court's findings, but at that moment, every heart in the room became a pounding gavel in the chest of each man and woman. *BAM! BAM! BAM!*

The chief justice continued. He had still not issued the final verdict. The court's findings, which included a lengthy summary of the evidence that had been presented during the case, took nearly half an hour to read. Nobody knew for sure what the outcome would be. As the clock in that courtroom ticked and ticked, the chief justice kept reading. News wire services eagerly awaited the decision. Finally, Justice Warren said slowly, "We conclude . . ."

Now all those beating hearts did double time. Nobody dared let out a breath.

When Justice Warren said, "Unanimously," some hearts nearly stopped beating. Then, concluding, the justice announced, "that in the field of public education the doctrine of 'separate but equal' has no place. Separate educational facilities are inherently unequal."

At that moment a collective gasp rose up, nearly sucking the air out of that courtroom.

The word *unanimously* echoed into the thick afternoon. *All* of the Supreme Court justices had agreed on the verdict.

Like a final exam given by the law's hardest teachers, each justice on the Supreme Court's bench had passed this test with two flying colors — black and white.

As Thurgood walked down the marble steps of the Supreme Court building, he turned back to take a satisfied look at the words etched into the building's front cornice: EQUAL JUSTICE UNDER LAW.

As powerful as those words were, it didn't take long for the folks who'd whined "Oh, no!" to protest the Supreme Court ruling. In many Southern towns and cities, people spoke out vehemently against the decision. Their attitude was, *You can tell us we gotta integrate, but we sure aren't gonna hurry.*

And they sure didn't have to. The Supreme Court's *yes* to integration, and their *no* to segregation, didn't include *when* white schools were required to let black students in.

In September 1954, when school bells throughout America rang to welcome children back to their classrooms, black students were eager for new books, sharpened pencils, and desks free of gum globs. These were simple desires that weren't so easy to have. Though schools were integrated by law, very few actually abided by this new ruling. After years of living under oppressive segregation laws — and enduring the hatred of racism — black parents weren't so quick to all of a sudden send their children to white schools. They feared for the safety of their children, who were at risk of being harmed by people who did not want them in their schools.

White parents who still firmly believed in segregation clung to "Oh, no!" They did not want their children coming into contact with black children. So, even though the law had changed, schools, for the most part, stayed the same. Black kids went back to tar-paper shacks with broken clocks and half-cracked pencils, while white kids enjoyed new books, and frankfurters and cherry Jell-O in the school cafeteria.

Though Thurgood had enjoyed such a notable victory in court, his fight for justice had just begun. He took a break from his legal activities, though, when his wife Vivian told him she had been diagnosed with cancer. She died in February 1955.

It was hard for Thurgood to return to his work, but he knew that his pursuit for equality was far from over. The year following Thurgood's triumph, the Supreme Court had ordered desegregation of schools "with all deliberate speed." Still, not many schools acted quickly. Progress was extremely slow.

Thurgood was fortunate to meet someone who helped make the situation less difficult. He began a courtship with Cecilia Suyat, a secretary for the NAACP. Cecilia and Thurgood married in December 1955. Their marriage was blessed with two sons, Thurgood Jr. and John William.

As an employee for the NAACP, the new Mrs. Marshall understood the importance of her husband's ongoing fight for justice. She was proud to be married to "Mr. Civil Rights" and encouraged his efforts in every way.

So, in 1957, when nine black students in Little Rock, Arkansas, took a bold stand by attempting to integrate the town's Central High School, Cecilia supported her husband's desire to help the students.

Known as the "Little Rock Nine," these students faced angry mobs and were barred by National Guardsmen sent by Arkansas governor Orval Faubus.

Thurgood went to Little Rock to comfort the students and their families and to give them guidance. When word spread that he would soon be in Little Rock, it was like the arrival of a great savior.

People shouted, "Thurgood is coming! Thurgood is coming!"

And Thurgood came. And offered advice. And spoke to Little Rock government officials on behalf of the students.

It wasn't until President Dwight D. Eisenhower ordered federal troops to protect the students that they were allowed to enter Central High

School safely. But school days were still a struggle for the Little Rock Nine. Each morning while entering school and each afternoon when leaving to go home, they faced threats, jeers, and a hatred that stung worse than a swarm of hornets.

Amid all of this, the students still had to somehow learn. Thurgood encouraged them to stay strong. With his support and that of the NAACP, the Little Rock Nine endured.

As government officials issued deadlines by which school districts were required to abide by the laws, more schools in more states became integrated. But change only came after great resistance. It would take more than a decade after the *Brown v. Board of Education* ruling for America's schools to become completely integrated.

The *Brown v. Board of Education* case gave Thurgood great confidence in his ability to argue cases before the Supreme Court. Over the next ten years, he successfully represented many clients. Of the thirty-two cases Thurgood argued in front of the Supreme Court throughout his career, he would win twenty-nine of them.

His track record was undeniable. By the early 1960s, Thurgood had shown the nation that he was an ace attorney. In 1961, President John F. Kennedy nominated Thurgood to be a judge on the Court of Appeals for the Second Circuit, one of America's higher courts.

Four years later, on a hot day in July, Thurgood was enjoying a sandwich and iced tea with some colleagues. An aide came to their table to tell him that the president was on the phone. Thurgood sipped his tea. "The president of what?" he asked.

The aide was quick to answer, "Of the United States, Mr. Marshall."

Thurgood spoke into the telephone, and sure enough, on the phone was President Lyndon B. Johnson, who had become president in November 1963 after President Kennedy was assassinated. The president was inviting Thurgood to Washington, D.C., for a meeting.

Days later, the president gave Thurgood a firm handshake and asked him to accept his nomination to the post of U.S. Solicitor General. As Solicitor General, Thurgood would decide which cases the Justice Department would ask the Supreme Court to review. And he would represent America in front of the Supreme Court for all cases in which the United States had an interest.

This was a big job and an important honor. Thurgood accepted the president's offer immediately. The president wasted no time. Two weeks after Thurgood's nomination was announced, confirmation hearings began that would solidify Thurgood's position. He was the first African American to serve as Solicitor General.

As always, Thurgood took his work seriously. He prepared well for each and every case. He spoke articulately on behalf of his country. His legal arguments were strong. He was a rock-solid Solicitor General.

President Johnson was pleased. In 1967 Thurgood Marshall was named the first African American Supreme Court justice. With Thurgood at his side, the president conducted a press conference from the White House rose garden. On that day, June 13, every rose in the nation must have been in full bloom, expressing the joy of this beautiful occasion.

When citing his reasons for nominating Thurgood Marshall to serve as a judge on the highest court of the land, President Johnson said, "He is best qualified." The president spoke with unmistakable force. "I believe

it is the right thing to do, the right time to do it, the right man, and the right place."

When Thurgood was sworn in, he set his hand on the Bible and made an oath. He promised to "administer justice without respect to persons, and do equal right to the poor and the rich." On his first day as a Supreme Court justice, Thurgood received the regal black robe worn by America's key legal decision makers.

It fit him perfectly.

It was the *right* robe for Thurgood Marshall—and the beginning of a whole new chapter in his career.

In Thurgood's first year, he heard more than one hundred cases. This was a vibrant start to Supreme Court service that would last nearly a quarter century.

One of the most notable cases during Thurgood's tenure involved the perceived civil rights of a white college student.

In 1973, Allan Bakke applied to the University of California Davis School of Medicine. Allan was a highly qualified candidate, but his application was rejected. He applied again in 1974 and was rejected for the second time.

The university had actively practiced a program known as affirmative action, a plan enacted to help create more opportunities for black students at colleges and universities, and in corporations. The purpose of affirmative action was to address both past and ongoing discrimination.

The idea behind affirmative action was that by opening more doors for minority candidates, the balance of black versus white students in colleges would become more equitable. To achieve this balance, the University of California had filled many of the open slots in its medical school with black candidates. So, when Allan Bakke applied, there was no room for him. To his way of thinking, he was being discriminated against—for being white. Allan sued the university for reverse discrimination.

The case, known as *Regents of the University of California*, reached the Supreme Court in 1978. Unlike in the *Brown v. Board of Education* case, the justices on the Supreme Court were not unanimous in their views. Thurgood and other justices believed it was fair for colleges to use race as a determining factor in selecting its student body, ensuring that universities remain racially diverse.

Other Supreme Court justices strongly disagreed. They believed that affirmative action quotas should not be allowed and that Allan Bakke had been discriminated against.

Thurgood took a strong stand in favor of the university. He said the Supreme Court had made a commitment to end racism in public life, but that by siding with Bakke, the court was backsliding on its commitment to racial justice.

But he could not convince enough of the justices who disagreed with this belief.

The Supreme Court ruled in favor of Allan Bakke, who was admitted to the University of California Davis School of Medicine, and graduated in 1982.

Though the outcome of the *Regents of the University of California* case was not to Thurgood's liking, he continued to support equality in education, as well as the constitutional rights for Americans of all races.

On June 27, 1991, Thurgood retired from the Supreme Court. The man once known as "Mr. Civil Rights" hung his black robe on a hanger for the last time. That robe had a special pride embodied in its threads. With his sharp intellect and keen command of the law, Thurgood Marshall had woven equality into the fabric of American justice.

His hands crossed the color line.

When he heard the call, "Play ball!"
he reached to the other side,
where he raced
'round the Dodgers' all-white diamond.

Stirred up second base.
Sent dirt's dust rising
        while he slid
        to the plate.

Brought baseball's new inning.

Bat held high.
Turning the other cheek.
Swinging righty.

Black-pride slugger
Number 42
Stealing home.
        Make no mistake—

"Safe!"

Jackie Robinson

b. January 31, 1919, Cairo, Georgia;
d. October 24, 1972, Stamford, Connecticut

Game-Changer

———◆◆◆———

Jack Roosevelt Robinson was a sharecropper's son, born on what some folks believed was the coldest day ever near Cairo, Georgia. He was the youngest of five children and he made his family especially proud by accomplishing great things.

Times were tough for the Robinsons. As a sharecropper, Jackie's daddy, Jerry Robinson, farmed land that he didn't own. He had to give half of every bushel of cukes, tomatoes, collards, and squash that he grew to the man who owned the farm. He worked hard and earned little to support his wife and children. One day Jerry walked off the farm, and he never came back. He left Jackie; Jackie's mother, Mallie; Jackie's brothers Edgar, Frank, and Mack; and Jackie's sister, Willa Mae. Jackie was still a baby at the time, but when his father abandoned him and his siblings, it hurt the entire family.

Jackie's mother was strong and determined. She moved her family to Pasadena, California, soon after Jackie turned one year old. Mallie and her children lived in a small apartment with no hot water. Jackie took his baths in a tin tub. Jackie's mother worked as a laundress.

As Jackie grew, he became very proud of his mother and her ability to support their family with limited means. More than anything, Mallie wanted Jackie to go to school and to attend college. When he was still a little kid, too young to enroll as a student, he tagged along to school with his sister, Willa Mae, until he was old enough to go to kindergarten. School was a place where he felt good about himself and his abilities.

In school, Jackie quickly learned that book smarts had nothing to do with skin color. If he could read well and master arithmetic, he could excel. But no matter how well he learned to read big words and memorize math facts, there were some things that didn't fully add up.

Jackie often wondered why it was that he and his black friends could only swim at the local pool on Tuesdays.

Why did he and his brothers and sisters have to sit in the part of the movie theater called "the buzzard's nest"—the seats way up high in a balcony, so far from the screen that even a buzzard with 20/20 vision wouldn't be able to see it clearly?

Here's something else Jackie's school textbook could not explain: Why, when the movie was over, were all the white kids able to hang out at Woolworth's drinking root beer and lemonade, when Jackie had to walk past Woolworth's WHITES ONLY sign to quench his thirst at a water fountain marked COLORED?

While none of this made sense to Jackie, there was little he could do to change it. This was the law of segregation. A law that told him and every other black child he knew that white people had privileges that were not extended to black people.

This made young Jackie angry. But it taught him something that no amount of homework or test-taking could help him learn. He discovered that, as a black child, he would have to *earn* the privileges white children got. A root beer and a front-row seat at the movies wouldn't be given to him. He'd have to work hard for any advantages—and for just plain fairness. He'd have to be smarter and tougher.

By the time Jackie was eight years old, he was taller and stronger than most boys his age. He had what folks called "limb-smarts." He was agile and coordinated. Even as a kid, Jackie had muscles. His legs could run fast. His hands were solid and filled with power.

Jackie came to see that he could put his limb-smarts to good use by playing sports, a skill that let him compete with white kids on the same terms. A field didn't care whose feet stomped on its turf. In a game, points were won by the best players. It didn't matter if their skin was black, white, blue, or greener than the field's grass after a season of grooming.

By the time Jackie was a fourth grader at Grover Cleveland Elementary School, he was scoring soccer goals by slamming the ball past sixth graders.

By the time Jackie got to George Washington Junior High, he was the top player at baseball, and at many other sports. "The more I played, the better I became," he once said about his abilities as a kid athlete. "In softball, handball, football, basketball . . . I played hard and always to win."

As a student at John Muir Technical High School, Jackie wore a *V* on his jacket for the *four* varsity teams he played on—football, basketball, baseball, and track. There was no stopping Jackie Robinson. He could punt, slam-dunk, race to a base, and run super-fast around a track.

After high school, Jackie took his sports talent to Pasadena Junior College, where, once again, his abilities were outstanding. At a track meet in May 1938, when it was his turn at the broad jump, his limb-smart legs propelled him 25 feet and 6½ inches, farther than any other junior-college athlete anywhere. And that same year, Jackie—now sporting a Pasadena *V*—put an even higher shine on that letter. He was named the most valuable junior college baseball player in Southern California.

Even as a superior athlete decorated with *V*'s and showing the world he was the best junior college broad-jumper, Jackie could not escape the sad reality of racism. Jackie's coaches and teammates cheered his abilities, but there were many times when players on opposing teams tried to knock Jackie off his game by yelling mean things to him about his skin color. They made fun of his family, too, by insulting his mother, and talking trash about the poor conditions under which Jackie and his family lived.

Those players on the other teams had no idea that they were actually helping Jackie. Every time they called him a degrading name, he grew more determined. When the curse words flew, he smacked the pitcher's ball with his baseball bat harder than hard—knocked the jelly out of that doughnut—and rounded the bases to home, where he quietly took in the victory of another run. Jackie ate words of prejudice like they were mounds of spinach. The insults were bitter, but they made him stronger!

In 1939, Jackie took his mighty resolve to UCLA, where he had received an athletic scholarship after attending Pasadena Junior College for two years. He once again showed folks that he was serious about playing and winning. He was the first athlete at UCLA to compete on all four of the school's varsity teams, for the same sports he'd mastered at Muir: basketball, baseball, football, and track.

In 1940, when Jackie was a senior, he was introduced to a freshman, Rachel Isum, a young woman he would come to love as much as he loved sports. Rachel became his steady girlfriend and most devoted fan.

Though sports had gained Jackie respect and notoriety, his mother was still living in poor conditions. This bothered him. Mallie Robinson wanted her son to complete college, but Jackie believed that, given the times, no amount of education would guarantee him a job that would earn him a good living. Jackie wanted to help his mother financially. He couldn't study for classes, compete on four varsity sports teams, and work to earn money at the same time. So, in 1941, Jackie decided to leave UCLA and get a job working with kids who'd come from poor families like his own.

The following year, with World War II raging, Jackie was drafted by the army. He was stationed at Fort Riley, Kansas, and Fort Hood, Texas. Through perseverance and hard work, he became a second lieutenant, a rare feat for a black man.

Like many institutions in Jackie's life, the army was segregated. Black soldiers and white soldiers were kept separate. Jackie hated this. Segregated movie theaters and restaurants were bad enough. And enduring racist comments from other athletes had toughened Jackie. But as a member of the U.S. Armed Forces, Jackie had become fed up with racism.

Here he was fighting for his country, yet being forced to deal with the injustice of segregation. Jackie stood up to this unfairness by refusing to abide by rules that kept him separate from white soldiers. Once, when Jackie rode a bus from the military base into town, the driver insisted that Jackie sit in the back. Jackie did not budge. He was a solider, and he felt he had the right to sit where he pleased. An argument broke out. Jackie was arrested and later forced to defend himself in military court. The court dismissed the charges.

While some soldiers respected Jackie's firm stance, the army saw it as defiance. A year after he became a second lieutenant, Jackie received an honorable discharge.

Returning to his love of sports, Jackie became a coach at Samuel Huston College in Austin, Texas. He was good at mentoring. Because of his experience as a college athlete, he could easily inspire student ballplayers. But Jackie missed being a player himself. As a coach he quickly came to see that the best way for him to inspire others was by playing *in* the game.

But every game worth playing was segregated. He could not escape the laws of racial separation. They were everywhere, including professional athletics. It didn't matter that Jackie had aced every sport he'd ever played—and that even though his full name was Jack Roosevelt Robinson, his other middle name could have been "Varsity-4" for all the school teams he'd graced. He had racked up hundreds of points on plenty of fields and had fans from Shasta to Burbank, California. But to play ball professionally, Jackie V-4 Robinson could not be on the same teams as white athletes. In professional sports the color line was so thick that not even a buzz saw could cut it.

At the time, black baseball players couldn't play in the major leagues. They were confined to the Negro Leagues, a group of all-black teams that had been established in 1888. Before 1888, blacks had played on integrated minor and major league teams.

The Negro Leagues had some great players, such as Josh Gibson, Satchel Paige, Willie Mays, and Hank Aaron. When Negro League teams traveled, folks came out to shout their praises.

Josh, Satchel, Willie, and Hank—they could sure play. But they had to stay on the black side of baseball's invisible color line. They earned less money than white players. Their playing schedule was not as professionally organized as the schedules in Major League Baseball. And after a day on the field of hard-hard playing, the Negro League players faced the same discrimination they suffered at other times. They had to drink up the cool quench of a sports victory from segregated water fountains marked COLORED. They were forced to sleep on their team buses, since white motels did not welcome them.

Luckily, there were often kind people in each town who allowed them

to stay at their homes, where hand-stitched quilts and solid bed pillows helped them sleep well before the next game. At breakfast time, these generous souls shared slices of honey toast to sweeten the bitter blow of what was known as "Jim Crow baseball."

During the 1945 season, Jackie played in the Negro Leagues for the Kansas City Monarchs, which allowed him to earn a living doing what he loved. But he hated the racial barriers that kept him out of the major leagues.

At this time, Branch Rickey, president of the Brooklyn Dodgers, had an idea that would shake baseball to its bones. He wanted to recruit black players into the major leagues. When Branch shared his idea with others, most people thought he was crazy. They encouraged him to bury his plan deep in left field. Judge Kenesaw Mountain Landis, the commissioner of baseball, was firmly against integrating the game.

But Branch was a bold man. He was smart, too, and, like Jackie, he wanted to win games. He knew that some of the best athletes in America were in the Negro Leagues. Black- and brown-skinned players deserved to play in the majors. They had the ability to help all-white teams score big. And they could attract fans to the stadium.

Branch Rickey believed in equality. Segregated sports disturbed him greatly. How, he wondered, could America be the land of the free and the home of the brave but also be a nation chained to the idea that black and white baseball players could not play on the same team? And why were so many people scared to integrate baseball? This was not freedom or bravery.

When A. B. Chandler became the new commissioner of baseball in 1945, he agreed with Branch. Excluding black players was wrong.

Branch wasted no time. He'd already been scouting the Negro Leagues for the most-talented players. But he needed a black man who had more than batting and throwing skills. He needed someone who had a solid backbone, strong morals, and the maturity to know that the importance of integrating baseball outweighed the ridicule an individual player would suffer day to day.

Inviting a black player into the major leagues was risky. Branch was putting his reputation on the line, but, more importantly, he would also be putting a player in potential danger. Prejudiced people might want to harm a black man for daring to integrate the sport.

Branch was about to introduce what would later be known as "The Noble Experiment." He was preparing a test to prove his theory that baseball could be successfully integrated.

Branch knew about Jackie's ability to smack a ball, play bases, and man the outfield. But he wasn't so sure about Jackie's willingness to stay calm in the face of racial taunts. The black player who would be at the center of The Noble Experiment would need to have incredible self-restraint. In no way could he give angry whites a reason to oust him. Those who didn't believe in integration would look for any excuse possible to kick a black player out of the major leagues. Since most Negro League players were excellent athletes, the easiest way to get rid of a black player would be to prove that he was a troublemaker.

On August 28, 1945, Branch Rickey and Jackie Robinson met in

Branch's office in Brooklyn, New York. Branch asked Jackie if he wanted to play with a Canadian team, the Montreal Royals, the top minor league team of the Brooklyn Dodgers.

Of course Jackie wanted to be a Royal. Playing for the Royals would put him closer to playing for the Dodgers and the major leagues. But asking Jackie if he wanted to become a Royal was the easy question. The tougher question was, Could Jackie stand up under the pressures of prejudice? Could he squash his anger every time some dumb person attacked his character or ridiculed him?

Jackie had to carefully consider this.

To Branch's way of thinking, the player he chose needed to be certain. There was no room for doubt.

To see if Jackie had what it took, Branch got up in Jackie's face. He snarled at Jackie. He bombed threats at him. With hateful words, Branch attacked Jackie's mother, Mallie, and Rachel, his fiancée. He made vicious jokes about Jackie's skin color, face, and race. At that moment, a bulldog had more grace than Branch Rickey. Branch was showing Jackie the kind of hatred and stupidity he'd be forced to endure every time he played alongside white players.

For much of their three-hour meeting, Branch didn't let up. He growled at Jackie, calling him names that were the ugliest of ugly. He said things cruel enough to make a grown man cry. Most grown men would have run home crying to their mamas, begging for a hankie right then. But not Jackie. He knew what Branch was doing.

When Branch barked, Jackie stayed calm. When Branch snapped, Jackie was cooler than cool. This was not easy for Jackie. He didn't like having to shy back from insults. But he understood that Branch's plan had a purpose. He knew that if he took this important step—while at the same time practicing nonviolence—he could change baseball forever by making it possible for other black players to play on all-white teams.

The heat rising in Branch's office was so hot on that day that it could have sparked a fire on the subway tracks of the Brooklyn-bound A train.

Jackie possessed a great amount of dignity. He was proud of all he'd accomplished and of how well he'd stood up to racism in sports and in the army. He wanted Branch to know he was no milksop.

Just to be clear, Jackie asked Branch, "Are you looking for a Negro who is afraid to fight back?"

This wasn't about fear. Branch told Jackie he needed a Negro player "with guts enough *not* to fight back."

The two men shook hands.

Jackie agreed to join the Royals for the 1946 season. In February 1946, Jackie married Rachel Isum, who stood by her husband as he was about to make history.

On April 18, 1946, Jackie was good and ready to play. This was the day he made his first public appearance as a Royal. The thirty-five thousand fans who'd come to watch were eager, too. The exciting game took place at Roosevelt Stadium in Jersey City, New Jersey. School was out on that day, so the stands were filled with kids—cheering, giddy, more jumpy than the popcorn flinging up from the stadium's snack bar popper.

On opening day, and throughout the season, Jackie's play with the

Royals brought many black fans into the stadium. They traveled from towns all over. Like every public place, baseball stadiums were segregated. African American spectators had to sit in bleachers and outfield seats that were so far away from the action that Jackie appeared as small as an action figure. This didn't matter to Jackie's followers. They packed those far-off seats like working folks pack a subway car at rush hour on payday. They sat elbow to elbow, knee to knee, all to see Jackie Robinson play.

His first game with the Royals began with the integrated team making its way onto the field at Roosevelt Stadium to play against the Jersey City Little Giants. The real giant of the day was Jackie. He played with power, speed, and grace.

And, oh, could Jackie throw. And run. And steal bases. And score—royally. The black fans, seated in the stadium's buzzard's-nest seats, cheered for Jackie from way up high.

Inside, Jackie felt pressure to play his best. Black people were counting on him to show the world that a brown-skinned man could hit, throw, and catch a stitched white ball as good as anybody.

While playing Jackie taught all the schoolkids in the stadium how to count, baseball style. He drove in *six* runs, scored *four* times, stroked *three* singles, stole *two* bases, and hit *one* home run. Thanks to him, the Royals beat the cleats off the Little Giants and won the game 14 to 1.

Jackie was off to a great beginning as a member of the Royals, but as the season unfolded, he faced immense prejudice. Though he showed amazing sportsmanship on the field, there were people who couldn't stand the idea of a black man playing with white men. Jackie started to get hate mail and prank telephone calls from racists who threatened to kill him if he kept playing for the Royals. Also, people threatened to boycott games in which he played.

During games, especially those played in the South, Jackie had to endure taunts and angry shouts while he stood in the batter's box or played the field. This made him red-hot mad. He wanted to shout back, but couldn't. He'd promised Branch Rickey that he'd keep his composure. To help himself stay calm, Jackie put his anger to good use.

The louder and meaner the hecklers got, the harder Jackie hit the ball and the faster he ran the bases. During the entire season, he kept his eye on the true prize he wanted: equality.

Jackie's determination paid off. The Royals won the International League pennant in 1946, and nabbed the Little World Series of the minor leagues. That year, Jackie was voted Most Valuable Player in the International League. He had shown Branch Rickey and his fans that even though baseball was a sport, he meant business.

On April 10, 1947, five days before the start of the new baseball season, the Montreal Royals played the Brooklyn Dodgers in an exhibition game. Jackie did not play his best that day. In the sixth inning he hit a pop fly into a double play, getting two of his teammates out. But Jackie won nonetheless. As soon as the inning ended, it was announced that Branch had signed him to play with the Brooklyn Dodgers. Major league baseball had cracked its bat down on Jim Crow's head! Jackie would be the first black athlete in modern times to play on an integrated major league team.

When the announcement was made, the cheering was loud enough to rattle the rivets on the Brooklyn Bridge. Happy shouts could be heard from Bushwick to Brownsville to Bed-Stuy, in every other Brooklyn neighborhood between, and throughout all the other boroughs of New York City.

On April 15, 1947, as Jackie Robinson came up from the dugout at Ebbets Field, the Dodgers' stadium in Brooklyn, his baseball cap was sporting a brand new *B*. As far as baseball was concerned, he was a Brooklynite now. The front of his jersey spelled out the big blue pride of Brooklyn—D-o-d-g-e-r-s. On his back, he sported the number that would become his legacy—42.

Jackie was crossing baseball's color line with style.

On that day, the Dodgers beat the Boston Braves. But more importantly, Jackie was taking the first steps toward beating back the club of segregation in sports.

Progress took time. While many people were glad to see a black man in the majors, there was a whole mess of folks who wanted African Americans to stay on the Negro League side of baseball's color line.

On April 22, 1947, when the Dodgers began a three-game series against the Philadelphia Phillies at Ebbets Field, the racist remarks from the Phillies flew faster than a speed-pitch greased with Crisco. Jackie let the wisecracks slide by. He kept playing the best he could, swallowing hard on those oily insults. His fortitude had the same effect as in the past. It made him a more focused player.

Finally, by the last game in the series, Jackie's teammate, Eddie Stanky, had had enough. He stuck up for Jackie by barking back at the hecklers. He encouraged the other Dodgers to rally around Jackie, to support him as they would any teammate. And they did. More of the Dodgers looked past the color line. They had come to see Jackie for the man he truly was—a stellar athlete, and a good guy.

Instead of weakening his ability to play, the Phillies' meanness strengthened Jackie's game and gave the Dodgers even more team spirit. With the encouragement of his fellow players, Jackie's game was even sharper. Sports commentator Red Barber told it like it was: "When Robinson was on base, every eye in the ballpark was on him."

By the time Jackie's first year with the Dodgers was ending, toward the close of 1947, there was no mistaking his talent and drive as a major leaguer. He was named Rookie of the Year by *Sporting News* and the Baseball Writers' Association.

As Jackie continued to play with the Dodgers, he kept hitting his stride. By 1949 he was at the top of his game. That year he broke all kinds of records and continued to break down Jim Crow baseball. Jackie was the Dodgers' second baseman. He played that base with such solid focus that if second base could talk, it'd be thanking Jackie for keeping it covered. In that same season, Jackie slammed the pants off some of the league's toughest pitchers by hitting sixteen home runs. He led the league with thirty-seven stolen bases, drove in one hundred and twenty-four runs, and led the league in batting with a .342 average. So it was no surprise that he won the National League's Most Valuable Player Award.

Even with so much success, there was still one prize Jackie wanted: the world championship for the Dodgers. His team had lost the World Series to the New York Yankees four times. After each defeat, the Dodgers chanted, "Wait till next year!" Finally, in 1955, the Dodgers turned their disappointment chant into a victory dance. Jackie and the Dodgers won the World Series against the New York Yankees! This slugged it all home for Jackie. He'd now achieved the greatest success any ballplayer could ever hope for. He was on the best baseball team in the world.

By 1956, things had started to change in Jackie's baseball career. Branch Rickey, his friend and ally, had left the Dodgers. In December of that year Jackie was traded to the Dodgers' rival team, the New York Giants. Jackie had put his heart into being a Dodger, and he didn't like the idea of having to swap his blue baseball cap with the proud letter *B* on its front for a black cap with the letters *NY*.

As the first black player in the major leagues, Jackie had held back so many of his true feelings about the discrimination he faced. When he was sad or angry, or when situations arose that he didn't like, he couldn't show it. Jackie pretended that he was fine with being traded. Like so many times before, he put on his game face and appeared to go along with the plan, even though he felt differently inside.

But Jackie was a smart, strategic player. He expressed his dissatisfaction in a way nobody expected. He had been secretly planning to end his baseball career so that he could try another line of work. Also, he and Rachel now had three children, Jack Jr., Sharon, and David. Jackie wanted to spend more time with his family.

While the Brooklyn Dodgers team officials were busy trading Jackie, he was busy getting a new job off the field. At this same time, his agent was quietly making a deal with *Look* magazine to print the news about Jackie's retirement from baseball.

When *Look* magazine hit newsstands in January 1957 with a feature story announcing Jackie's retirement, the world knew they would never see Jackie Robinson wearing a New York Giants jersey.

Without saying a word, and with the quiet dignity that was his way, Jackie had announced the news that he was leaving baseball for a new game.

He became an executive at the Chock Full o'Nuts coffee company, where he helped the company brew up ways to hire more black employees.

Though Jackie had chosen to end his baseball career, he still scored big for civil rights causes. Folks still cheered him on, too. Along with his job at Chock Full o'Nuts, he worked on behalf of the National Association for the Advancement of Colored People (NAACP) as chair of the NAACP Freedom Fund Drive. He traveled to cities throughout America, speaking about the importance of equality. His fans from Brooklyn to Pasadena—and even folks from the Southern towns that had once protested his playing in the major leagues—now came to hear what he had to say about fair play in sports, business, education, politics, and on any other playing field where black people and white people had opportunities to make progress together.

Jackie was a persuasive speaker who convinced people to make donations to the NAACP. In one year's time, he helped raise one million dollars for the organization.

On January 23, 1962, Jackie earned a tribute that made his struggles on the field and his work on behalf of social justice worth it. He was inducted into the Baseball Hall of Fame, the first black man to attain that honor. This was a personal triumph for Jackie, a victory for sports lovers, and a win for African Americans.

Jackie's work with the NAACP and his inclusion in the Hall of Fame proved that Americans were becoming more committed to justice. His success demonstrated that African Americans could garner acknowledgement for their achievements. He also showed that when black people rallied together, they had the power to bring about big changes.

These truths sparked an idea in Jackie. He pooled his resources with a group of other like-minded activists. Together they founded the Freedom National Bank, a black-run bank that opened in Harlem on January 4, 1965. On that day, Jackie once again illustrated to the world that freedom comes through hard work, teamwork, and going to bat for what's right.

His hands lit a fuse

on black anger's *tick-tick-ticking . . .*
time bomb.

Ready to explode
with a vengeance so hot,
it built a Nation

"By any means necessary!"

Set seething city streets
ablaze.

Igniting riots,

resistance,

rage!

His elocution electrified.
Filled fallen angels
with heart-pounding pride.

Malcolm Little, turned X
to mark the spot where Mecca's wisdom
changed his ways from militant
to Muslim,

anointing him a minister,

then a Martyr.

Malcolm X

b. May 19, 1925, Omaha, Nebraska;
d. February 21, 1965, New York City

Spark-Light

———•❈•———

LITTLE MALCOLM LITTLE KICKED his way into this world. Birthing him was no easy feat. He was a scrawny baby with sharp elbows, pointy knees, bony heels, flat feet, and a hard-hard head. Malcolm's mother, Louise, a creamy-skinned woman, was pleased to see the beautiful face on her nut-colored babe. He was the fourth of her eight children.

Malcolm's father, Earl, was a Baptist preacher. Both of Malcolm's parents were followers of Marcus Garvey, a militant activist who promoted black unity through nationalism, the belief that black people from all over the world could make the greatest impact when they formed a unified nation.

Earl Little was anything *but* little. He was a bear of man. Big. Loud. Proud. Had a complexion black-black-strong as the richest coffee.

Weeks before Malcolm was born, his family faced a violent attack by the Ku Klux Klan, a hate group of white supremacists. While Malcolm's father was away preaching in another town, members of the Klan came to the Littles' home on horseback. It was a night as dark as tar. Hot for the month of May in Nebraska.

The men wore the Ku Klux Klan uniform of white robes and hoods, which hid their identities. They looked like Halloween ghosts, only ten times scarier, with angry eyes shining through the holes of their hoods.

Each man carried a rifle. They had arrived with an evil plan—to lynch Reverend Little in front of his wife, their sons, Wilfred and Philbert, and their daughter, Hilda.

Louise Little was a woman with a strong will. Of course she was terrified, but when the Klansmen demanded to see Reverend Earl, she came onto her front porch and faced them squarely. Louise told the hooded horsemen that her husband was not at home. That wasn't enough to satisfy their hatred. They took turns smashing the windows of the family's house, using the butts of their guns to shatter glass. Before they rode off, they told Louise this was the beginning of the end for her and her family.

Some say this awful incident upset Malcolm's mother so much that its effects somehow riled Malcolm, who was in his mother's womb, waiting to be born. He had been terrorized by white people before he was even held in his mother's arms. After such a frightening incident, Earl Little moved his family from Omaha, Nebraska, to Lansing, Michigan. He hoped that by leaving Nebraska he would also be protecting his family from the racist hatred they'd experienced. Not everyone in Omaha agreed with Earl's views on black nationalism. Some people felt threatened by him and his preaching.

But even relocating his family couldn't fully protect them. This was America in the 1920s. Prejudice was everywhere.

Malcolm was four years old when hooded night riders inflicted another attack on his family. This time they were robed in black, making them almost invisible in the dark night. It was the pounding hooves of their horses and their burning torches that let the Little family know danger had come to their front lawn. The men set Malcolm's house on fire, lighting the neighborhood with their hatred. Malcolm's mother held tightly to Yvonne, Malcolm's new baby sister, who whimpered and choked as smoke filled her tiny lungs. Malcolm's little brothers, Reginald, Wesley, and Robert, clung to their mama and wailed.

Thankfully, the Little family escaped the flames, but the horror had burned itself into Malcolm's memory. And more horror followed weeks later, when his father was found beaten and run over on East Lansing's trolley tracks. White officials in town tried to convince Louise that her husband had taken his own life. But she knew the truth. The father of her sons and daughters had been brutally murdered.

Now Louise was on her own with a brood of restless children. It was 1929, and times were harder than hard in America. Jobs were scarce, and she had no skills. She could not support her family. Dinner was dandelion greens, cornmeal, and "mud meat," a concoction made of dirt, water, spices, and anything else that could add flavor to the gloppy mixture.

As Malcolm grew, so did his desire to help his family. He and his brother Philbert played in fields of tall grass, where they snapped up bullfrogs and rabbits to eat. When they returned home, their mother fried the frogs in cooking grease, skinned and roasted the rabbits. At least this provided meat to serve along with their weedy greens. Somehow, Malcolm and his siblings survived on such meager meals. There couldn't have been much protein in a frog's leg or a rabbit's shank, especially when these were rationed among a family of nine hungry children.

Malcolm was skinny. Long. Bony. And, like his father, loudmouthed and outspoken. His hair was a copper cap, topping off freckled skin. The boy's smile could charm with its broad hello of teeth.

Despite Malcolm's good looks, he was restless, irritable, discontent.

By age ten, Malcolm was as jumpy and as wild as the frogs and rabbits he hunted for dinner. He started to steal from local merchants, a habit that would stay with him for years to come. When Malcolm was caught over and over again with stolen candy, jacks, playing cards, and other items in his pockets, the police contacted Lansing's child welfare services. The authorities determined that Louise Little was an unfit mother who could not control her son. Malcolm was sent to live with a foster family. The other Little children became wards of the state. They were split up and placed with different foster families.

Malcolm's mother, overcome with grief from losing her husband and children, and from being the victim of so much hardship, was committed to a mental hospital. She would end up staying at the hospital for twenty-six years.

Being separated from his family plunged Malcolm into a sadness so deep he felt as though he was drowning. Like a person gasping for air, fighting a harsh current, Malcolm started to thrash about in his everyday life. At school he acted up, disrupting the classroom and talking back to his teachers. He was defiant, oppositional, and filled with rage.

As a result, Malcolm fell behind in school. This made him even angrier. He came to hate reading. Soon *B-O-O-K* was the foulest of all four-letter words. He got a bad reputation and a label: PROBLEM KID. The school expelled him. In 1937, state officials sent Malcolm to a juvenile detention center twelve miles from home. He was thirteen years old. At first, the center and its directors, the Swerlin family, were a comfort to him. The place served balanced meals. Everyone ate together. Sometimes Mrs. Swerlin even made pies for dessert. It was like the family Malcolm wanted but had lost.

He started to do well in school. He was small for his age, but he made friends easily. The other students liked his quick humor. The teachers appreciated his charm. Malcolm applied himself to his studies.

Now *B-O-O-K* was *G-O-O-D*.

Little Malcolm Little ranked third in his grade. He was even elected class president. When Malcolm told one of his teachers that he wanted to become a lawyer, the man looked over the top of his glasses and frowned. He was quick to tell Malcolm that his dream would never come true. Negroes, he said, could not be lawyers. Black people were better suited to menial jobs such as janitors. The teacher thought he was helping the boy by not allowing him to set his hopes on something he believed was not attainable. To make Malcolm feel better, he encouraged him to consider becoming a carpenter. Malcolm persisted by saying he wanted to be an attorney. The teacher shushed him. He refused to argue with this kid.

Things started to turn sour at home with the Swerlins, too. As Malcolm grew more aware of his surroundings, he noticed that the Swerlins, a white family, talked about black people as if they were dirty dogs. They made all kinds of derogatory and racist comments right in front of him, as if he were invisible. After putting up with this for months, it didn't matter to Malcolm that the Swerlins served solid meals and sat around their table together. This was no kind of family for him.

One day Malcolm got a letter in the mail that would change the course of his life forever. His half sister, Ella, a daughter from Earl's first marriage, had heard through the family grapevine that he was struggling.

When Malcolm was about fifteen, she wrote to him, inviting him to spend the summer with her in Boston, where she lived. Ella was a lady with class, and very smart. She took pride in being of a dignified sort, a socialite, and a churchgoing sister. She arranged with the officials in charge of Malcolm's care to allow him to visit her.

And Boston—well, well. For little Malcolm Little, a boy from the rural Michigan sticks, Boston's big-city culture and happening nightlife was ten times sweeter than the Swerlins' desserts. Ella lived in a neighborhood called Roxbury, the rich part of town with a bustling black community. On Saturday nights, she took Malcolm to local dance halls to hear big-band music performed by Duke Ellington and Count Basie. The jazz music touched Malcolm two ways at once. It soothed his soul and sparked his imagination. For the first time in a long time, he was happy.

He begged Ella to let him stay, but she couldn't keep him in Roxbury without first notifying the proper authorities in Michigan. They had to approve his move to Boston. Malcolm's good grades and improved behavior helped Ella convince the child welfare officials to let him live with her.

The following summer, Malcolm left the Swerlins' home with no more than a set of clean underpants, a cotton nightshirt, and raggedy shoes the same color as the mud meat he once ate for dinner.

To the Swerlins he said good-bye. What he wanted to say, but didn't, was good riddance.

Roxbury's high life was an irresistible magnet for Malcolm. The city's excitement pulled him in quick. He was still only a teenager when he told Ella he was quitting school to find a job. He'd rather learn on the streets than at a desk, he said. Ella didn't approve of this, but she'd agree to it if he could secure work that was respectable and paid well.

Malcolm wasted no time getting a job—and getting into trouble. He met a guy named Shorty, a kid not much older than he was, who had also come to Roxbury from Lansing, Michigan. Shorty hooked him up as a shoeshine boy at Boston's Roseland State Ballroom, a dance hall filled with hot jazz, loose women, and hard drinks.

Malcolm's employment did not put a smile on sister Ella's face. Hanging out with Shorty and Boston's party people wasn't her idea of reputable. But she had a hard time controlling Malcolm. He was earning a salary and pocketing hefty tips. He could afford to stay out late and have fun with Shorty. What Ella didn't know was that her little brother was supplementing his shoeshine income by selling drugs. This illegal activity earned him more than tips. With his drug money he was sporting a silver clip packed with a thick wad of fifty-dollar bills. The cash and the thrill enticed him to use drugs in addition to selling them.

That's when his downward spiral started. He began running with thugs and sunk quickly into the fast, high life of a criminal. To fit in, Malcolm peeled off some of his fifty-dollar bills and bought himself a powder-blue zoot suit, a suit with blousy pants, a long jacket, and padded shoulders. He also purchased a shiny gold watch and pair of wing-tipped shoes.

He topped off his cool-blue style by "conking" his hair, a chemical process that turned his pretty-boy cotton-kink to slick-daddy bone-straight. Conking was popular among street thugs and clubsters. They thought smooth hair made them look more like a white person, and therefore more attractive.

Malcolm colored his conked hair, too. As little Malcolm Little, he was a ragamuffin with a copper top. Now, as Wanna-Be-a-Man Malcolm, his slick strands were brighter than fire.

Unlike the red of a stop sign that signals a halt, Malcolm's new look encouraged him to move at full speed toward more recklessness. He began working in train yards at age sixteen. When he turned seventeen, he boarded the Yankee Clipper, a train that ran between Boston and New York. He lied to the train's hiring manager about his age. With his slick conked do and pointy shoes, he could pass for twenty years old. The Yankee Clipper man handed him an apron and a tray, and hired him to sell sandwiches on the train.

Malcolm's drug use increased. So did his criminal instincts. While serving ham-and-cheese on the Yankee Clipper, Malcolm, often under the influence of drugs, insulted the passengers, jumped on the seats, and spilled drinks on people's crisp travel clothes. He was fired from his job as a sandwich salesman and moved quickly onto a fast track to more bad behavior.

He settled in New York's Harlem, where he felt he'd entered heaven.

With its vibrant black culture and beautiful people, Heavenly Harlem had an immediate hold on Malcolm. He talked his way into a job as a waiter at Small's Paradise, a swanky nightspot. But for every bit of swank at Small's, there was even more sweat and grime—and crime. It was as if Malcolm wore a sign that said LOOKING FOR TROUBLE.

It sure didn't take long for Do-Bad to find him. Though Harlem was enjoying a renaissance filled with black literature, music, poetry, and art, it was also a hotbed of sinful activity. Criminals and gangsters stuck to Small's Paradise like flies on a sticky strip. They lured Malcolm into their nest of unsavory behavior by teaching him a whole new brand of crime: hustling. These men took pride in "the hustle"—conning people out of their money, organizing illegal gambling schemes, picking the pockets of some innocent person while smiling in his face.

Malcolm caught on quickly and became a skilled hustler whom his gangster friends nicknamed Detroit Red on account of Malcolm's Michigan roots and his brightly colored hair.

The close-knit ring of criminals served as a kind of family that eighteen-year-old Malcolm still longed for. In addition to perfecting "the hustle," he went back to peddling drugs, this time on the streets of New York, where drug-loving customers were in abundant supply.

The police force in New York kept a very close eye on Harlem's underworld. That had not been true in Boston. With his hot-top of hair and standout looks, Detroit Red was hard to miss. He couldn't get lost in a crowd. Or even hide out in back alleys or dark doorways.

He was a watched fox, scurrying into hiding whenever possible. Because of the threat of being caught, Malcolm was forced to stop peddling drugs. He'd become addicted to narcotics, though, which impair judgment. While it would make sense that the fear of being nabbed would motivate him to get out of the gangster business, Malcolm increased his chances of getting caught by embarking on even more dangerous criminal acts. He purchased several guns and started pulling stickups in towns outside of New York. He robbed stores, private homes, and any unfortunate soul who happened to run into him on a dark street corner.

Now, no matter where Malcolm was, the police were after him. He couldn't even go to the post office to mail a letter to Ella. His picture was plastered on the post office walls. Under the drawing of his deadpan gaze was a warning: WANTED FOR ARMED ROBBERY!!

Splitting his time between Harlem and nearby towns, Malcolm got involved in gambling, illegal lottery games, double the robbery, and triple the drugs. Detroit Red was a hot mess.

Malcolm's friend Shorty had heard about his decline, and he came to Harlem to help. One day, Shorty pulled up in a car and drove slowly beside Malcolm, who was stoned and stumbling down a city street. Shorty told his friend to get into the car. Malcolm was relieved to see Shorty. He wanted to be back in Boston where the streets seemed tamer and where his sister's love was nearby.

While Malcolm slept, Shorty drove back to Roxbury. Shorty hoped the change of scene would change Malcolm's bad habits.

But it was too late for that. With so many drugs in his blood, Malcolm seemed powerless over his destructive actions. In Roxbury, he went right back to numbers-running. He launched a burglary ring. He added dollar bills to his money clip by selling stolen stuff to pawnshops.

On an afternoon when the sun was shining and the sky was as blue as his zoot suit, Malcolm walked into a jewelry repair shop to pick up a stolen watch that he'd taken to get fixed. He didn't leave with the watch, though. Instead, he was given something new and shiny for his wrists—handcuffs. The police had been waiting for him. They arrested him in front of everyone at the store. A judge sentenced little Malcolm Little, a.k.a. Detroit Red, to ten years in Charlestown State Prison. He would be staying in Boston, behind bars.

For Malcolm, jail was hell. Even the devil himself feared being sent to Charlestown State Prison. It was a broken-down facility, swarming with roaches, mice, and stink.

As soon as he got to Charlestown, Malcolm was stripped of his flashy suit and given a plain pair of pants and a simple shirt. The prison barber shaved off his conked hair and quickly swept its feathery remains into the trash. Malcolm's pretty-boy clothes and pointy-sharp shoes also ended up in the garbage can.

He was forced into a tiny cell with a single pee-hole that was his "bathroom." Like a caged wild animal, Malcolm bucked as soon as the door clanged shut on him. He hollered and cursed at anyone who came near him. He spat at the guards. He kicked inside his cell. He was creating his own hell within himself. This went on for two years. Malcolm's defiant attitude earned him a new nickname among the other inmates and the prison staff. They called him Satan.

In an effort to tame Malcolm, the prison authorities locked him in solitary confinement, an all-dark cube with only room enough for him to sit and breathe the little bit of stale air that came through a small opening in the wall.

Alone in that cramped place, Malcolm focused on the slice of sunlight forcing itself into his darkness. That shred of brightness must have been the eye of an angel watching him. Its tiny beauty inspired him to think deeply about his life up to that point. He wanted to change, but didn't know how. One night, when no light shone, Malcolm whispered what would be his first prayer in jail: *Help!*

The plea worked. After he was released from solitary confinement, he met an inmate named John Elton Bembry, an older man who was called Bimbi. Once a hustler like Malcolm, Bimbi had transformed himself into a gentleman in prison. The other inmates respected his strong, quiet demeanor, and the articulate, compelling way in which he spoke. Bimbi was a man who felt good about himself. This impressed Malcolm. He asked Bimbi how he, too, could become a powerful, persuasive speaker.

Bimbi's answer was simple: *Read*. But reading was a struggle for Malcolm. He had quit school in the eighth grade, which made academics challenging. Bimbi told him that he didn't have to *like* reading, he just had to *try* it. This, Bimbi advised, could be Malcolm's beginning.

As resistant as Malcolm was, he took Bimbi's advice. He went to the prison library, where, for the first few days, all he did was sit quietly. When another inmate showed him some of his favorite books, Malcolm took one.

Slowly Malcolm stumbled through the books. There were big words he couldn't pronounce or understand. But he *tried*. When Malcolm struggled

with a sentence, he asked the man who organized the prison library to help him. Bimbi helped too. Malcolm's curiosity kept him going. Over time he learned Latin and world history. His reading improved. He got to be a regular in the Charlestown prison library.

Now books were better than *G-O-O-D*. They were the nourishing ingredient to Malcolm's salvation. For him, reading became *F-O-O-D*.

Malcolm was encouraged to enroll in an English grammar course that was administered through the mail. When it was time for prisoners to receive letters from loved ones, Malcolm always had a bunch of envelopes. His mail included something he loved—the English lessons from his correspondence course. His half sister, Ella, his brothers Reginald and Philbert, and his sister Hilda wrote to him frequently too. Their letters lifted his spirits.

Ella mailed a request to state prison officials asking that Malcolm be transferred to a better prison facility. He was first sent to Concord, Massachusetts, then to a jail in Norfolk, Massachusetts. It was 1948. Malcolm was twenty-three years old, and still as skinny as the bars on his jail cell. But something was changing in him. As a result of his studies, he was thinking differently about himself and his future.

In Norfolk, letters kept coming from Malcolm's family. His brothers and sisters told him they had become Black Muslims, members of a religious group known as the Nation of Islam. His brother Reginald was especially enthusiastic about his association with what members sometimes called "the Nation." He wrote to Malcolm every day. He explained that, as a Black Muslim, he'd given up pork to cleanse his body and mind. He urged Malcolm to join the Nation of Islam.

Feeling healthier by not eating bacon and ham wasn't enough to convince Malcolm. Up to this point, he had shunned religion. The way he saw it, his life had been a mess. His daddy had been killed. His mama was still in a mental institution. He'd been beaten down by drugs and crime, and forced to call jail his home. For Malcolm, no kind of religon was going to make things better. He expressed this in his letters back to Reginald.

Reginald visited Malcolm in jail to explain, face-to-face, how Islam had changed him. He sat with Malcolm, gently holding both of his hands, and talked quietly about the beliefs of the Black Muslims. Malcolm listened, but he still had no interest in joining. Then Reginald said something that sliced through Malcolm's cynicism. He told Malcolm that Black Muslims believed white people are devils that have brainwashed black people. Reginald described the white race as evil.

According to Black Muslim theology, Reginald said, the black race consisted of special people chosen by an all-powerful being called Allah. Whether this idea was right or wrong, it appealed to Malcolm. The logic of the Black Muslims made sense to him. Looking back over his troubled childhood, it did seem that white people were devils. Had Malcolm made a list of the evils inflicted on him by white people, it could have cited:

1. The Ku Klux Klan had set his house on fire.

2. His foster family had taken great pleasure in their racist remarks.

3. A school teacher had insisted that black people were not fit to become attorneys.

4. White government officials had sent his mama away.

5. Though it was never proved, it was very likely that white men had killed his daddy.

He thought carefully about some of the beliefs he'd held in the past, and how they supported the idea that he'd been brainwashed by whites. For example, straightening his hair was Malcolm's attempt to deny his black heritage by trying to look "more white."

Malcolm recalled his father's firm commitment to civil rights. Earl Little's willingness to take a stand on behalf of his entire race now made it seem to Malcolm that his father was one of the chosen people.

These realizations made Malcolm feel like a blind man who had suddenly been granted the gift of sight. White prison guards had once called him Satan; he now believed this was another example of their brainwashing.

He wasn't the devil; *they* were.

Reginald continued writing daily to his brother. He urged Malcolm to surrender to Allah's all-powerful guidance, and to abandon himself to a man named Elijah Muhammad, the Nation of Islam's leader and Allah's supreme prophet.

Whew! Even though he liked the Nation of Islam's ideas, putting himself in the hands of some power he couldn't see and a man he'd never met was hard for Malcolm to accept. Deep down, he still had one of the strongest instincts of a hustler: never ever let anybody rule over you.

Reginald transcribed some of Elijah Muhammad's sermons and sent them to Malcolm. Black Muslims called Elijah "the Messenger." Elijah promised his followers liberation in a place he called the Kingdom of Allah. In this mighty kingdom, Elijah said, black people would find salvation.

Malcolm looked up this word in the prison library dictionary. *Salvation:* Deliverance. Rescue. Recovery. Escape. These words were a sweet balm for all that had wounded Malcolm.

One night in his cell he returned to the prayer he had uttered while in solitary confinement at Charlestown Prison: *Help.*

At that moment, though he wasn't confined in a dark room, Malcolm realized that his soul had been trapped in darkness for a very long time. *Help* unlocked the door. He experienced a powerful conversion. The little bit of light that had broken through Malcolm's solitary confinement cell years before was now a bolt of hope streaming into the windows of his heart. He was ready to surrender, to give up the attitudes that had held him back from what he wanted more than anything: Deliverance. Rescue. Recovery. Escape. *Salvation.*

Malcolm wrote to Reginald, Ella, Philbert, and Hilda immediately. His words read like a simple yet powerful poem. *I have accepted Allah.*

Malcolm's brothers and sisters advised him to write to Elijah Muhammad. He wrote draft after draft, struggling to find the best words to express his urgent desire to follow the Nation of Islam's ways. Finally, after twenty-five drafts, Malcolm mailed a letter that he was proud of.

Muhammad wrote back immediately. His words were filled with promise. He told Malcolm to shut the door on his past, to humbly ask Allah to forgive him for the wrongs he'd done, and to promise that he would give up crime for good.

Malcolm wept when he read the Messenger's letter. He then whispered another prayer: *Thank you.*

In keeping with the Nation of Islam's practice, in which some followers modify their names, Malcolm gave up his surname and added the letter X. Members of the Nation of Islam adopted the X to symbolize original African names that had been erased through slavery.

He was no longer Malcolm Little.

Or Detroit Red.

Or Satan.

He was now Malcolm X.

Malcolm embraced Islam. He adhered closely to the religion's customs.

Saying good-bye to bacon, booze, and cigarettes was easy. But it was hard for him to bow down in prayer several times each day. As a street hustler, Malcolm had been taught that lowering oneself was for weaklings. Sissies and milksops got down on their knees when they were begging a kingpin criminal for mercy. A real man never kneeled.

But Malcolm knew that to fully accept the power of Allah and embrace Elijah Muhammad's wisdom, he would have to humble himself. This became easier over time. When he practiced prayer each day, he experienced it as a sign of strength, not weakness.

As a Black Muslim, Malcolm was seized with an urgent desire to help black people break free of racist oppression by white people. And he was determined to understand the teachings of Elijah Muhammad. He continued to expand his thinking by reading to an even greater degree. He studied history, science, philosophy, and religion. He even started to memorize each page of the dictionary. By doing this, he learned that words have great power, and that the command of language could make him a stronger spokesperson for the Nation of Islam.

In jail, he entered into heated and affecting debates about the state of the black race. He became a prison preacher. The other inmates listened to him as he told them about the beauty and power of Allah and the Nation of Islam. Young inmates sought his advice, and because of him, they became Black Muslims. At Norfolk Malcolm grew a community of believers. And, just as important, he grew into a man he liked and respected.

In 1952, because of his model behavior, Malcolm was released from prison four years early. He left Massachusetts and returned to Michigan. His brother Wilfred helped him get a job working as a salesman in a furniture store in Detroit. When Malcolm learned that the store's white owners were taking advantage of black customers by selling them sofas and chairs on credit at very high interest rates, he left the job and found work in an automobile factory.

Some of Malcolm's hustler buddies remembered him, though he wasn't easily recognizable at first. He had strained his eyes from so much reading in jail, and now wore glasses. And his conk was long gone. The zoot suit and sharp-toed shoes had been replaced with dignified black slacks, a jacket, a pressed white shirt, a bow tie, and loafers. People still called him Detroit Red, but he quickly corrected them, pointing out the X in his name and his devotion to the Nation of Islam.

When these junkyard thugs tried to entice him back into their shady dealings, Malcolm preached the word of Allah and kept stepping. But hustlers are hard-core when it comes to pulling people down. They tried to "brother" Malcolm—referring to him as "brother" in an attempt to lure him back to burglary. Not even the "brother" bait could tempt Malcolm to stray from the practices of his religion.

In Detroit, Malcolm joined a mosque, the Nation of Islam's Temple Number One. There he found the fellowship of other Black Muslims who shared his beliefs and welcomed him. The warmth of the people comforted Malcolm. But it was their pride in being black that affected him the most. For the first time ever, he felt like he belonged. Like he mattered. Like he had come to a new beginning.

It was autumn 1952. One aspect of Temple Number One bothered Malcolm, though. There weren't a lot of members. At worship meetings, many seats stayed empty. As Malcolm listened to the religious discussions that filled him with so much hope, he looked around at the sparse hall and wished all the chairs in the room had people sitting in them.

Weeks later, Malcolm X met Elijah Muhammad at the prophet's home in Chicago. Malcolm and other Black Muslims often referred to him as "the Messenger" and as the Honorable Elijah Muhammad. They believed him to be a man of great wisdom and high moral character. It was a privilege for Malcolm to finally meet this honorable man.

In the presence of Elijah Muhammad, Malcolm was overcome with emotion. He couldn't speak. It was as if he were trying to write those twenty-five drafts again. There seemed to be no words to express his gratitude.

Elijah took an immediate liking to Malcolm. Once Malcolm found the right way to express his thankfulness, he and Elijah began to talk. Elijah saw that Malcolm had a gift for speaking. And that he possessed a special kind of charisma. Malcolm told Elijah that he'd come to Detroit hoping to find more Black Muslims. Elijah agreed that the Nation of Islam's pool needed more fish. He gave Malcolm an assignment—to "go fishing," a term the Black Muslims used for recruiting new members.

Malcolm went to Detroit's blackest and bleakest parts of town. He fished for the most troubled guppies, young men and women who lived in neighborhoods filled with drug pushers, barflies, hustle kings, and armed robbers. He focused on the ones who were just beginning to spiral into crime, those who were denying their blackness by sporting conked hair, and those who'd been wronged by whites and were enraged because of it.

Malcolm *knew* these young men and women. He had suffered the same hardships and attitudes. Like them, Malcolm had been slick. Quick. Sharp. Street-smart. He understood how to appeal to these people.

With his gift for preaching, Malcolm visited pool halls, honky-tonks, conk salons, and street corners ruled by card sharks.

He didn't just speak, he *sparked*. With humor, intelligence, and his hot-buttered way with words, Malcolm told Detroit's drifters about the salvation he'd found as a Black Muslim. He emphasized the Nation of Islam's belief that the white race was comprised of devils, and that black people had been chosen by Allah as special and superior.

Malcolm's sizzling speeches worked. The membership at Temple Number One tripled. Men and women arrived at the mosque early and stayed all day. If you got there late, you'd better be wearing comfortable shoes, 'cause the place had become standing room only. Black people from all over Detroit came to hear Malcolm address the congregation. His popularity and persuasive delivery earned him the position of assistant minister at Temple Number One. He quit his job at the automotive factory to devote himself to his work within the Nation of Islam.

Malcolm X was a magnet pulling in new members wherever he went. It became clear to Elijah Muhammad that he had the ability to build the Nation of Islam into a powerful force. In 1953, he gave Malcolm a charge: to organize a temple in Boston. Malcolm returned to his old stomping ground with a whole new outlook. Where once he arrived in Boston as a juvenile delinquent, then as an inmate, he was now entering the city as a religious leader.

The same thing happened in Boston as in Detroit. Malcolm's former cronies tried to drag him into crime. But he refused to let them. He organized Temple Eleven, where he quickly attracted a following. During the next few years, Malcolm opened temples in New York, San Francisco, Los Angeles, Philadelphia, and Atlanta, each with packed-house success. In his sermons, Malcolm drew on his command of language, history, and philosophy to spread the doctrine of Elijah Muhammad. Every time Malcolm spoke, he attacked white people and praised his black brothers and sisters. He always stressed the importance of black unity and empowerment. In one sermon he said, "We never can win freedom and justice and equality until we are doing something for ourselves."

That *something* came in many different forms. In several American cities, the Nation of Islam organized temple schools for their children. They opened a Nation of Islam restaurant, and launched a newspaper called *Muhammad Speaks*. The publication featured quotations by the Honorable Elijah Muhammad. Malcolm's evenings were spent in his basement, printing copies of the publication. Each week, once the papers were stacked, male members of the Nation came to collect the bundles. Malcolm instructed them to sell papers on street corners to attract new members and to raise money.

The newspaper was embraced by the black community. It grew to have the largest circulation of any black publication in America, reaching more than half a million readers.

The popularity of *Muhammad Speaks*, along with Malcolm's electrifying sermons, inspired people to pack Black Muslim mosques. The Nation's membership continued to grow in large numbers. Malcolm organized several national conventions and hosted rallies attended by hundreds of men and women. He often ignited these meetings by making very provocative statements. In one speech he referred to the early American settlers who'd arrived on the *Mayflower*. He sent a ripple of laughter and applause through the crowd when he shouted into the microphone: "We didn't land on Plymouth Rock, my brothers and sisters. Plymouth Rock was landed on us!"

Once Malcolm's listeners were warmed up and primed to receive more of the Nation's doctrine, Malcolm introduced the Honorable Elijah Muhammad, who continued to promote his belief that white people were "blue-eyed devils." He warned that whites would someday meet their doom under divine retribution. Elijah and Malcolm also preached their belief that black Americans could only gain total liberation by remaining completely separate from white people. These militant views lit a fuse with black folks whose wrath against whites needed an outlet. With Malcolm and Elijah Muhammad working as a team, the Nation of Islam started to explode into a revolutionary force.

With so many temples opening in major cities, Malcolm's notoriety grew within the black community. But an incident in 1957 brought Malcolm to the attention of the general public. On April 26 of that year, Johnson Hinton, a young member of the Nation of Islam, was beaten by two white police officers in Harlem when he tried to help a black man who was being assaulted by the same two cops.

When Johnson and the other man were hauled to the police station, Malcolm came right away and asked that Johnson be taken to Harlem Hospital so that doctors could examine his bloodied, swollen head and the purple bruises on his face. Johnson was taken by ambulance to the hospital, where a surgeon determined that the police had caused damage to his brain when they clubbed him. Johnson needed to stay in the hospital, but the police took him back to the precinct.

Word spread quickly among New York's Black Muslim community. By this time, the Nation of Islam had become highly organized, thanks to Malcolm's leadership. It didn't take long for Black Muslims to gather outside the 28th Precinct. Harlem's sidewalks and streets were soon filled with four thousand members of the Nation of Islam who had come to support Johnson and to protest his having to spend the night sleeping on a rickety precinct cot with no pillow.

The scene on the street—Muslim men in dignified suits, the Nation's women robed in white—created a mosaic of solidarity. This impressive image of unity appeared in newspapers and on television news broadcasts. When people saw that the Nation of Islam was a powerful unified group, they took notice. But it was Malcolm's control of the throng that piqued the greatest interest.

The police came onto the street to tell the enraged mob that Johnson would be not be released until the following day. Malcolm knew the police would not budge from their position, and that for Johnson's safety it was best that the crowd disperse. Malcolm silently raised his hands to indicate that those gathered should retreat. That's all it took. The mosaic

broke up quietly as the crowd moved off. Referring to Malcolm, one of the policemen told a newspaper reporter, "No one man should have that much power."

But that one man did have power—lots of it.

When the story of the incident broke, neighbors phoned each other, saying, "Did you hear about this guy named Malcolm X?"

People wondered what Malcolm would do next. The Black Muslims had become a topic of conversation in barbershops, on playgrounds, and at family dinner tables throughout America. In some communities the Nation of Islam's membership increased as a result of Malcolm's actions surrounding Johnson's beating. He had become a militant with muscle.

Malcolm's influence made law enforcement authorities nervous. They began watching Malcolm and the Nation of Islam's activities closely.

Six months after the assault on Johnson Hinton, a grand jury acquitted the policemen who'd brutally beaten Johnson. This miscarriage of justice, in Malcolm's eyes, sent him into a rage. The attack on Johnson brought back memories of the racial inequities Malcolm had suffered during his childhood. He grew more bitter than ever, and spoke about the evilness of white people with even more fervor.

Adding to this fervor, Malcolm crafted an irate telegram to the police commissioner, expressing his views on the mistreatment of Johnson Hinton and how this affected race relations. Unlike his twenty-five attempts to write a letter to Elijah Muhammad, Malcolm articulated his views on the first try. His furious words sparked even greater suspicion among law enforcement officials, who now kept a constant eye on him.

Thankfully, he had the comfort and support of a loving woman. In 1958, Malcolm married Betty X, a nurse and teacher at the Nation's temple school in New York. Malcolm was devoted to Betty. In marrying her he furthered his commitment to the Black Muslims' ethical code of faithful allegiance to one woman. Betty and Malcolm would have six daughters. Malcolm was determined to give his children something he didn't have for most of his childhood—a stable, close-knit family.

Spending time with his wife and his daughters was a good way for Malcolm to relieve the stress of his public life. His family loved him unconditionally, but not all black Americans supported Malcolm's views. His caustic remarks shocked and frightened many people, black and white alike. Some thought Malcolm was a crazy demon. Only the cruelest of men, they reasoned, could spew so much hatred.

There were black people who were ashamed of Malcolm's opinions and the public recognition he was gaining. According to them, he made the race look bad. His hatefulness was delaying racial progress, they believed, not helping make things better.

At this same time, America was entering a period of increased civil rights activity, much of it led by Reverend Martin Luther King, Jr. Like Malcolm, Martin was a powerful public speaker whose philosophy was underscored in his sermons.

Martin believed that equality would come to African Americans through patience and peace, and that black citizens should strive primarily for *integration*—for opportunities to live *among* white Americans and to be *equal* to them. This ideal was in direct conflict with the separatist beliefs held by Malcolm and the Nation of Islam.

Malcolm was very outspoken in his criticism of Martin's approach to racial equality. To Malcolm, this struggle was not about peace. Black people were at war against a white foe.

Peace, Malcolm believed, was a waste of time. He told folks that black Americans had to *fight* for what they wanted—and they needed to defend themselves against the cruelty of white oppression "by any means necessary."

Malcolm's in-your-face attitude led him to confront Elijah Muhammad about rumors that had begun to spread about "the Messenger." Two female members of the Nation of Islam came forward saying that Elijah was the father of their children. If this was true, it meant that Elijah had violated the Nation of Islam's code of conduct and had ignored the religious doctrine regarding fidelity.

When Malcolm asked Elijah if the rumors were true, Elijah didn't confirm or deny them, and he had a hard time looking Malcolm in the eye when Malcolm pressed the question.

Malcolm asked the women about the accusations. They each presented proof. All someone had to do was take a good look at their children to see that they had Elijah's features, coloring, and mannerisms. There was no doubt in Malcolm's mind that these kids resembled their daddy.

Suddenly the Honorable Elijah Muhammad wasn't so honorable. To Malcolm, Elijah's acts of adultery were more sinful than eating two plates piled with bacon or smoking a carton of cigarettes.

This discovery crushed Malcolm. He could no longer trust his mentor. Elijah Muhammad wasn't a positive presence; he was a weak-willed man who had given in to lust. Elijah's promiscuous behavior created a rift between him and Malcolm, which in turn made Malcolm question his involvement in the Nation of Islam.

Maybe it was a kind of vulnerability that pushed Malcolm to act carelessly following Elijah's indiscretion. Soon after he learned of Elijah's involvement with the two women, he himself behaved irresponsibly. A loose lip—and shooting from the hip—got him into trouble.

In 1963, when President John F. Kennedy was assassinated, Malcolm stated publicly that his murder was an example of "chickens coming home to roost." This was his way of saying that violence against the president was retribution for so much aggression perpetrated on black citizens by white people over the course of America's history. White society was getting what it deserved.

This comment outraged many people. Once again folks on street corners and in living rooms were talking about this guy named Malcolm X. But this time they weren't impressed or intrigued by Malcolm's actions—they were incensed. Americans were now shaking their heads and calling him stupid.

Elijah Muhammad was one of them. Malcolm's comment had brought bad publicity to the Nation of Islam, which issued a public statement of condolence to Mrs. Kennedy and her children.

Elijah Muhammad suspended Malcolm from his role within the Black Muslims for ninety days. The ground rules were simple:

No public speaking.

Stay out of the limelight.

Keep a low profile.

Malcolm was still angry about Elijah's betrayal of the Black Muslims' religious observance of fidelity. This, coupled with Elijah ordering him into silence, further weakened his commitment to the Nation of Islam.

In some ways, Malcolm felt it was Elijah Muhammad who had committed an act of violence—against Malcolm and against himself. It was murder by character assassination. Malcolm had lost his faith in "the Messenger" and in the Black Muslims. To make matters worse, he started to hear more bad rumors about Elijah Muhammad. Some of his fellow Black Muslims were whispering that Elijah Muhammad wanted Malcolm X dead.

Malcolm started to question the Nation of Islam's beliefs in promoting hatred and condoning violence. These values were hurting too many people. Malcolm's goal was to unify black Americans by instilling racial pride among them. Now, though, within his religious community, pride and unity were breaking down.

On a cold day in early 1964, Malcolm X knelt to pray. He issued an urgent plea to Allah: *Show me.*

Sometimes prayers are answered quickly. Other times slowly. Malcolm received guidance right away. In March 1964, he announced that he was leaving the Nation of Islam to form a group called Muslim Mosque, Incorporated. The organization's goal was to bring together black people of all religions who would work on building strong black communities. In outlining his ideals for the Muslim Mosque, he cited his belief that black Americans had the political strength and power that it would take to change their destiny overnight.

Malcolm began to read the Koran, a holy book that the larger Muslim community believes is the true word of Allah. The Koran's wisdom inspired him. He realized that his devotion to the Black Muslims had limited his thinking. The Koran showed Malcolm that in true Islam there are no "blue-eyed devils" and that all white people aren't evil.

Malcolm's prayer for guidance continued to be answered. *Show me* became *take me*. Malcolm had reached a new surrender, which was aligned with Islam, a word that in Arabic means "submission." A voice deep within him responded to his longing. It led him with a simple direction: *hajj*.

The *hajj* is a journey to the Middle Eastern Islamic holy city of Mecca, in Saudi Arabia. Malcolm didn't have to question whether to make this pilgrimage. Upon hearing the word, he went. His wife, Betty, stayed at home with their daughters, knowing her husband was making an important spiritual journey.

Malcolm X was ready to change. For him, Mecca was a place filled with light, love, hope. Muslims of every race welcomed Malcolm. Some were blacker than blackest. Others were blond, blue-eyed, beautiful souls who embraced Malcolm as they would a brother. Malcolm's long-held hatred of white people melted away. This *hajj* had healed Malcolm's anger. He wrote a letter to the press saying that he was "spellbound by the graciousness" shown to him by "people of all colors."

This was a revelation for Malcolm. He was so moved by all that this *hajj* had presented to him, that he took an Islamic name, El-Hajj Malik El-Shabazz. Shabazz is the name of an ancient black scientist who, some Muslims believe, founded the populations of Africa.

He returned to America with a new identity and a quiet, peaceful heart. Malcolm had renewed his commitment to racial unity. This time, his vision was to bring black people together throughout the world to build economic empowerment. This was a big plan. To carry it out,

Malcolm helped form a group called the Organization of Afro-American Unity (OAAU). The OAAU was not a religious organization; it was a nationalist one.

To share his mission for the OAAU, Malcolm traveled throughout Africa, speaking to black people of many religions and social customs. Their common bond was the color of their skin. During his travels he told his African brothers and sisters that they shared a common quest for racial equality with black Americans. "Our problems are your problems," he said.

Malcolm also promoted the OAAU's objectives at rallies in American cities and at universities. People liked the new Malcolm and his broad ideas. He attracted followers of all races, including white people. At the same time, though, he openly condemned Elijah Muhammad and the Nation of Islam's practices. Throughout his travels, both the Nation of Islam and federal authorities had continued to keep a close watch on Malcolm's activities.

His new open-mindedness was not met with the same enthusiasm among the Black Muslims and the Nation of Islam. A burning hostility had grown between him and his former friends. As 1964 drew to a close, death threats came to Malcolm's home. Betty received scary anonymous phone calls, letting her know that her husband's life was in danger.

On February 21, 1965, Malcolm was dressed in a starched white shirt, a necktie, and one of his best suits. It was a Sunday. The winter sky was a crisp, cold shock of blue. Malcolm was scheduled to speak at a meeting of the OAAU at Harlem's Audubon Ballroom that afternoon.

He began his remarks with the Muslim salutation: "*Assalaikum*, brothers and sisters!" a greeting that means *peace be with you.*

The packed ballroom called back to brother Malcolm: "*Wa alaikum assalam!*"—a response that means *and peace be with you.*

Malcolm was pleased to see so many members of the OAAU.

A strange calm settled down on the room.

Peace be with you.

Malcolm spoke deliberately and with great assurance. His presence alone was an inspiration to his listeners. He had hardly begun his remarks when several gunshots were fired. The room erupted into shrieks and cries for mercy.

Three assassins were out to kill Malcolm.

After the shooting, the men raced out of the Audubon Ballroom into the day's biting air. Malcolm was rushed to the hospital, but by the time he arrived, it was too late. He was dead.

The three men who had opened fire on Malcolm—Talmadge Hayer, Norman 3X Butler, and Thomas 15X Johnson—were found guilty of murder. Both Thomas 15X Johnson and Norman 3X Butler were identified as being members of the Nation of Islam.

Malcolm had overcome many obstacles in his life. Through hardship, hard work, and hard lessons, Malcolm had given black people the gift of knowing that any individual can change for the better.

Malcolm had instilled pride in black men and women. He gave many lost souls purpose and direction through the building of the Nation of Islam and the organizations he founded before his death.

Today, Malcolm's memory endures in many ways. In New York City's Harlem, Malcolm X Boulevard is a main street in one of America's leading black communities. There are many schools and civic organizations that bear his name. In 1992, Warner Bros released a motion picture based on *The Autobiography of Malcolm X*, a best-selling book published in 1965 on which Alex Haley collaborated with Malcolm and completed after Malcom's death. The film was co-written, co-produced, and directed by Spike Lee, and starred Denzel Washington in the title role.

Malcolm's life was a powerful example of the words that spurred him to make an incredible personal transformation and that marked his legacy:

Deliverance.

Rescue.

Recovery.

Escape.

Salvation.

Praying hands

put this man
on the path to justice.

Preacher

Scholar

Writer

Teaching peace

Holding fast
to his Dream.

Speaking up and out.
Leading us to shout, hands raised:

"Free at last!
"Free at last!

"Thank God Almighty!"

Martin Luther King, Jr.

b. January 15, 1929, Atlanta, Georgia;
d. April 4, 1968, Memphis, Tennessee

Nonviolent Visionary

————◆•◆•◆————

THE BABY BOY WAS born at high noon in his grandparents' home on Auburn Avenue in Atlanta, Georgia. He was the second child of Reverend Martin Luther King, Sr., and Alberta Williams King. They named the child Martin Luther King, Jr., after his daddy.

The King family had already been blessed with a daughter, Willie Christine, born two years before Martin. When Martin's little brother, Alfred Daniel Williams, came a year and half after Martin, the King family was complete.

Each of the Kings had a nickname. Martin's was M.L. Willie Christine was called Christine for short. Alfred Daniel was A.D. The reverend was Daddy King. Alberta was referred to as Mother Dear.

Daddy King was a proud man. Strong, too. Same for Mother Dear. She had the fortitude of ten, the conviction of twenty. Daddy King and Mother Dear instilled this strength in each of their children. Goodness knows, they needed it. Growing up in the segregated South was not for the weak-willed or fainthearted.

Jim Crow, the law of the land, had a mighty wingspan. He cast his darker-than-dark shadow over much of Atlanta. M.L. and his family were forced to live by Jim's rules, known as segregation.

There were signs posted in public places to make Jim's laws super-clear. The signs said: WHITES ONLY and COLORED. While segregation laws were referred to as Jim Crow, it was *people* who enacted them. These people hung reminders at water fountains, restaurants, hotels, libraries, pools.

Those signs seemed to be everywhere. Once, when Daddy King took M.L. to buy a new pair of shoes at a white-owned store, the clerk was quick to make M.L. and his father move to the back of the shop. The clerk would not wait on them otherwise. Daddy King left that place quick. He was not going to stay put for such foolishness. This type of prejudice happened many times in M.L.'s young life.

Inside Atlanta's Ebenezer Baptist Church, Jim Crow's tune was tempered by faith's beautiful music. Every Sunday, Reverend Martin Luther King, Sr., Ebenezer's pastor, and Alberta, the church musical director, blessed their congregants with sermon and song.

Reverend King, he sure could preach! His delivery thundered that church down to its bones. Alberta graced Ebenezer with the hymns she played on a pipe organ whose music filled every corner—and every soul—of their holy home.

As the son of Ebenezer's preacher, M.L. spent all day on Sunday at his daddy's church. On weeknights he was there too, helping keep the church tidy, watching his mother practice her organ, listening to his daddy work on sermons for the coming Sunday. Ebenezer provided its congregation with more than just the gospel. Church was the place black folks went to find strength, quiet, fellowship, and an escape from the weight of segregation.

For M.L., church was as comforting as a hand-stitched quilt. Even before he was old enough to go to school, M.L. was learning at church. His first book was the Bible, its words helping teach him to read and providing his earliest lessons. By watching his daddy preach, M.L. saw how an effective speaker can help people. His mother's organ music, and the chorus of Ebenezer's choir, were the greatest reassurances of all. Hymns put Jim Crow in his place. Spirituals shot him out of the sky. When the power of Reverend King's prayers were added to the joyful noise made by Alberta's organ, Jim Crow cowered.

By the time M.L. was five, he was singing at church socials. This strengthened his voice, which, soon after his twelfth birthday, took on the low tone of a rich baritone. It soon became clear to everyone at Ebenezer that M.L. King had been blessed with each of his parents' gifts. He could sing with the might of a Christian solider, and speak with the conviction of the Lord's most devoted messenger.

Because he'd learned to read when he was very young, M.L. became proficient at it. He could comprehend complex ideas. This helped him advance more quickly in school than other children. He skipped ninth grade, and would later skip twelfth grade. By the time he was fourteen, he was in the eleventh grade and already thinking about college.

M.L.'s talents for speech and song made him a popular student at Booker T. Washington High School. During his junior year, he entered a statewide oratorical contest, sponsored by the Negro Elks, a civic organization. The event took place in Dublin, Georgia, several miles from his home in Atlanta. His teacher, Mrs. Bradley, accompanied him to Dublin. She was prouder than proud when her student stepped to the stage.

There was no sweat to that competition. As soon as M.L. began to articulate his views on "The Negro and the Constitution," the contest judges were unclasping the first-place ribbon, preparing to pin it on his tweed lapel. He walked away with the grand prize, and with folks congratulating him for a speech delivered like a man with years of oratory experience. Mrs. Bradley beamed. She couldn't wait to get home to share the good news with the principal at Booker T. High, and with the other students and teachers.

But soon after M.L.'s win, he and Mrs. Bradley experienced a blow. On their way home, the two were riding a bus bound for Atlanta. The bus stopped at a small town to pick up more passengers. When a group of white people got on, the driver yelled at M.L. and his teacher. He demanded that they give up their seats so that the white passengers could sit down.

Jim Crow laws had swooped in!

Segregation rained down on the joy M.L. felt from taking first place in the contest. His blue ribbon made him feel bigger than Jim Crow laws. He was a winner. He was not about to let segregation's humiliation take away his pride. He refused to move. Mrs. Bradley feared a fight. She gently made M.L. obey the law.

M.L. and Mrs. Bradley were forced to stand for the rest of their ride. For ninety miles, they listened to the bus's rickety engine.

M.L. never forgot that long bus ride. Even though he graduated from Booker T. High at the top of his class. Even though he was considered among the brightest and the best of all students in Atlanta. Even though his singing continued to shine on sermon Sundays at Ebenezer. The law was the law.

White people *here.*

Black people *there.*

No mixing.

No sharing.

No crossing the line.

M.L. was determined to get away from Jim Crow laws. After he graduated, he took a summer job in Connecticut working on a tobacco farm. As a preacher's son who'd spent much of his time in pressed pants and neckties, he didn't take too well to farming. But spending time in the North opened his eyes to a whole new world. The first thing he saw was the sunlight of equality. Jim Crow's wings did not stretch to the North. In Hartford, Connecticut, the state's capital, M.L. and his fellow black field hands rode on any bus they pleased. There were no WHITES ONLY signs.

When the summer ended and M.L. returned home to Atlanta, "Colored" took on its old hue. On the train ride back to Georgia, he could sit in any seat he chose, but only as the train raced through the northeast. Once that iron horse crossed over into Virginia, Jim Crow laws were waiting. When M.L. went to the dining car, the waiter showed him to his seat at the back of the cabin, where he pulled a curtain around M.L. to cover him so that white passengers would not have to witness a black man eating. This kind of humiliation made his meal tough to chew and even harder to swallow. The situation served up a powerful intention for him. He would do whatever it took to pull segregation's curtain down on Jim Crow's head. Let the bird eat his seed behind a veil!

M.L. knew that one of the first steps to gaining the knowledge needed to help end segregation was to get a college education. In 1944, at age fifteen, M.L. entered Morehouse College, an all-male, all-black institution in Atlanta. He had passed the Morehouse admissions exam and was now the youngest student in the freshman class.

Reverend King and Alberta loved to tell the congregants at Ebenezer all about M.L.'s studies at Morehouse. While his parents didn't like bragging, they couldn't help but sing their son's praises. Their teenage boy was a college man! And he was enrolled in the same college Daddy King had attended.

Daddy King also enjoyed pointing out that his son had the skills to become the next minister at Ebenezer. Since M.L. had followed in his father's college footsteps, his daddy assumed he would do the same thing by becoming his successor.

The parishioners at Reverend King's church liked this idea, but whenever Daddy King mentioned it to M.L., he got quiet. At college M.L. learned about many career choices. He imagined becoming a lawyer or a doctor. He respected his father, but he was beginning to question religion. Compared to his college courses about philosophy, history, and literature, sermon Sundays at Ebenezer were starting to seem all about emotion rather than concrete knowledge.

Church had offered M.L. so much as a child, but he now had doubts about what preaching and praying had to do with one's intellect. To M.L., the thunder that rumbled each week at Ebenezer had little to do with black progress.

Dr. Benjamin Mays, the president of Morehouse, showed him that spirituality and smarts could exist hand in hand. He gave M.L. a new view of religion. Dr. Mays was a minister who spoke with quiet, powerful poise. Each Tuesday at the Morehouse chapel, Dr. Mays presented his views for social change. He tied his sermons into the Bible's stories, relating these to the plight of black people. M.L. often sat in the front row of Dr. Mays's discussions. In Dr. Mays he saw that Christianity was filled with wisdom, and its tenets could be applied to the struggle for racial equality.

M.L. told his parents what he'd learned from Dr. Mays and that he was ready to become a minister at Ebenezer. That night before bed,

Daddy King got on his knees and thanked the Lord for leading M.L. onto what he believed was the right road. To keep him on this path, Daddy King wasted no time. He saw to it that his son got ordained immediately. On February 25, 1948, M.L. became a minister and the assistant pastor at Ebenezer.

Though M.L was following in his father's footsteps, he was walking to his own rhythm. As soon as he graduated from Morehouse, he applied to the Crozer Theological Seminary, a theology school in Upland, Pennsylvania. M.L. was only nineteen years old, but already becoming a seasoned clergyman. At first, Daddy King objected to his son attending Crozer. He was too young, Daddy King believed. M.L. loved his father, and he respected Daddy King's robust style of preaching. But he recognized that if he wanted to become a minister like Dr. Mays—a minister who sought to improve conditions for black people—he couldn't just "get religion." He had to study theology as an intellectual discipline.

Eventually, Daddy King gave M.L. his blessing. As he and Mother Dear helped him pack for Crozer, Daddy King looked forward to the day M.L. would return to Atlanta and apply what he'd learned at Crozer to his work as the head minister at Ebenezer.

Crozer was an integrated school, where, for the first time ever, M.L. shared classrooms with white students. He wanted to make a good impression and was intent on showing his white classmates that a black student was respectable. M.L. always made sure to dress his best. He spoke with only the best diction. To be certain that he would be taken seriously, he introduced himself as Martin. The white students at Crozer treated him as they would anyone else.

Through his class reading Martin learned about the teachings of Indian leader Mahatma Gandhi. Gandhi believed that the best way to approach opposition is through a concept known as *satyagraha*—resolving conflicts by peaceful nonviolent protest. Gandhi encouraged his followers to approach their enemies with the same love they would bestow upon a friend. This philosophy struck a chord with Martin.

He wondered:

Could satyagraha *be applied to the racial hatred between black and white people?*

Would satyagraha *help end segregation?*

What if, rather than seek to break Jim Crow's beak, he and others practiced peace?

Martin spent hours reading about Gandhi's approach. He studied it carefully. He wanted to see exactly how it worked.

The idea was simple: *Meet hate with love.*

In time, Martin's questions turned to intentions. There *was* nothing to question. Peace, he believed, was the only answer to solving the problems of prejudice.

In 1951, Martin received his bachelor's degree in theology from Crozer. As the valedictorian of his class, he was awarded a scholarship to continue his education at a graduate school. Crozer had shown Martin the depth of theological study. He learned that God could be found in his textbooks! So, to find more of God through his education, Martin chose to pursue a PhD at Boston University's School of Theology.

In Boston, Martin met Coretta Scott, a vocal student at the New England Conservatory of Music. Coretta was a Southern lady from Alabama. She was educated, refined, and could sing sweeter than peach cobbler tastes.

Soon after Martin and Coretta were introduced, they knew God meant them to be together. They married on June 18, 1953.

As Martin worked on his doctoral dissertation, he thought hard about the best way to use his degree to serve others. Daddy King and Mother Dear had been waiting patiently for his return. So had the parishioners at Ebenezer. By earning so many educational degrees in the study of religion, their local boy had done a whole lot of good. The people in Atlanta loved to talk about all that Martin was accomplishing. But at Christmastime in 1953, Martin received a special gift. He was invited to deliver a sermon at the Dexter Avenue Baptist Church in Montgomery, Alabama.

Martin preached with assured dignity. He shared what he'd learned at Crozer and Boston University. The parishioners at Dexter were impressed. Their attitudes about religion were similar to his. Like Martin, the members saw the black church as a means for furthering the cause for civil rights. They felt he could help their congregation foster these beliefs by bringing the perspective he'd gained through his years of theological study. When they offered him a job as their new pastor, he accepted.

Daddy King was not happy about this. Neither were the folks at Ebenezer. They wanted Martin. But Martin wanted a church to call his own. His father had no choice but to wish his son well. From one reverend to another, Martin Luther King, Sr., congratulated Martin Luther King, Jr., on his new post at Dexter.

Montgomery, Alabama, welcomed Martin. The town was steeped in segregation. Its white residents boasted that Montgomery had done a good job upholding the South's tradition of white supremacy.

Right away, Martin set out to improve the race struggle in Montgomery. This he would do by "pulpit and pew."

He used his *pulpit* to persuade those in Dexter's congregation to join America's leading civil rights organization, the National Association for the Advancement of Colored People (NAACP). With his rousing sermons, Martin pulled people from their *pews*—he inspired them to take action.

He insisted that Dexter's members register to vote. This was not easy. Jim Crow worked hard at voting poll sites. Discrimination by white officials made voting very difficult for black citizens. The people who monitored voting stations forced black people to take ridiculous, unfair "exams" that were supposed to "test" their ability to register as voters. For example, if a black man or woman wanted to become a registered voter, a white polling representative would ask the person to tell them how many dried beans there were in a jar filled to the top. This kind of silly guessing game was meant to determine a black person's aptitude.

Or, a prospective black voter was given a written test with "official" questions such as "Write out all the words to the Declaration of Independence."

This had nothing to do with registering to vote, and it was illegal to prevent any qualified person from voting. The primary requirements for registering to vote were that the individual be a U.S. citizen and could write his or her name on the voter registration form.

When Martin's parishioners went to the polls, they politely told Jim Crow to bug off. Some were permitted to vote. Others were turned away because they hadn't passed the bean-counting-guess test.

Martin urged people to persevere despite these setbacks. When a discouraged soul wanted to lash out at such indignity, Martin instilled his strong beliefs in peace. He told his parishioners to combat bigotry by opening their Bibles. Answers to racial progress, through love, could be found in the Good Book's scriptures:

"Thou shalt love thy neighbor as thyself."—Matthew 22:39

"A soft answer turneth away wrath: but grievous words stir up anger."—Proverbs 15:1

"Walk in love. . . . Walk as children of light."—Ephesians 5:2, 8

These were the words that would make for change, Martin believed. Peace and love would knock out segregation, he said.

As passionate as Martin was, not everyone agreed with his philosophy. Some of the most religious-minded people felt that the best way to protest Jim Crow was by meeting Jim where he lived—on the mean side of the sky. They proposed an aggressive approach, fighting fire with fire. To these people, Martin pointed out that hatred is the hottest fire there is, and that by lighting a violent torch to spread its flame, *everybody* gets burned, not just Jim Crow.

In 1955, when Martin completed his doctoral dissertation, Boston University awarded him a PhD in theology. This earned him the distinction of being addressed as Dr. King. But to folks who knew him well, he was still Martin. Having worked so hard on the study of religion and its positive impact on people, he remained convinced that his nonviolent approach was more than just a concept—it was a *calling*. Also, he determined that peace was his moral obligation to advancing the cause for equality.

In December 1955, Martin put this calling into practice. On the evening of December 1, Rosa Parks, a black seamstress and long-time member of the NAACP, got on a Montgomery, Alabama, city bus and sat down a few rows behind the driver. It had been a long day at work. Rosa was bone-tired. When a white passenger boarded the bus, he expected Rosa to move to a seat farther back so that he could sit down. Rosa clutched her handbag. With quiet determination, she shook her head.

The white man insisted.

Rosa persisted.

She stayed seated. The white man yelled at her. So did the driver. This kind of confrontation was nothing new.

A policeman came. He arrested Rosa and put her in jail. This outraged the black residents of Montgomery, who immediately rallied together and decided they would boycott the city buses—for as long as Jim Crow laws were alive, they would not ride. News of Rosa's arrest and the boycott plans reached Martin. Rosa was tried and found guilty of breaking the law. She was fined and released, but she wasn't truly free. With Jim Crow laws still around, Rosa and every black person living under Jim Crow's wing were confined to the ways of segregation.

Montgomery's black residents were as weary as Rosa had been when she'd refused to give up her seat. For Martin, the situation brought back the memory of his own degrading experience as a bus passenger returning from the oratory contest with his schoolteacher, Mrs. Bradley. Like Rosa, he and Mrs. Bradley had been asked to give up their seats so that a white passenger could sit down. Mrs. Bradley had relented. As a teenager, Martin had little choice but to obey Mrs. Bradley and follow her to the aisle of the bus so that they could stand, while white people sat in the seats that had been theirs. Now, as a grown-up, he had the power to stand up in a new way. He could take a stand against this kind of humiliation.

Just days after Rosa's trial, when a bus pulled up to the South Jackson Street stop outside Martin's house, Coretta called her husband to come see. The rush-hour bus was practically empty. There were no black riders. A boycott had begun.

To organize the boycott, black members of Montgomery's NAACP formed the Montgomery Improvement Association. They appointed Martin as their president. On the evening of December 5, 1955, a meeting was held at Montgomery's Holt Street Baptist Church, where Martin had been asked to speak and to offer direction for the boycott.

To inspire those gathered, he did what he knew. He exercised the power of "pulpit and pew."

And Lord, that pulpit stood ready, with a microphone and speakers to project sound to the streets outside. As for the pews, every single one of them was filled. Nearly a thousand people had gathered inside the church.

Those who were forced to stand in the aisles didn't mind it one bit. They were there to hear Martin Luther King, Jr. His words would give them strength.

Thousands more people filled the streets outside, also excited to hear Martin. He addressed the crowd with unmistakable power. He began: "We are here this evening to say to those who have mistreated us so long, that we are tired. Tired of being segregated and humiliated; tired of being kicked about by the brutal feet of oppression."

At this, some people stomped *their* feet while they applauded Martin's speech. His delivery grew louder, stronger. With the speakers' volume turned up high, his sermon rang through Montgomery's streets. He urged everyone listening to practice peace as the boycott proceeded. "Love must be our regulating ideal," he said.

With love leading the way, the people of Montgomery walked every day. The official name of their protest was the Montgomery Bus Boycott. African American Montgomery residents refused to ride city buses. They stayed on foot.

Even when their feet ached.

Even when their backs felt like breaking.

Even when hard rain stung their heads.

They would not ride those buses until segregation laws changed.

The impact of the boycott was immediate. Bus companies were losing business—and money. All those dimes black riders had spent on bus fare were going into their piggy banks instead of into coin collection boxes on city buses. Black folks were saving their cash, and protecting their dignity.

But progress took time. Things got worse before they got better. For each day that Montgomery's black residents kept up with their peaceful demonstration, the white citizens grew angrier.

In January 1956, Martin and Coretta's home was bombed. Fortunately, no one was harmed. But the act of violence enraged black people, some of whom showed up at Martin's house carrying clubs. They were ready to strike back! In their minds, even though the boycott had only lasted a few weeks at that point, it had gone on long enough. Jim Crow was still overhead. Segregation still hung in the air. The heck with nonviolence! Peaceful protest—forget about it!

Martin asked the marchers to keep the peace, no matter what. He told them to continue "using the weapon of love" in their fight. As hard as this was, it was even harder to ignore the conviction of Martin Luther King, Jr. His leadership helped the boycotters stick to their course. It was nonviolence all the way.

The Montgomery Bus Boycott continued for more than a year.

After months of black folks *walking, walking, walking*; after seasons of white-owned bus companies watching their revenues *falling, falling, falling*, Jim Crow's wings started to wither.

On November 13, 1956, the United States Supreme Court ruled that laws requiring segregation on Montgomery, Alabama's city buses were unconstitutional. It was now illegal to force a black man, woman, boy, or girl to sit in the back of a bus, or ride in the aisle.

The protesters' adherence to Martin's nonviolent approach had worked. Though Jim Crow's segregationist ways still persisted throughout the South, as far as the buses in Montgomery were concerned, Jim Crow laws were now taking a backseat to justice.

But the fight for fairness was far from over. Black people were still subject to job and housing discrimination. WHITES ONLY and COLORED signs still hung in restaurants and other public places. If a black person wanted to drink from a fountain, he was made to sip "colored" water. Then, when nature called and that person needed to use a public restroom, the same was true—he or she could only find relief on the "colored" side of things.

With the success of the Montgomery Bus Boycott, Martin had become more than a minister. He was now a civil rights crusader. Black Americans were looking to him for direction.

As a clergyman, Martin always stuck close to his Christian beliefs. While he led the cause for racial equality, he was *being* led by the wise teachings he'd learned in divinity school. There were several prevailing principles that he clung to: faith, love, hope, and prayer. These, he believed, were the fundamental virtues that would bring about positive changes.

In February 1957, Martin's portrait appeared on the cover of *Time* magazine. Inside the issue there was an article about him in which he shared his Christian views and spoke about nonviolence and his beliefs about peace. The magazine article referred to Martin as a "scholarly Negro Baptist minister." The profile in *Time* brought him widespread acclaim. He was becoming the most notable black man in America.

President Dwight D. Eisenhower had certainly heard of Martin, but seeing him on the cover of one of the nation's leading news publications showed him and other high-ranking government officials that the fight for civil rights was growing into an unstoppable movement. President Eisenhower supported Martin's cause. He sent a civil rights bill to Congress. The bill outlined the formation of a civil rights commission that would investigate racist acts against black people. Also, the bill called for the Justice Department to take action on behalf of black citizens who had been denied the right to vote. If Congress approved the bill, there would be no more bean-counting and phony tests given at voting polls.

Martin was keen for this bill to pass. On May 17, 1957, twenty-five thousand people came together under Martin's leadership to take part in the Prayer Pilgrimage for Freedom. A crowd of white people and black people gathered in Washington, D.C., in front of the Lincoln Memorial. Martin gave a speech that was a prayer of sorts. It was an urgent plea to Congress. "Give us the ballot!" he said.

Martin's words rang throughout Washington. Congress heard them. It took some time, but Congress did approve the Civil Rights Act of 1957. But they only approved certain aspects of the president's original bill. Missing from the final act was the enforcement of voting equality. So, yes, there was now an official new Civil Rights Act. But as far as Martin—and every black citizen who'd ever been forced to guess at the number of beans in a jar—were concerned, the Civil Rights Act of 1957 was only *half* an act. The act didn't go far enough.

That same year, Martin brought together several notable civil rights leaders to form the Southern Christian Leadership Conference (SCLC), an organization whose mission was to use spiritual principles to promote social justice. The SCLC established its headquarters in Atlanta. Martin traveled between Montgomery and his hometown to work on various SCLC initiatives. One that was particularly important to Martin was the SCLC voter registration campaign.

Traveling back and forth between Montgomery and Atlanta took a toll on Martin. He and Coretta now had two young children, Yolanda, a daughter, and Martin III, a son. Martin looked forward to spending time with his family, and he wanted his daughter and son to live closer to his own parents. To make this possible, in January 1960, Martin left his position as the head pastor at Montgomery's Dexter Avenue Baptist Church. It was hard for him and Coretta to say good-bye. In his farewell remarks Martin told the parishioners at Dexter, "History has thrust something upon me from which I cannot turn away."

When Martin, Coretta, and their children returned to Atlanta, Daddy King and Mother Dear were overjoyed to have them back. Martin assumed the role of co-pastor at Ebenezer Baptist Church, working alongside his father. In 1961, Coretta gave birth to the third baby King, Dexter, a boy, named after the church in Montgomery.

Martin continued to work tirelessly toward progress for black Americans. With Coretta often at his side, he marched. He preached. He led a charge that grew mightier each day.

By 1962, Martin's work with the SCLC had become a full-fledged crusade. Jim Crow's loyal followers felt threatened by the increasing magnitude of civil rights activists who were committed to stomping out Jim Crow laws for good. This set fear and violence in motion. More and more, black people became the victims of brutal attacks, lynchings, bombings, and other hate crimes. White segregationists redoubled their efforts to frighten black Americans.

Birmingham, Alabama, was considered by many to be the most racist town in the South. The place had become a hotbed of violent activity. When an act of abuse against a black man or woman happened in Birmingham, Martin was called. He joined several racial protests in this town, and his nonviolent approach was doubly challenged.

In March 1963, Martin's fourth child was born, a daughter he and Coretta named Bernice. Now more than ever, Martin wanted to put out the blistering flames of hatred that were still ablaze. As a father, it was very important to him to achieve racial equality. He wanted a better future for his children.

On April 3, 1963, Martin issued a "Birmingham Manifesto," a demand that public places in the town be desegregated. To gain support for this proposal, he and SCLC members marched through the city's streets. After several demonstrations, the government issued an injunction that forbade any more marching. If the protesters continued, they'd be arrested.

Martin was not about to turn back. On April 12, 1963, he led a group of demonstrators to Birmingham's City Hall. The fifty marchers proceeded quietly, but Birmingham's police were ready to cart them away. They handcuffed Martin and threw him in the Birmingham jail, where he would be locked up for eight days. He used the time spent in his cell to write one of the most defining documents of his career, his "Letter from Birmingham Jail."

Martin's letter was hotter than any hate-flame ignited by Birmingham's racists. Its words served as a beacon, lighting the way to equality. In his letter he wrote, "segregation distorts the soul and damages the personality."

The "Letter from Birmingham Jail" was issued as a pamphlet distributed by the American Friends Service Committee. It also appeared as a magazine article in periodicals such as *Christian Century*, *Christianity and*

Crisis, the *New York Post,* and *Ebony.* Through these publications, the letter circulated to nearly a million people.

Being jailed didn't dampen Martin's spirit. Once released, he was even more determined to continue his fight, peacefully, nonviolently, forcefully.

The movement gained momentum in the summer of 1963. August had pressed its heat onto America's towns and cities more heavily than the nose of an iron bears weight onto a shirt collar. Maybe the heat rose from bigotry's oppressiveness, which was still in the air.

Neither high temperatures nor high tempers stopped the plans for what would become one of the largest and most memorable civil rights demonstrations in America's history. The March on Washington for Jobs and Freedom took place on August 28, 1963. On this day, two hundred and fifty thousand people gathered in the nation's capital to protest the inequalities that remained so much a part of America's landscape.

Martin had a dream that someday there would be no Jim Crow laws. He was eager to share this dream so that others could see the possibilities of an equal society and could continue to work hard to achieve freedom.

The organizers of the march had specific goals, which they outlined for government officials. Mainly, they sought job training and employment opportunities for black people who were out of work; they wanted a law preventing housing and job discrimination, and they wanted fair voting practices.

Folks from every state in the nation came to Washington to participate in the march. Some walked. Some rode buses. Some laced up their skates and rolled. They would get to the march any way they could. There were black people and white people, men and women, Christians and Jews, Northerners, Southerners, boys, girls. They arrived with love in their hearts and with peace in each and every step they took. They walked together, arm in arm, as brothers and sisters, singing spirituals to celebrate the day's glory.

"Woke Up This Morning with My Mind Stayed on Freedom" rose up, marking this as a morning filled with the sweet music of progress.

The march began at the Washington Monument, then made its way

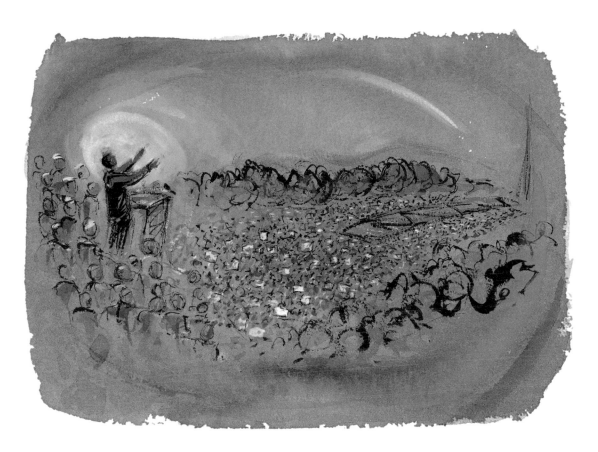

to the Lincoln Memorial, where civil rights speakers graced the day with their speeches. As the afternoon's sun swept its tawny sleeve across the sky, Martin prepared to speak.

He stepped to the podium, starting off slow, steady, ready. He began by telling the crowd that this day was the greatest freedom demonstration in the history of our nation. We are at a beginning, Martin said. "We cannot turn back."

At that moment, something grabbed ahold of Martin—something powerful.

He shared his dream. It was a dream that someday his children and all children would "not be judged by the color of their skin, but instead by the content of their character."

In Martin's beautiful vision, black boys and girls would be able to join hands with white boys and girls.

As he continued, Martin's speech took on a mighty roar. It was a sermon, a prayer, a promise. He expressed himself so eloquently, that everyone could see the future. He was painting its beauty right in front of them!

Again and again, he told the crowd, "I have a dream! I have a dream today!"

He spoke of the faith that could turn our nation into a "beautiful symphony of brotherhood," where people of all races could live together peacefully.

"Let freedom ring!" he declared.

To end his speech, Martin proclaimed the words from an old Negro spiritual:

"Free at last! Free at last! Thank God Almighty, we are free at last!"

Martin's listeners shouted their praises.

"Amen, Martin!"

"Glory be for peace!"

"Hallelujah, brother King!"

On July 2, 1964, President Lyndon B. Johnson struck a final blow to Jim Crow. He signed the Civil Rights Act of 1964 into law, banning racial segregation in schools and other public places.

Martin was pleased to see Jim Crow laws go, but segregation's shadow lingered. Though signs saying WHITES ONLY and COLORED were no longer permitted, discrimination of other kinds still existed.

As Martin had said in his March on Washington speech, "This is no time to engage in the luxury of cooling off."

He stayed focused on his dream. In October 1964, he learned that he'd won the Nobel Peace Prize, one of the highest honors in the world. He was the youngest person to ever receive a Nobel citation. The prize showed that Martin's commitment to peace was making an important impact across the globe.

Martin continued to advance the freedom struggle in the United States. On April 3, 1968, he delivered a speech at a Mason temple in Memphis, Tennessee. That evening he returned to the Lorraine Motel, where he and fellow SCLC members Ralph Abernathy and Andrew Young were staying, along with Martin's aide, Jesse Jackson, and student activist Bernard Lee.

The next day the men prepared for an upcoming march in support of fair wages and improved work conditions for the local garbage collectors. Martin was tired but happy. He'd been traveling and speaking nonstop, always holding fast to his vision for a better world. Always clinging to his hope for a society completely free of bigotry.

At six o'clock that evening, Martin and his friends stepped onto the balcony of the Lorraine Motel. They were leaving the motel to attend a dinner at the home of Samuel Kyles, a local minister.

Almost as soon as the men walked onto the balcony, they heard a loud *POP!* Martin fell. He'd been shot. Someone had tried to kill him!

The assassin was a man named James Earl Ray, a white racist whose heart was full of hatred. James had succeeded. Martin Luther King, Jr., was dead.

After Martin's death, President Johnson called for a National Day of Mourning. On this day, April 7, 1968, America's schools, public libraries, and businesses were closed. The next day, Martin's widow, Coretta, and other family members marched in Memphis to honor him and to support the town's sanitation workers.

Martin's body was sent to Atlanta, where one hundred thousand mourners surrounded the Ebenezer Baptist Church on April 9, 1968, the day of his funeral. Americans cried as they said good-bye to one of the greatest civil rights leaders of all time.

In 1983 President Ronald Reagan declared the third Monday in January of each year Martin Luther King, Jr., Day. This federal holiday marks Martin's birthday and honors the tremendous contributions he made.

On October 16, 2011, the Martin Luther King, Jr., Memorial was formally dedicated on the National Mall in Washington, D.C. It is the first national monument created in honor of an African American leader. That monument stands tall. That monument stands proud. That monument stands for everything Martin stood for—not backing down in the face of injustice.

Though Martin didn't live to see his dream come true, its promise prevailed. His leadership, and his love, lifted the world to a higher ideal.

His hands seized

what some believed to be
      the impossible American Dream.

A black boy in the White House?

What are the chances?
Dare we hope?
Will our vote
      elect this impossibility?

Biracial child
      of two worlds, both strong.

One of Kenyans from the African Continent.
The other, Kansas folk.

Long-gone daddy.
Strong mama.

An inner constitution
      that lifted him above the odds.

Let him dream of becoming
      Commander-in-Chief.

Refused to give way
      to *"No, we won't."*

Held tight to The Audacity of Hope.

Pumped-up America with

"*Yes, we can!*"

Barack H. Obama II

---

b. August 4, 1961, Honolulu, Hawaii

Holding on to Hope

———◆◆◆———

WHEN BARACK HUSSEIN OBAMA II was born, his parents gave him a Swahili name, Barack, which means "one who is blessed by God." And the middle name Hussein, which, in Arabic, means "beautiful."

Barack's father, Barack Obama, Sr., lived up to the meaning of his own name and the name he bestowed on his son. Barack Sr. was blessed with brains and ambition. And he had a true appreciation for beauty. He had been born near Kenya's Lake Victoria, where the sunsets and crystal waters are among God's most extraordinary gifts to the world. Barack, Sr., a member of the Luo tribe, grew up witnessing these wonders.

When Barack Sr. was awarded a scholarship to attend the University of Hawaii, he knew he'd been blessed with another gift. Hawaii, like Kenya, was a land filled with beautiful birds, wide skies, and the sweet-sweet of sugarcane juice. It was a new state, adding color and diversity to America's mainland mosaic.

At college, Barack Sr. met a special girl in his Russian class. Her name was Ann Dunham. Ann was nothing like the girls he'd known back in Kenya. For one thing, she was white. Ann had been raised in Kansas, one of the more conservative states, where black folks and white folks didn't keep company. And in Kansas, Africans were more rare than blackbirds at a dove convention.

Barack Sr. was the first and only African student at the University of Hawaii. As soon as he and Ann got to talking, the two had eyes for each other. Ann—who at sixteen had been accepted to the University of Chicago, but whose parents would not allow her to attend because of her age—was smarter than smart, and was taken with Barack's confidence, easy way of speaking, and his knowledge of American politics.

Ann's mother, Madelyn, and her father, Stanley, were living in Honolulu while Ann attended college. Though people from many races called Hawaii their home, the Dunhams' interactions with, and perceptions of, people of color was limited to what they had known in Kansas. Back in Wichita, their hometown, black people lived on one side of the fence, whites lived on the other. Madelyn and Stanley had always frowned on racism, but whenever they tried to help or befriend a black person, their neighbors scolded by wagging a finger and muttering, "Uh-uh-uh."

That was one of the reasons the Dunhams had moved to Honolulu— to escape such narrow-mindedness. When their daughter Ann brought Barack home for dinner, they saw in him what Ann saw. He was a brilliant thinker and told colorful stories about his life back in Kenya. They liked him.

But when Ann told her parents that she and Barack planned to marry, they weren't so happy with the idea. They worried about their daughter's future. It was 1960, a time of great racial upset in America. In many states, it was illegal for white people to marry "Negroes." And attitudes about race extended far beyond finger wagging and "Uh-uh-uh."

To lots of people, a black person and a white person exchanging wedding vows was as unnatural as mixing blackbirds and doves.

Barack's family in Kenya felt the same way. Upon hearing that his son intended to marry Ann Dunham, Barack's father, Hussein Onyango Obama, did not mince words. *"Uh-uh-uh"* was too mild for the way he felt about their union. He came right out and spoke his mind—*"No! No! No!"*

There were some pitfalls in marrying Barack that Ann didn't fully realize. In his tribe, it was customary for a man to have several wives. Barack had a first wife in Kenya, a Luo woman named Kezia. Onyango, as most people called him, asked his son straight-out if Ann would be willing to move to Kenya with her new husband, where she would share

Barack with Kezia. (Barack had told Ann about Kezia, but indicated that they were separated.)

Onyango was a proud African. He believed that marriage was an agreement between families, and that Ann's father, Stanley, should get on a plane, come to Kenya, and ask if his daughter could marry his son.

Onyango's attitudes and Barack's other wife complicated matters. But all of that, coupled with a bunch of *uh-uh-uh*'s and *No! No! No!*'s, didn't prevent Ann and Barack from saying, "I do."

Soon after they were married, Barack Hussein Obama II was born, in August 1961. His family called him Barry, for short.

Barack Sr. loved his wife and new son but had his sights set on continuing his education. While Ann changed baby Barack's tiny diapers and warmed his bottles of milk, her husband worked hard to finish his four-year undergraduate studies. He was so enthralled with his schooling that he wanted to go further by earning a PhD. When Barack Sr. was offered a full academic scholarship to Harvard University in Massachusetts, he ran after that opportunity. In many respects Barack Sr. was in a kind of race of his own. As one of very few Africans in his town able to get the stellar education offered by Harvard, he was seized with a sense of urgency to get an advanced degree that would make his father and his tribe proud.

It was 1963 when Barack Sr. left for Massachusetts. Little Barry was a toddler, and like every other child his age, he got into a lot of mischief. Ann was essentially a single mother. Now *she* was the one warning, "No! No! No!" and working hard to keep her curious son away from electrical outlets, potted plants, and hot kettles bubbling on the stove.

Thankfully, Ann's parents helped care for Barry in Honolulu. Barry called his grandma "Toot," a name that came from *tutu*, the Hawaiian word for grandmother. Grandpa was called "Gramps."

As Barry grew, Ann knew she would never go to Kenya with her husband, once he finished at Harvard. Onyango had been right. She could not abide by Kenyan custom and be Barack Sr.'s second wife. Also, her parents didn't want their daughter and grandson to live so far away in a country that was going through a political rebellion for independence. It was too dangerous.

Barack Sr.'s family also had strong opinions. Onyango believed that Barack Sr. had an obligation to use his education to help the people of Kenya modernize the country by sharing information about government, politics, technology, and the changing world.

So, Ann and Barack Sr. divorced. Barry and his mom stayed in the United States, while Barack Sr. returned to Kenya, where Kezia and Onyango were waiting for him.

Ann, Toot, and Gramps worked hard to keep Barack Sr.'s memory alive for Barry. It was easy to paint a colorful picture of the charismatic Barack Sr. in the stories they told. A favorite family tale was about the time Barack Sr. was with Gramps in a bar. A white man came up to him, made fun of his dark skin color, and called him a derogatory term. Gramps thought Barack Sr. was going to haul off and hit the guy. But Barack Sr. was too smart and too much of a gentleman. Instead, he leaned in close to the racist man and lectured him on why bigotry is a bad thing. Barack Sr. spoke so persuasively that the prejudiced guy handed Barack Sr. one hundred dollars as an apology for his actions.

This kind of story turned Barry's daddy into a hero. But to Barry, who had no memory of his father, he was a mystery. Even as a little boy he couldn't help but wonder, *How great can a man be if he leaves his wife and son?*

His father's absence was heightened by the fact that Barry resembled his dad in many ways. He had Barack Sr.'s broad smile, Kenyan nose, and a head full of what some people described as "ethnic hair."

At quick glance, Barry's physical appearance was different from his mom's and grandparents'. Barry's mother was white, and his father's dark coloring had given him the complexion of someone who, in the eyes of most people, was *not white.*

Wherever Ann walked her ginger-colored son around the neighborhood on his tricycle, or wheeled him through the grocery store in a supermarket cart, nosy people asked her, "Whose baby is *that*?"

Ann answered simply: "Mine."

Gramps took another tack. At the beach, when tourists stared, Gramps told them Barry was the great-grandson of King Kamehameha, one of the great rulers of the Hawaiian islands. That's when their zoom-lens cameras came out. These gullible tourists started snapping pictures of Barry (a.k.a. "The Royal Great-grandson") for their vacation memory albums!

Gramps's joke was funny, but its humor only went so far. From the time he was very young, Barry, who by most standards was a child of color, felt like a "different" kid in his all-white family.

The differences kept coming. When Barry was four years old, his mother met an Indonesian man named Lolo Soetoro, who was attending the University of Hawaii. After two years of dating, Lolo asked Ann to marry him. She said yes right away. But, because he was not a citizen of the United States, Lolo was forced to return to Indonesia. This time Ann would follow her husband. She was not going to leave Barry without a father figure in his life again.

Ann packed her belongings, the few toys Barry owned, his favorite sneakers and shirts, and traveled to Jakarta, Indonesia, to start a new life with her six-year-old son and her husband.

Lolo was a quiet man and very generous. When his new stepson arrived at their red-tiled home, Lolo had a gift waiting for him, a wild ape named Tata, who swung out from a tree branch to greet Barry. With his new pet, Barry explored the wonders that lived right in his own backyard. Chickens, baby crocodiles, and cockatoos were all glad to see him. Now they had a playmate, a brown-skinned boy who was curious about his new surroundings.

The neighborhood in Jakarta where the Soetoro family lived was far from paradise, though. Barry's home had no refrigerator or air-conditioning. There was no flush toilet. Electricity had arrived not much before Barry and Ann had. The houses surrounding Barry's were made of shabby wood and bamboo. For lunch and dinner the family ate roasted grasshoppers, fried snake, or grilled dogmeat. Barry longed for his life in Honolulu. Even though Lolo was a kind man, Barry missed Gramps and Toot. And, once again, Barry wasn't like any of the other kids around him. On top of having "ethnic hair" and an African nose, he didn't speak Indonesian.

On his first day of school, Barry walked into Ms. Darmawan's first grade classroom, wishing he could translate what was being said. This was one of Barry's first lessons in paying close attention to others so that he could understand them. It didn't take long for him to learn that listening works. In six months he could speak Indonesian well enough to participate in class. But Barry was a shy boy. He sat in the back of the room and didn't raise his hand much. He could express himself through writing, though. When Ms. Darmawan asked students to write an essay on what they wanted to be when they grew up, Barry had no trouble spelling out his plan. The title of his essay was "I Want to Become President."

By the time Barry was in third grade, he spoke Indonesian fluently. And he never lost sight of the dream he'd put to paper in first grade. Now, at age eight, when his teacher, Ms. Sinaga, asked her students to complete an assignment called "My Dream: What I Want to Be in the Future," Barry finished the homework immediately. He had a one-word answer to "What I Want to Be in the Future": *President.*

Barry was very clear about his aspirations. More and more, his mother started calling him Barack, rather than his nickname, Barry. Seeing that her son had such big dreams, Ann began to teach him about Martin Luther King, Jr.'s dream for racial equality. She encouraged Barack to read about civil rights pioneers such as Rosa Parks, and she explained important events led by Martin and Rosa, such as the March on Washington and the Montgomery Bus Boycott. Also, Ann began talking more and more to her son about his father. How kindhearted and upstanding he was. How filled with racial pride. How smart. How charming.

Young Barack didn't know it then, but his mother's marriage to Lolo was failing. She had given birth to a baby girl, Maya Soetoro, Barack's half sister. But the new baby didn't help the troubles in their relationship.

Maya's birth made Barack feel like even more of an outcast in his Indonesian surroundings. At least Maya was living in the same country and the same house as *her* father.

Questions about his absent father pelted Barry like a hailstorm.

How come this upstanding, kindhearted, filled-with-racial-pride father of his was nowhere in his life?

How would he ever feel like he belonged?

And how was he supposed to believe in the power of a man he'd only met once?

These troubling questions were never far from Barack's mind. His mother must have sensed some kind of longing in her son. Ann purchased a plane ticket for Barack and sent him, all alone, back to Hawaii to live with his grandparents. He was only ten years old when he boarded the plane from Jakarta for Honolulu.

Barack was so glad to see Toot and Gramps. He didn't care that people at the airport stared at the sight of a black boy traveling by himself, hugging two older white people at the airline terminal.

Through a contact at his job at a life insurance agency, Gramps had arranged for Barack to attend Honolulu's Punahou Academy, an upscale prep school. Gramps took Barack to his fifth-grade classroom, where Miss Hefty, his teacher, greeted him happily. As soon as he walked into the room, Barack felt that he didn't belong. Among the first things the other kids noticed were his shabby feet. In this prestigious place full of starched collars and pressed pants, Barack's brown Indonesian sandals stuck out.

Unlike when he was a baby, nobody mistook Barack for being Hawaiian. He was the kid regarded as *new and few*. He was entering a school where most of the other students had grown up together, and he was among a handful of black children at Punahou.

To fit in, Barack introduced himself as Barry. But Miss Hefty was quick to call him by his real name. She encouraged the other students to welcome Barack Obama to their classroom. Miss Hefty had been a teacher in Kenya. Gramps had enrolled him at Punahou using his complete name, and had told the teacher about the elder Barack Obama.

Miss Hefty invited Barack Jr. to tell the class about his father. He was hesitant. The whole time, Barack secretly wished that Miss Hefty had a little less heft in her Kenyan pride. When she asked which tribe his father came from, Barack told her what he knew of the Luo people. As soon as Barack mentioned Luo, he was struck with feelings of Oh, no!

It might have been better to just say, "I don't know."

When Barack talked about the Luo people, the other kids let their laughter roll. Barack's description of the tribe brought on all kinds of goofy monkey imitations and wisecracks from boys and girls who had false ideas about living in Africa and being black. These were kids who'd had very limited contact with black people.

Days at school got worse before they got better. Some of the same ignorant kids who thought *Luo* was just so funny, also figured it would be even more entertaining to see what Barack's "ethnic hair" felt like. They took turns asking Barack if they could pat his afro. At least they asked. But there was no mistaking Barack's answer: *Uh, uh, uh! No! No! No!*

Having to deal with so much stupidity, Barack had no choice but to try and impress. At Miss Hefty's urging, he continued to talk about Barack Obama, Sr. He told every tall tale he'd ever heard about his father, adding his own spin to each of the stories. Some of the kids giggled. One boy assumed that Africans were cannibals and asked Barack if his father ever ate people!

Punahou was a school that bragged about how intelligent its students were, yet these were the kinds of idiotic questions they asked!

A few weeks into the school year, Toot received a telegram saying that Barack's father would be coming to visit at Christmastime. Barack's mother and half sister, Maya, were also scheduled to return to Hawaii from Indonesia during the holidays. It was 1971.

Barack was excited and nervous to finally meet his father. Miss Hefty was so eager on his behalf that she let him go home early on the day Barack Sr. was scheduled to arrive. But young Barack didn't hurry home. He dawdled and kicked at stones in front of Toot and Gramps's house before going inside. Finally, he walked in. Barack Sr. was standing there. He'd been waiting all afternoon to greet his son. When the younger Barack saw his father, his heart leaped, then sank fast.

Young Barack had heard so many stories about this larger-than-life man, but just by looking, Barack could see that he was no Superman. His skinny neck poked out from his shirt collar like a protruding pencil. He wore thick glasses. His complexion was as black as the skin on a raisin.

Barack expected his father to be a towering giant, but the top of Barack's head reached his father's shoulder. In a few years, he'd be as tall as this man.

Miss Hefty, so full of enthusiasm about having a member of the Luo tribe right in their town, had invited Barack Sr. to come speak to her class. Of course Barack II couldn't tell his teacher or his father that he hated this idea. He was dreading the visit. As the day approached, young

Barack braced himself to become the brunt of every joke known in the history of middle-school life. He was ready to take up permanent residence in Fifth Grade's Snicker City.

But the opposite happened. Barack Sr. made his son proud. In the cadenced rhythms of his homeland, he told the students how mankind rose from Africa's soil. He entertained them with tales of Kenya's lions. He explained Kenya's history and the nation's fight for its independence.

In addition to *what* Barack Sr. said, he appealed to his son's classmates and teachers with *how* he said it. He spoke with such articulation. His presentation showed Barack's classmates that Africans were educated, cultured people. Miss Hefty was as pleased as young Barack. She and her students were smiling. From that moment on, Barack no longer had to endure monkey imitations and questions about Africans eating people. Barack Sr. had given his son an important gift. He'd demonstrated that one's heritage is a source of strength.

In some respects, Barack Sr. had behaved like the superhero his son had hoped for—he'd swept in to save his child's reputation.

Then—*poof!*—he disappeared, leaving Barack to wonder, *Who was that black man?*

Soon after speaking in front of his classmates, Barack's father returned to Kenya. It was the last time Barack Obama Sr. and Barack Obama II would ever see each other. For young Barack, all that was left of his father was a memory and a basketball that the elder Barack had given him for Christmas before he left for good. Barack loved that basketball, but it was no substitute for the love a son experiences each day when his father is there to give it.

Barack tried to find comfort in the family he had. His mother was now separated from Lolo and brought baby Maya to Hawaii for a visit. His grandparents were always close by, so this helped ease the ache of growing up without a father. But the absence of a daddy had left a hole in Barack's life. He often felt as though something was missing. Being fatherless was like moving through each day without a limb. It was debilitating. It hurt. And it seemed everyone noticed.

At school events it was Gramps and Toot who showed up to support Barack, not his mom and dad. After Christmas, his mother and Maya had returned to Indonesia so that Ann could complete a course of academic study and finalize her separation with Lolo. Barack refused to go with his mother. He was tired of shuttling back and forth between countries and cultures. And he was sick of walking into a school of strangers, of being the kid who was *new and few.*

Over time, Barack settled in at Punahou. Although he still felt like an outsider, he excelled in middle school. In high school, inspired by the basketball his father had bought for him years earlier, he joined Punahou's varsity basketball team. Turns out, Barack Obama II could play some fierce B-ball. He had a long jump shot that helped his senior class team win the state championship. The way he worked that ball earned him the nickname "Barry O'Bomber."

The best part of basketball for Barry O'Bomber was that it seemed to matter less that he was a brown-skinned player in Punahou's buff-colored uniform. He could get to the net and score. That's what counted most— the points he earned for his team, not the color he added to the varsity roster. Also, every team needs a player who, along with the team's coach, can rally the athletes, solve conflicts between players, and inspire fellow teammates to perform their best. Barack had all of these skills. He was good at fostering camaraderie and helping to make the Punahou team a strong, unified group.

This was Barack's first experience in being an effective organizer of people and working toward a win. He liked to do it. He was good at it. His teammates agreed.

Even with his talent for team-building, and the acceptance of his teammates, questions about his racial identity plagued Barack. He knew where he stood on his school's basketball team, but as far as race was concerned, he wondered if he should be trying to fit into a particular ethic group.

Was he African American?

Biracial?

A Kenya/Kansas blend, with some Indonesian flavor thrown into the mix of his multiethnic upbringing?

Like many teenagers, Barack began to ask himself, *Who am I?*

He looked for the answer to this question by reading the works of notable black writers and thinkers who'd made an impact on race in America.

210

There were essays by scholar and historian W.E.B. DuBois, whose book *The Souls of Black Folk* described Barack's racial tug-of-war.

The Autobiography of Malcolm X, coauthored with Alex Haley, told the story of one of America's most controversial and outspoken race radicals. These and other books inspired Barack to identify himself as African American.

Barack graduated high school from Punahou Academy in 1979, eager to be black-identified. The following September, he enrolled at Occidental College in Los Angeles.

He didn't have Miss Hefty's enthusiasm to bolster his Africanness, but he now insisted on being called Barack all the time. Barry O'Bomber no longer existed. Having read so many books about the importance of racial pride, Barack Hussein Obama II was *Barack*. As a college freshman, whenever he introduced himself, he said his name with conviction. He was so focused on being black that he seemed to lose sight of the larger goal for attending college, which is to get an education by learning from others.

It took a fellow student to set him straight. He told Barack that while it was admirable to be so black-identified, worrying about who was African American and who wasn't and whether *he* was or wasn't a "real" black man missed the point. There was no "Official African American Identity Handbook." Racial pride was less about skin color and ethnic makeup than about one's intentions for advancing the race.

This concept made Barack think even more deeply about his own racial character. It was at this time he started to develop an interest in government and politics as they relate to race.

He gave a speech at a campus rally about the injustice of South Africa's apartheid system of racial segregation. As Barack spoke, the power of his father's ability to articulate flowed through him. From Barack Sr. he'd inherited the gift of effective public speaking and the ability to move people with his delivery.

At this rally he grabbed his listeners by their earlobes within the first three sentences of his speech. Referring to the evils of apartheid, he began: "It's happening an ocean away. But it's a struggle that touches each and every one of us. Whether we know it or not."

His remarks brought people to their feet. They were roused by his forceful delivery. Their reaction showed Barack what his classmate had tried to explain—it was his commitment to social justice, rather than his obsession with his own family tree, that made him a "real" black man.

By Barack's sophomore year at Occidental, he realized that if he was going to pursue the broader issues of race and politics, he'd need a more rigorous course of study to prepare him for a larger arena. In 1981, Barack transferred to New York City's Columbia University, a college at the edge of Harlem, America's center of black life and culture.

Harlem's pulse intrigued Barack. This upper Manhattan neighborhood had once enjoyed a heyday of black creative expression. During the 1920s, it was glistening with black poets, writers, musicians, and intellectuals. When he arrived in New York, Barack thought Harlem's streets would be burgeoning with the likes of poets as notable as Langston Hughes and jazz geniuses on par with Duke Ellington.

What he found was that while Harlem still boasted a proliferation of black creativity, its streets no longer glistened. Row homes that had once been jewels of the neighborhood had fallen into disrepair. Also, racial discrimination was prevalent, not only in Harlem, but throughout New York. For example, taxi drivers often refused to pick up black passengers. Sometimes, if a white cabbie did pull over for a black man or woman who'd been standing out on a rainy street corner with a hand raised to hail the cab, the driver would speed off quickly when the prospective passenger lowered his or her umbrella, leaned into the driver's open window, and said, "I'm going to Harlem." Some drivers didn't want to travel to what some of them referred to among themselves as "colored town."

This was just one example of prejudice in New York. Others included housing and employment discrimination.

Parts of the apartheid speech he'd given at Occidental applied to life in the United States. Racial hatred wasn't just happening oceans away. Its struggle was touching everyone in America, white and black, whether they knew it or not.

More and more, Barack was beginning to see that his question about where he fit in among the black race—*Who am I?*—was limiting. The real question was: *Who are WE?*

Barack was now taking a broader view of race in America. He started to question how he could help improve the injustices black people faced.

In November 1982, a little more than a year after he'd arrived at Columbia University, Barack received an upsetting phone call from a relative he didn't know well. His aunt Jane from Nairobi told him that his father had been killed in a car accident. Barack was stunned, but he didn't cry. How could he mourn a man he hardly knew? He was mostly sad for his mother, who wept when he called to tell her what had happened. He didn't attend his father's funeral. Instead he wrote a condolence letter to his aunt Jane and his father's family.

His father's accident was a wake-up call. Barack realized that life was precious, and that he needed to make *his* life count for something greater than himself.

Barack plunged into his studies. He was a political science major. At Columbia he became active in the Black Students Organization and continued to support the antiapartheid movement. He went into race-pride overdrive, working long hours on behalf of black causes.

It seemed Barack was rushing to catch a fast-moving train, while at the same time running away from an oncoming locomotive. A year after Barack's father died, his feelings of grief caught up with him.

One night, Barack woke up with a tear-stained face. He'd had a vivid dream about his father. A dream that broke open the sadness he wasn't allowing himself to feel about his father's death. In the dream, Barack's father was locked in a jail cell. Barack opened the door to set him free. The older Barack told his son that he loved him. Hearing this, Barack II urged his dad to leave the jail with him. Barack Sr. shook his head. He was staying back. He wanted his son to go alone. Barack had never fully mourned the loss of his father until that moment. This dream played in his sleep like a large-screen movie. And it made him weep all night long.

The dream was a powerful one. It was as if Barack's father was telling him to leave the burdens of their relationship (or lack of relationship) behind—to walk away from the issues that had confined him for so long. His father was encouraging Barack to free himself.

Barack took heed of this message. He turned his grief into a deep and genuine desire to work on behalf of the larger black community.

After Barack graduated from Columbia in 1983, he looked for work as a community organizer. Community organizers brought neighborhood people together to appeal to government leaders so that these men and women would address problems such as lack of employment, faulty schools, and run-down housing.

Barack had no official experience as a community organizer, but from his days as a basketball player, he knew what it took to bring people together for a common cause. He understood team-building.

After receiving several rejections for this type of work, Barack got a job offer from the Developing Communities Project (DCP), an organization in Chicago whose primary purpose was to improve conditions in black neighborhoods.

To start his work with the DCP, Barack bought a battered blue Honda. That car sure was rickety. But it had four tires filled with air, solid steering, and an engine that worked. Though his salary was small, he earned enough to keep his gas tank filled. It's a good thing too, because to make inroads with the residents of Chicago's South Side, he needed to get around.

Before he could help people, he first had to find out what their most pressing concerns were. To do this, he needed to talk with them. But he was a stranger to these folks. He didn't grow up in their neighborhoods. None of them knew this recent college graduate with big hopes. Many South Siders hadn't finished high school. Some had tried to appeal to local politicians to improve their living conditions and schools, but their appeals had been ignored. By the time Barack arrived, they'd resigned themselves to living under shabby circumstances with no help from local politicians.

What, they wondered, could this guy do to help? They were skeptical. Barack had to gain their trust. This took time. Rather than swoop in and tell the people his ideas for change, he began by letting *them* talk about their concerns while *he* listened.

Chicago's South Siders had a long list of issues, all stemming from the recent closing of a steel plant. Many had lost their jobs. People were fleeing their neighborhoods and leaving them in a state of disrepair. The playgrounds stood empty and had become the hangout for drug dealers and gangs. Parents wouldn't let their kids go out and play. Schools were overcrowded and broken-down. The nightly news reported an increase in car robberies.

Barack had to find a way to galvanize the neighborhood residents and motivate them to act on their own behalf. To visit with the locals, he drove his Honda from black churches to community centers to Laundromats, all the time wondering how he could organize people who felt so powerless in the face of such big problems.

As soon as he saw the Altgeld Gardens public housing project, Barack knew where to start. To show Chicago that change was possible, he had to focus on one concern. Something that was measurable, that folks could see.

People sure could see the mess at Altgeld Gardens. They could smell it, too. The apartments at Altgeld sat in the middle of several waste sites, the Midwest's largest landfill, and a sewage plant. *Whew*, did that place ever stink! How Altgeld ever got "Gardens" added to its name was a mystery. The only things growing at Altgeld were brown grass and the frustrations of those living there.

The foul odor filled the air outside and also inside the apartments. When Barack entered one of the buildings, he saw cracked walls and broken windows. In people's homes the toilets didn't flush. This added to the stinky lives the Altgeld residents led. The environment at Altgeld was as bad as the living conditions he had seen in Indonesia and those he'd read about in the most depressed parts of South Africa. But this wasn't a Third World nation. It was South Chicago—America!

Barack immediately called a community meeting to be held at a local church. He gathered ideas from neighborhood residents and listened to their concerns. They told him that jobs would raise the quality of the neighborhood, and also increase their morale. He and the DCP took action to bring shops and restaurants closer to Altgeld. This brought jobs, and it motivated people to follow Barack's lead as he organized neighborhood cleanups, crime-watch programs, and street repairs.

Slowly, Altgeld Gardens improved. Barack's big victory on behalf of the neighborhood, though, came when someone discovered that the Altgeld apartments might contain asbestos, a harmful material that causes cancer. Barack and one of the Altgeld residents asked the manager of the apartments about the asbestos. The manager told them not to worry. He assured them that the apartments had been tested. There was no asbestos, he said. Barack asked to see a report showing when the tests were conducted, and what the results showed. This was like asking for a report on when the tooth fairy had made her last pillow visit and what she'd found! When Barack and the Altgeld neighbors pressed the issue, all they got were excuses.

So they boarded a city bus and showed up at the offices of Chicago city officials. Somebody had called the press. A bunch of television news crews arrived to film the scene. Newspaper reporters came, too. The city officials had Barack in their face, along with a bouquet of microphones and news people asking for a quote about the Altgeld Gardens asbestos report. Officials were forced to admit that no asbestos testing had taken place. This was all captured on video.

One reporter asked, "When will the asbestos examination begin?"

The answer came loud and clear through those microphones. "Today."

That "today" shaped Barack in an important way. He'd achieved what he'd set out to do as a community organizer. He'd won the confidence of everyday citizens and had effectively rallied them to bring positive changes to their lives.

As it turned out, Altgeld did deserve to be called a garden. Its residents and improved surroundings had planted seeds of experience for Barack. They shaped his view of public service, an ideal that would someday bear even more beautiful fruit.

The success of Altgeld Gardens also led Barack to finding a spiritual life. Up to that point, he hadn't embraced religion. He was all about finding solutions through his intellect. But he couldn't deny the power of the black church. This was evident while he worked as a community organizer. Black churches had been instrumental in bringing people together to help and work with him.

Churches were communities in themselves. They fostered unity among black people and strengthened African American families. The black church provided so much more than sermons on Sundays. Churches served as a cultural centerpiece in neighborhoods throughout Chicago and America. Chicago's Trinity United Church of Christ was one of the places Barack visited while gaining support for his work with the DCP. Trinity's pastor, Reverend Jeremiah A. Wright, Jr., was a smart man who impressed Barack. Reverend Wright's congregation was engaged in a practical spirituality. They understood that God could be found through hard work and education. Trinity members focused on progress for black people. The church sponsored after-school tutoring sessions, drug-counseling programs, legal assistance, and job training.

One Sunday, Barack attended a Trinity service in which Reverend Wright delivered a sermon called "The Audacity to Hope." He talked about keeping one's faith intact during the toughest times. He told his congregants that light can pierce even the darkest night. That's what hope is—believing in the power of that light. The reverend acknowledged that it takes a bold soul to believe. Faith requires *audacity*, courage. It was as if Reverend Wright was speaking directly to Barack.

"The Audacity to Hope" spurred Barack to make an even greater commitment to improving the plight of African Americans. Through his community organization work he saw that if he was to be an effective leader in the struggle for black advancement, he would need more education.

At the DCP, Barack had dealt with attorneys, bankers, politicians, and business people. He wanted a better understanding of how these men and women conducted their work. He wanted to know what made them and their professions tick. To acquire this knowledge he applied to Harvard Law School, one of the most rigorous academic environments in the world. He was accepted almost immediately.

Attending Harvard presented an irony for Barack. His father had once abandoned him and his mother to go to Harvard, and now he was walking down the same campus pathways and corridors that had once been occupied by his dad.

Barack was a hard worker who focused on his studies. He wanted to make the most of the top-notch education he was receiving. Also, he never lost sight of his reason for attending law school. He was there to gain the knowledge needed to serve the black community in the best possible way. On campus, Barack was an active supporter of the antiapartheid movement. He rallied to get more diversity among Harvard's teaching faculty, and he wrote articles for the university's *Harvard Civil Rights–Civil Liberties Law Review*. Getting published in this journal wasn't easy. The editors were very selective, and having a piece chosen was a big accomplishment.

By the end of his first year at Harvard, Barack was a vital member of the school community. Through his articles for the *Harvard Civil Rights–Civil Liberties Law Review,* more and more people had come to know Barack Obama's name.

In the summer of 1988, Barack returned to Chicago as a summer associate in the law firm Sidley Austin. He wasn't thrilled to be working in corporate law. As someone with a yen for public service, Barack wanted to practice a strand of law that put him in touch with people he could help.

As Barack would soon discover, though, working at Sidley Austin would present him with a gift he was not expecting. On his first day at the firm, Barack was introduced to the attorney who would be his supervisor for the summer. Her name was Michelle Robinson.

Barack took an immediate liking to this bright young lawyer. For weeks he asked her to go out with him. For weeks she turned him down.

Michelle found Barack attractive, but she was there to work, not get a boyfriend. Besides, how would it look to her colleagues if they knew she was dating this guy she was supposed to be mentoring?

As a lawyer-in-training, and as someone who was hoping to someday win the respect and confidence of people who could impact his community service work, Barack was very persuasive. Every time Michelle turned down one of his invitations, he tried a new approach. Finally Michelle agreed to meet Barack for ice cream at Baskin-Robbins.

Over two scoops of chocolate, Barack learned a lot about Michelle. She'd grown up on Chicago's South Side with her mom and dad and older brother, Craig. She'd received an undergraduate degree from Princeton University. After Princeton, Michelle had gone directly to Harvard Law School, from which she'd earned a law degree. She was younger than Barack but had finished school sooner. What impressed Barack most, though, was that Michelle was deeply committed to her family and community, two values that were important to him.

One night Barack invited Michelle to a training seminar in a church basement on Chicago's South Side. He was speaking to a group of young single mothers. It was Barack at his best—articulate, charming, and very committed to this cause. Michelle knew then that this man had a promising future. He was an effective communicator. He was humble. He listened. He cared about the future of people who had once been her neighbors.

It was clear to everyone in that church basement that this skinny student, with a name nobody could pronounce, was special. And now Michelle was in love with him.

By the end of the summer, Barack and Michelle were committed to each other. Barack returned to Harvard to continue his studies, though he and Michelle kept dating.

Back at Harvard, he was as fired up as ever to gain the knowledge he needed to get his law degree. He served as an editor of the *Harvard Law Review*, one of America's leading law publications. In addition to becoming an excellent speaker about legal issues, he had grown into a skilled writer and a smart, critical thinker.

In 1990, Barack's friends convinced him to run for president of the

Harvard Law Review. They might as well have been telling him to climb Mount Everest. Attempting to become president of the *Harvard Law Review* was as steep a feat, and just as treacherous. This wasn't just a matter of getting people to vote for you. It involved meeting with eighty *Law Review* editors—some of the sharpest legal minds in the nation—and enduring a series of interviews to test each candidate's legal know-how as well as his or her intellectual abilities and social skills. One very important quality for the *Law Review* president is that the person be fair-minded. The publication's president needed to see all sides of an issue, and had to remain impartial to views that differed from his or her own. Also, because writers and editors of varying opinions contribute to the *Law Review*, the president should be able to build consensus among the publication's team.

Barack was one of nineteen candidates competing for the position. After hours of grilling potential presidents, the interviewers whittled down their pool until they finally named Barack Obama the winner.

It was Barack's ability to listen carefully and to consider all factors in making decisions about which articles would appear in the prestigious publication that won him the presidential seat. He became the first black president of the *Harvard Law Review*, a journal that, at the time, was one hundred and four years old.

Barack's post at the *Harvard Law Review* garnered him a lot of national media attention. A major book publisher offered him a contract for his life story. The *New York Times* profiled him and his accomplishments.

High-status law firms throughout the nation were calling him, urging him to work for them, once he finished school. Barack kept a list of the companies who wanted to hire him. There were six hundred and seven of them! Of these, one appealed most: Davis, Miner, Barnhill & Galland. It was one of the lesser-known firms on the list, but it handled civil rights and discrimination cases. Also, it was located in Chicago, which meant Barack could be with Michelle.

Barack graduated with high honors from Harvard Law School in 1991. One year later he and Michelle were married at Trinity United Church of Christ by Reverend Wright. The Obamas started their lives as husband and wife on Chicago's South Side, the place where they both had roots and were ready to grow together.

Before starting his job at Davis, Miner, Barnhill & Galland, Barack worked on the Project Vote registration drive in Illinois. There were many people in the state who didn't understand how elections worked and had never voted. He sat down with them. He explained that by *not* voting, they *were* voting. They were electing to have no choice in who their government leaders would be, and were thereby choosing to let others make decisions that affected their lives. With this rationale Barack encouraged more people to get to the polls. He was part of an initiative that registered one hundred fifty thousand voters in time for the 1992 presidential election.

While registering voters, Barack worked on his memoir. He wrote about his childhood, his family, the sadness of losing his father, his schooling, and his hopes for the future. Writing helped Barack express his feelings about all he'd been through in his life. He put his pain and his hopes onto the pages. The book was entitled *Dreams from My Father: A Story of Race and Inheritance*. When it was published in summer 1995, it sold modestly. The sales didn't matter to Barack. Most important to him was that he'd told his story. Sharing it helped him get perspective on his life and experiences, and it led him to realize that one of the dreams his father instilled in him—serving others—could be achieved by entering politics.

On the cover of his book, Barack didn't include II as part of his name. And, as he gained more renown, he publicly identified himself simply as Barack Obama.

In November 1995, Barack's mother, Ann, died of cancer. Barack told the press that his mother's death was the worst experience of his life. He didn't know she would die quickly from her illness and didn't make it to the hospital in Hawaii in time to say good-bye.

Ann's death and the insight he'd gained from crafting his memoir encouraged Barack to think even more deeply about his life's direction. He now had his law degree. He had experience as a community organizer. He was married to a woman who shared his values. And he'd written a book that told readers his life story. Barack had revealed the deepest parts of himself to the world.

The time was right to seek public office. In 1996, Barack ran for the Illinois State Senate and won. As a state senator he could serve all kinds of Illinois residents in many ways. He helped people living in ghettos, folks running bean farms, immigrants who barely spoke English, and heads of banks whose pinstriped suits were bluer than blue and perfectly pressed. All of these citizens had concerns, ideas, and needs. Each of them looked to their government's leaders to improve the quality of their everyday lives.

Barack held the office of state senator from 1997 to 2004. During these seven years he accomplished many things. He got health care for families who couldn't afford doctors. He secured funding for after-school programs and AIDS prevention. He arranged to have harmful lead removed from people's homes.

Barack was making Illinois a better place to live for the state's residents. And he was helping Illinois grow into a safer, cleaner, and more prosperous place. His life at home was growing, too. Michelle gave birth to their first daughter in 1998. They called her Malia, a name that is both Hawaiian and African. Malia is often said to mean "calm" in Hawaiian and "queen" in Swahili. Three years later, baby Natasha was born. Barack and Michelle called her Sasha for short.

Now Michelle and Barack had a family. Barack was more than a politician—he was a dad! Caring for his daughters made him look at his work differently. Whenever he got a bill passed or lobbied for equal rights, he wasn't just working on behalf of the public. He was affecting the future of his own children. When Malia was diagnosed with asthma, Barack took a strong stand on legislation to prevent air pollution in Illinois. But he wanted to do even more to serve Americans. He needed a larger political forum, and he was eager to take this step.

In 2000, Barack ran for the United States House of Representatives. He didn't win this time, but the loss taught him a valuable lesson about politics. To get votes, you have to *get known*. During the congressional race, a poll was conducted to find out how well voters knew each candidate. Barack learned that his name recognition was only eleven percent. His opponent, Bobby Rush, boasted name recognition of sixty percent. Despite all the work he'd done in the state senate, not enough people knew that the man behind so many positive changes was Barack Obama.

Barack was ready to change that. In 2002, he decided to run for another high-profile office. This time it was the U.S. Senate.

By losing the congressional race to Bobby Rush, Barack had won something important—wisdom. He now understood that winning an election required a more aggressive campaign. If he wanted votes, he had to toot his own horn so loudly and so often that every voter able to pull the curtain at the polling booth would be quick to select the name they knew was the best candidate for the job: Barack Obama.

But horn-tooting takes time. And before a political candidate can shout the good news about himself, he first has to listen to the needs of prospective voters. Barack began his campaign using some of the same strategies that had brought him success as a community organizer and state senator. He met voters where they lived.

He traveled throughout Illinois, meeting people in their churches, backyards, knitting clubs, barbershops. Many times he would drive through rural areas on snowy nights, or to city side streets on hot-as-heck days. He would attend a community event, car wash, or pancake supper, hoping to meet potential voters. Sometimes just a handful of folks showed up. Barack would be there with two or three church ladies who were ready to feed him one of their pies. The only other buzz in the room would be the few flies who'd also come to meet this candidate and to perch on the crusts he'd left on his plate.

At first it didn't matter to Barack if his campaigning turned up two people or two hundred. He was making inroads slowly, but effectively, by letting people talk about issues important to the quality of their lives.

In addition to listening to people's concerns, one important aspect to Barack's campaign was sharing his life story. Popularity polls showed that people responded favorably to him when he talked about the struggles he'd faced while growing up, and the accomplishments he'd been able to achieve despite many personal obstacles. When he arrived at a church social or other neighborhood event, residents wanted to hear about Barack's biracial roots; the racism he'd encountered during his childhood in Hawaii; his years in Indonesia, Punahou, and Harvard; and his feelings of being an outcast much of the time.

Some folks started to compare Barack's story to that of Abraham Lincoln. Like Lincoln, Barack came from modest beginnings. Both men were self-made lawyers. Each had become a politician for the sake of helping others, not for their own personal gain.

As Barack's campaign unfolded, his name recognition increased. In March 2004, he won the senatorial election primary. He'd racked up more than fifty-two percent of the vote across the state. He was on his way.

In order to get the Senate seat, Barack now needed to win the general election. If he won, he'd be the only black Senate member. This, along with his success in the primary, attracted the attention of the national media. He no longer had to toot his horn all by himself. Reporters and broadcasters were helping to spread the word about him.

When it was time for the Democratic party to choose a keynote speaker for their 2004 national convention to be held in Boston, Barack received a call from Senator John Kerry's campaign organization. Kerry, a presidential candidate, had been paying close attention to Barack's trajectory.

This was a big deal. As each presidential election approaches, the major political parties, the Republicans and the Democrats, each host a convention. Millions of Americans watch the gatherings on television to hear from various elected officials, the keynote speaker, and the presidential and vice-presidential nominees. The keynote address is a high-profile speech that sets the tone for each convention and encourages viewers to vote for the presidential candidate.

On July 27, 2004, Barack did more than "warm up" the millions of United States citizens who were watching the convention. His presence lit up the night.

The title of his speech was "The Audacity of Hope," inspired by the sermon he'd heard years before from Reverend Wright. Barack told America that hope is God's greatest gift to the nation. That hope is "the belief in things not seen; a belief that there are better days ahead."

Barack's speech began with details about his life. These were the stories that had struck a chord with so many during his campaign travels. Standing before a national audience, he talked about the roots of his family tree, which spread between Kenya and Kansas. He told of Gramps and Toot. He let people know about his mother and father. Their hard work, their sacrifices, and their triumphs. Barack explained how his biracial heritage played a key role in shaping the man he'd become.

At this point in his speech nearly nine million televisions in America were tuned in. Barack's words were a magnet, pulling his listeners—and also pushing them to think deeply about race in America.

He said, "I stand here today, grateful for the diversity of my heritage, aware that my parents' dreams live on in my precious daughters. I stand here knowing that my story is part of the larger American story . . . that in no other country on Earth is my story even possible."

Barack's speech ignited a spark in the souls of Americans. He painted a powerful picture of America's unique diversity, and how, rather than dividing citizens, it served to unify. He said, "There's not a black America and white America and Latino America and Asian America; there's the United States of America."

At that moment, people of all races *in* America cheered!

The next day, the same viewers lined up at bookstores to purchase Barack's memoir, *Dreams from My Father*. The book sold out and became a best seller.

Barack's keynote address sealed his own election. Four months after the Democratic National Convention, he was elected to the U.S. Senate. He'd received seventy percent of the vote. His win would make him only the third black individual to serve as a United States senator since Reconstruction.

Soon after Barack was sworn into office as a U.S. Senator, his oldest daughter, Malia, asked her daddy if he was going to be the president. She wasn't the only one wondering if he would enter the presidential race in 2008. After his speech at the Democratic National Convention, many Americans wanted him to run. Barack's closest friends and the media pressed the question.

His primary focus, though, was to fulfill his role as senator. He got right to work in his new job. He sponsored legislation to improve schools and to make health care affordable. He opposed a proposal that would force voters to present photo identification before being allowed to vote in elections. Barack worried that this kind of scrutiny would discourage poor people who didn't have a driver's license or passport from going to the polls. He continued to strive for ideals he'd always believed in—equality, improved conditions for underprivileged citizens, better schools.

Two years into his senatorial term, Barack published his second book, which drew its title from a concept that had served him well. Inspired by Reverend Wright's sermon "The Audacity to Hope," Barack entitled it *The Audacity of Hope: Thoughts on Reclaiming the American Dream.* In this book he sent his readers a clear message. He was ready for "a new kind of politics." To make this possible, he had a plan that would "pull us together as Americans."

The Audacity of Hope was an instant best seller. The *best* part of its *best-sellerdom* is that it convinced many Americans that Barack Obama would make the *best* next president of the United States.

Barack started to receive letters and phone calls from men and women offering to work on his presidential campaign. Some of these same Democrats also asked him to consider hiring them when he took his place in the White House. They weren't asking *if* Barack was going to run. Their letters said *when* he ran, as if it were already happening.

For Barack, though, there were several considerations in running for president. Campaigning would mean spending countless hours away from his family. Presidential candidates need a tremendous amount of financial support to make their campaigns viable. Also, compared to others who were vying to become the Democratic nominee, Barack had little experience as a Washington, D.C., politician. One of the Democratic hopefuls was Senator Hillary Clinton, wife of former president Bill Clinton. Senator Clinton's years of working at a high level of government far outnumbered Barack's. People questioned whether he would be as formidable a candidate as Hillary.

Barack spent many days and nights thinking about running for president. He and Michelle talked for hours upon hours about the possibility. Little Malia still wondered if her father would be the president. Sasha was beginning to wonder, too. When Barack thought deeply about the impact he could make as president, and his ideas for bringing positive changes to America, he started to ask himself how he could *not* run.

While he had less government experience than others, it was still within his right to seek presidential office. As for his family, Barack and

Michelle agreed that he would make time for them and that running for president was a means by which he could build a better future for his children and other families as well.

About the money needed to run a campaign, there was only one way to find out whether funds would become available. Barack had to practice what he preached—*the audacity of hope*. He would have to go on sheer faith that he'd get the backing he needed.

Hope—a small word that packs big power.

For Barack and his family, it was that simple. They had to keep hope at the forefront of their plans. Through an immense amount of work and dedication, they had achieved so much. They agreed that if they continued to strive while clinging to hope, hope would take them to even greater heights.

On February 10, 2007—with a big dose of *hope* tucked firmly into every pocket of his being—Barack Obama announced his decision to seek the Democratic nomination for president of the United States. It was a little more than a week into Black History Month when he and Michelle stood on the steps of the Old State Capitol in Springfield, Illinois, to officially announce his intentions to the public. The wind blew a bone-chilling cold over the city, but *hope* kept Barack and Michelle warm.

Hope made Barack more ready than ever to seek the presidency.

Hope could stand up against winter's frosty white sky.

Once he'd made his decision, Barack discovered what most faith-abiding people learn at some point. Even with hope, doubters gather like ants when the sweetness of conviction appears. Naysayers can always be found swarming near a pot of optimism.

While many people applauded Barack's decision to seek the Democratic nomination, others were ready to yank him down. Right away the question of Barack's lack of experience sprung up from the press. He had an answer handy: "I know that I haven't spent a lot of time learning the ways of Washington. But I've been there long enough to know that the ways of Washington must change."

Still, his dissenters wondered if he was prepared to take such a big step. And even those who believed in Barack couldn't help but ask if America was ready for a black president.

When asked if he thought the time had come for a black man to be president, Barack told a *Newsweek* magazine reporter, "I absolutely think America is ready."

Despite his positive outlook, there remained a swarm of folks who took pleasure in chanting a negative refrain. It was a chant Barack had heard before in his lifetime: *Uh, uh, uh! No! No! No!*

But *hope* shone past all that down-in-the mouth pessimism. The *audacity of hope* chanted louder than *Uh, uh, uh. No! No! No!*

When the nonbelievers questioned how Barack would raise enough money to launch and sustain his campaign, people began to write him checks of support. Big checks came in from millionaires eager to see him win. Small checks came in from non-wealthy donors who were also excited to help Barack.

By early 2008, the two frontrunners for the Democratic nomination were Hillary Clinton and Barack Obama. Hillary stressed her experience as a senator and First Lady. Barack reminded voters of his ability to bring a fresh perspective to America's government.

Soon Hillary and Barack were competitors in a very tight primary race, each winning certain states and losing others.

They were close rivals who had gone head-to-head for much of the primary. Barack lost the race in New Hampshire but used the defeat as an opportunity to deliver a powerful campaign refrain that would sway even some of the most negative voters. In a speech following the primary, Barack turned *No! No! No!* into *Yes, we can!*

He proclaimed: "When we faced impossible odds. . . Americans have responded with a simple creed . . . Yes, we can. Yes, we can. Yes, we can . . . together we will begin the next great chapter in the American story, with three words that will ring from coast to coast, from sea to shining sea: Yes, we can."

Once again, Barack had used his gift as an orator to inspire.

Yes, we can! became a battle cry for many American Democrats.

By spring 2008, Barack had emerged as the leading Democratic candidate. On June 7, 2008, Hilary Clinton announced that she was stepping out of the race and endorsed Barack Obama as the Democratic presidential candidate. This put Barack one step closer to becoming America's president. Now he would go up against the Republican candidate, Senator John McCain.

The Republican Party had ruled in the White House for eight years. George W. Bush had served as president since 2001. It would take Barack double the diligence, triple the money, and four times the fortitude to run against a candidate whose party had been in power for the prior two presidential terms.

In order to win, Barack's campaign would now have to be a finely tuned machine. Although many Americans were ready for a change, and even though Barack had tremendous support for his candidacy, there were no guarantees that he would win. An election isn't over until all votes are counted. Barack was popular, but whether he'd become the president came down to the number of Americans who would select the voting tab with Barack's name next to it.

This was no ordinary election. This was Obama '08—the first time in America's history that a black man was so close to taking up residence in the White House. The excitement created a current that ran from Maine to New York, to Florida, to Louisiana, to Utah.

The charge crackled its way from Kansas, the home state of Barack's mother and grandparents, to his current home in Illinois, and spread all the way to Hawaii, where Barack had been born. Barack, Michelle, and their girls leaped onto a campaign trail that sizzled with the thrill of Obama '08.

The Obama family traveled to towns so small that a stroll down Main Street was a main event. They visited cities so big that rush-hour traffic was a daily spectator sport. In each place, Barack was greeted with the gift he had offered to Americans. Folks chanted "Yes, we can!" when they saw him and his campaign team come onto the scene. In more and more states, "Yes, we can!" was leading the parade.

On the night of the election, when each state's votes were being tallied, it became apparent by 9 p.m. Eastern Standard Time that Barack Obama was the winner. By 11 p.m. Eastern Standard Time it was official—he had won.

Rejoicing filled the streets, yards, and homes of his supporters.

On the South Side of Chicago, neighbors hugged each other and danced a hallelujah jig.

Barack hugged Michelle.

Malia and Sasha hugged their mom and dad.

And oh, how the joy-tears flowed. Grown men and women cried from a happiness that wouldn't quit.

Barack Hussein Obama, whose name means "one who is blessed by God," turned *Yes, we can!* into a celebration call.

On November 4, 2008, more than half of the voters in the land enabled Barack to make history again. He was elected the forty-fourth president of the United States of America, and the first black president.

The next morning, as the sun rose on a day filled with hope, many Americans reveled in a new refrain: *Yes, we did!*

Thousands of people flocked to Washington, D.C., to witness the occasion of Barack's swearing-in ceremony on January 20, 2009. Many of them participated in concerts, parades, and prayer services in the days immediately before and after.

The partying couldn't last long, though. There was too much work to be done. The country was suffering through a deep recession when Barack took office. Millions of people had lost their jobs in the months before, banks were on the verge of going out of business, and the automobile industry was failing. One of his first actions was to pass a stimulus plan that created jobs, stabilized the banks, and made automobile manufacturers more responsible and successful.

President Obama then turned his attention to health care reform, which was meant to provide medical coverage to millions of Americans who were uninsured. He also instituted federal funding for science and research labs in order to increase knowledge about how to cure certain diseases.

With such a rich cultural background, Barack knew how important it was to build alliances with many nations. He visited more countries and met with more world leaders than any president in his first six months in office. In 2009, he was awarded the Nobel Peace Prize "for his extraordinary efforts to strengthen international diplomacy and cooperation between peoples."

Barack added more strength and diversity to the Supreme Court by appointing the first Latina to the bench, Sonia Sotomayor.

As commander-in-chief he approved military actions that crippled the terrorist organization Al Queda, which had executed attacks on the United States on September 11, 2001. He announced plans to end combat missions in Iraq and Afghanistan. He secured funding for health care and other services for veterans.

Barack Obama showed the world that America lives up to its distinction as a democracy, and that any child who wishes to become president of the United States can do so, if he or she is dedicated enough. While economic turbulence, global political upheaval, and a lack of cooperation between Democratic and Republican leaders made his presidency challenging, Barack's many achievements prove that holding fast to hope despite obstacles is the first step toward making any dream come true.

Time Line

1731   Benjamin Banneker born on November 9 in the British colony of Maryland.

1775   The American Revolutionary War begins.

1776   On July 4, the Declaration of Independence is signed by America's founding fathers, declaring the thirteen American colonies independent entities from the British Empire. The document cites the belief that "all men are created equal."

1788   The Constitution of the United States is ratified on June 21, providing a structure for America's government.

1792   Benjamin Banneker publishes his first almanac.

1806   Benjamin Banneker dies in Baltimore County, Maryland.

1817 or 1818   (exact date unknown) Frederick Douglass is born a slave on February 14 in Tuckahoe, Maryland.

1845   *Narrative of the Life of Frederick Douglass, an American Slave* is published to widespread attention.

1856   Booker T. Washington is born on April 5 near Hale's Ford, Virginia.

1861   Abraham Lincoln becomes the sixteenth president of the United States. He is inaugurated on March 4.

1861   The Civil War begins on April 12 when Confederate troops attack Fort Sumter, South Carolina.

1862   Partly through the efforts of Frederick Douglass's "Colored Men to Arms" crusade, African Americans are permitted to join the Union Army.

1863	On January 1 at midnight, President Abraham Lincoln's Emancipation Proclamation becomes official, freeing all enslaved people in the Southern rebel states, meaning those states that did not return to the Union.
1865	The Civil War ends April 9, when Confederate General Robert E. Lee surrenders to Union forces. President Abraham Lincoln is assassinated by John Wilkes Booth on April 15.
1868	William Burghardt (W.E.B.) DuBois is born on February 23 in Great Barrington, Massachusetts.
1876	Jim Crow segregation laws begin to be put into effect, mandating that citizens be separated by race in public places such as restaurants, movie theaters, schools, pools, and drinking fountains.
1881	Booker T. Washington founds Tuskegee Normal and Industrial Institute, in Tuskegee, Alabama.
1889	Asa Philip Randolph is born on April 15 in Crescent City, Florida.
1895	Frederick Douglass dies on February 20 in Washington, D.C.
1896	W.E.B. DuBois is the first African American to receive a doctorate degree from Harvard University.
1901	Booker T. Washington's *Up from Slavery* is published; Booker T. Washington dines at the White House with President Theodore Roosevelt on October 16.
1903	*The Souls of Black Folk,* by W.E.B. DuBois, is published.
1908	Thurgood Marshall is born in Baltimore, Maryland, on July 2.
1915	Booker T. Washington dies on November 14 in Tuskegee, Alabama.
1917	The United States enters World War I. A. Philip Randolph launches publication of *The Messenger.*
1918	World War I ends.
1919	Jackie Robinson is born on January 31 in Cairo, Georgia.

1925   On May 19, in Omaha, Nebraska, Malcolm X is born as Malcolm Little.

1929   Martin Luther King, Jr., is born in Atlanta, Georgia, on January 15. The Great Depression begins when the United States stock market crashes.

1937   The Brotherhood of Sleeping Car Porters wins labor equality when they sign an agreement with the Pullman Company.

1947   On April 15, Jackie Robinson crosses baseball's color line by becoming the first black athlete to play in Major League Baseball since the 1880s.

1954   The Supreme Court rules segregation of public schools unconstitutional in the court case known as *Brown v. Board of Education of Topeka.* The case was argued and won by a legal team led by Thurgood Marshall. School integration becomes the law on May 17.

1955   On December 1, Rosa Parks, an African American NAACP member and seamstress, refuses to give up her seat to a white passenger at the front of a segregated bus in Montgomery, Alabama, igniting the Montgomery Bus Boycott.

1956   Buses in Montgomery, Alabama, become desegregated after a Supreme Court ruling is made final on December 21.

1957   During January and February of this year, Dr. Martin Luther King, Jr., helps establish the Southern Christian Leadership Conference (SCLC) and becomes its first president. On September 23, the "Little Rock Nine," a group of nine black students in Little Rock, Arkansas, enroll in Central High School despite initially being barred from entry by Arkansas Governor Orval Faubus.

1960   Four black college students stage a nonviolent protest by sitting at a Greensboro, North Carolina, segregated Woolworth's lunch counter on February 1. The Student Nonviolent Coordinating Committee (SNCC) is founded at Shaw University during the month of April.

1961	Barack H. Obama II is born on August 4 in Honolulu, Hawaii.
1963	Dr. Martin Luther King, Jr. is arrested on April 12 during a protest in Birmingham, Alabama. He is put in jail, where, on April 16, he writes his "Letter from Birmingham Jail" in which he underscores the importance of justice. W.E.B. DuBois dies in Accra, Ghana, on August 27. A. Philip Randolph helps lead the March on Washington, where on August 28, Dr. Martin Luther King, Jr., delivers his world-famous "I Have a Dream" speech while thousands of listeners gather at the Lincoln Memorial.
1964	The Civil Rights Act of 1964, which outlaws racial segregation in public places, is signed into law by President Lyndon B. Johnson and put into effect on July 2.
1965	Malcolm X is assassinated on February 21 in New York City.
1967	President Lyndon B. Johnson appoints Thurgood Marshall a Supreme Court Justice on June 13. Thurgood is the first African American to serve on the Supreme Court.
1968	Martin Luther King, Jr., is assassinated in Memphis, Tennessee, on April 4.
1972	Jackie Robinson dies on October 24 in Stamford, Connecticut.
1979	A. Philip Randolph dies on May 16 in New York City.
1993	Thurgood Marshall dies in Bethesda, Maryland, on January 24.
1995	Barack Obama's autobiography, *Dreams from My Father*, is published.
2004	On March 16, Barack Obama wins the Illinois Democratic senatorial primary. This same year he delivers the keynote address at the Democratic National Convention in Boston, Massachusetts, on July 27, and on November 2 is elected U.S. senator.
2006	*The Audacity of Hope*, by Barack Obama, is published.
2009	Barack Hussein Obama becomes the forty-fourth president of the United States of America, and the first black president.

Sources/Further Reading

Books

Abraham, Henry J. *Justices and Presidents: A Political History of Appointments to the Supreme Court*. New York: Oxford University Press, 1974.

Adelman, Bob, and Charles Johnson. *Mine Eyes Have Seen: Bearing Witness to the Struggle for Civil Rights*. New York: Time Home Entertainment Books, 2007.

Aldred, Lisa. *Thurgood Marshall: Supreme Court Justice*. Black Americans of Achievement Series. New York/Philadelphia: Chelsea House, 2005.

Altman, Susan. *Extraordinary African-Americans*. New York: Children's Press, 2001.

Beals, Melba Pattillo. *Warriors Don't Cry: A Searing Memoir of the Battle to Integrate Little Rock's Central High*. New York: Washington Square Press, 1994.

Bedini, Silvio A. *The Life of Benjamin Banneker*. New York: Scribners, 1971.

Bergman, Irwin B. *Jackie Robinson: Breaking Baseball's Color Barrier*. A Junior Black Americans of Achievement Book. New York/Philadelphia: Chelsea House, 1994.

Bolden, Tonya. *MLK—Journey of a King*. New York: Harry N. Abrams, 2007.

Branch, Taylor. *Parting the Waters: America in the King Years 1954–1963*. New York: Simon & Schuster, 1988.

Bridges, Ruby. *Through My Eyes*. New York: Scholastic, 1999.

Butler, B.N. "Booker T. Washington, W.E.B. Du Bois, Black Americans and the NAACP," *Crisis* 85 (August 1978): 22–30.

Carson, Clayborne, David J. Garrow, Gerald Gill, Vincent Harding, and Darlene Clark Hine. *The Eyes on the Prize Civil Rights Reader*. New York: Viking Penguin, 1991.

Carson, Clayborne and Kris Shepard. *A Call to Conscience: The Landmark Speeches of Dr. Martin Luther King, Jr.* New York: Warner Books, 2001.

Conley, Kevin. *Benjamin Banneker: Scientist and Mathematician.* Black Americans of Achievement Series. New York/Philadelphia: Chelsea House, 1989.

Douglass, Frederick. *Narrative of the Life of Frederick Douglass, an American Slave.* New Haven: Yale University Press, 2001.

DuBois, W.E.B. *The Souls of Black Folk: Essays and Sketches.* 1903 Reprint. New York: Vintage Books/Library of America, 1990.

Foner, Philip S. *W.E.B. DuBois Speaks: Speeches and Addresses.* 2 vols. New York: Pathfinder Press, 1988.

Hanley, Sally. *A. Philip Randolph: Labor Leader.* Black Americans of Achievement Series. New York/Philadelphia: Chelsea House, 1989.

Harlan, Louis R. *Booker T. Washington: The Wizard of Tuskegee, 1901–1915.* New York: Oxford University Press, 1983.

Harris, William. *Keeping the Faith: A. Philip Randolph, Milton P. Webster, and the Brotherhood of Sleeping Car Porters, 1925–1937.* Champaign: University of Illinois Press, 1977.

Hoose, Phillip. *Claudette Colvin: Twice Toward Justice.* New York: Melanie Kroupa Books/Ferrar Strauss Giroux, 2009.

Morrison, Toni. *Remember: The Journey to School Integration.* Boston: Houghton Mifflin, 2004.

Myers, Walter Dean. *Malcolm X: By Any Means Necessary.* New York: Scholastic, 1983.

Obama, Barack. *The Audacity of Hope: Thoughts on Reclaiming the American Dream.* New York: Crown Publishers, 2006.

_____. *Dreams from My Father: A Story of Race and Inheritance.* New York: Times Books, 1995.

Patterson, Lillie. *Benjamin Banneker: Genius of Early America.* Nashville: Abingdon Press, 1978.

Robinson, Sharon. *Jackie's Nine: Jackie Robinson's Values to Live By.* New York: Scholastic, 2001.

_____. *Promises to Keep: How Jackie Robinson Changed America.* New York: Scholastic, 2004.

Schroeder, Alan. *Booker T. Washington: Educator and Racial Spokesman*. Black Americans of Achievement Series. New York/Philadelphia: Chelsea House, 1992.

Strafford, Mark. *W.E.B. Du Bois: Scholar and Activist*. Black Americans of Achievement Series. New York/Philadelphia: Chelsea House, 1989.

Thomas, Garen. *Yes We Can: A Biography of President Barack Obama*. New York: Macmillan, 2008.

Washington, Booker T. *Up from Slavery: An Autobiography*. 1901. Reprint. New York: Viking Penguin, 1986.

Washington, E. Davidson, ed. *Selected Speeches of Booker T. Washington*. Garden City, N.Y.: Doubleday, 1932.

_____, ed. *Writings in Periodicals Edited by W.E.B. DuBois: Selections from the Crisis*. 2 vols. Millwood, N.Y.: Kraus-Thompson, 1983.

X, Malcolm, as told to Alex Haley. *The Autobiography of Malcolm X*. New York: Ballantine, 1964.

DVDs

Baber, Jerry; Fabian, Rhonda; Schlessinger, Andrew. *W.E.B. Du Bois*. The Black Americans of Achievement Video Collection II. Bala Cynwyd, Pa.: Schlessinger Video Productions, a division of Library Video Productions, 1994.

Biography: Frederick Douglass. New York: ABC News Productions and A&E Television Networks, 1994.

Biography: Thurgood Marshall: Justice for All. New York: ABC News Productions and A&E Television Networks, 1997.

Hampton, Henry. *Eyes on the Prize: America's Civil Rights Movement*. Blackside, Inc. New York: PBS Video, 2006.

Acknowledgments

*I*T TOOK SOME MIGHTY hands to create this book. I would like to thank the following individuals and institutions for their immense help in the completion of *Hand in Hand*: Thank you, Dr. Alfred Tatum and the literacy institute at the University of Illinois at Chicago, for igniting this book's purpose, and for ensuring the positive future of black boys through literacy. Thank you to everyone at the Smithsonian Institute's National Museum of African American Heritage and Culture, and Harlem's Schomburg Center for Research in Black Culture, for providing a vast trove of research material. Thanks to Samuel R. Rubin and Esther Kohn, education specialists, John F. Kennedy Library and Museum, in Boston, for fielding my ongoing queries.

Deep gratitude goes to my mother, Gwendolyn Davis, who shared primary source material and memories from her involvement with the League of Women Voters, the NAACP, and National Urban League, working alongside my father, the late Philip J. Davis, who in 1959 was selected as one of the first African American student interns in the U.S. House of Representatives, and was later named by the White House as the U.S. Deputy Assistant Secretary of Labor, and Director of the Office of Federal Contract Compliance.

Thanks to both my parents for showing me that by putting one hand into another, together we can do what we could never do alone.

Exceeding thanks to my extraordinary editor, Stephanie Owens Lurie, for believing in this project from its very beginning, and for skilled editorial hands that shaped this book with the utmost care. Thanks to researcher Catherine S. Frank, for nailing down some of the most important facts, and for asking all the right questions in all the right places. Thank you, copy editors Mark Amundsen and Monica Mayper, for expertly crossing every *T* and dotting every *I* through many drafts of the manuscript. Appreciation as well goes to Joshua B. Guild, Assistant Professor of History and African American Studies at Princeton University. This book's impeccable design could not have been achieved without the creative talents of art director Joann Hill and designer Whitney Manger, who both saw *Hand in Hand*'s creative vision so clearly.

Gratitude goes to my agent, Rebecca Sherman, whose good orderly direction always keeps me on the right road. Thank you, Peter Hassinger and Rosemarie Wyman, for your constant guidance and support. And finally, thank you is too small a sentiment for my husband, Brian Pinkney, whose evocative paintings grace this book, and whose loving hands are always there to hold me.

Index

241

His hands REACHED for the stars.

His Hands, big as hams reache

the color line   His hands rang

hands sei

His hands dug up

His two hands brought

ONENESS

HIS HANDS SEIZED the